Confessions of a once Fashionable Mum

Confessions of a ~~once~~ Fashionable Mum

GEORGIA MADDEN

NERO

Published by Nero,

an imprint of Schwartz Publishing Pty Ltd

37–39 Langridge Street

Collingwood VIC 3066 Australia

email: enquiries@blackincbooks.com

www.nerobooks.com.au

National Library of Australia Cataloguing-in-Publication entry:

    Madden, Georgia, author.

    Confessions of a once fashionable mum / Georgia Madden.

    9781863957366 (paperback)

    9781925203158 (ebook)

    Stay-at-home mothers – Fiction.

    Mothers – Social life and customs – Fiction.

    Motherhood – Fiction.

    A823.4

Cover and text design: Peter Long

Cover photograph: Getty Images

Printed in Australia by Griffin Press. The paper this book is printed on is certified against the Forest Stewardship Council® Standards. Griffin Press holds FSC chain of custody certification SGS-COC-005088. FSC promotes environmentally responsible, socially beneficial and economically viable management of the world's forests.

FSC
www.fsc.org
MIX
Paper from
responsible sources
FSC® C009448

To my very own Three Amigos –
Lewis, Elliot and Maia

1

#FashMum #playgrouphell #remindmewhyI'mhereagain?

Nine forty-five, Tuesday morning. In normal life I'd be:

a. knocking back my second grande soy latte of the day, courtesy of the work-experience girl who's now sulking in the samples cupboard because coffee runs really aren't part of her job description

b. busy convincing some puffed-up fashion editor that fluoro-print parachute pants really are about to make a comeback, even though in truth none of us would be caught dead in them

c. sending out a press release that would literally change the face of fashion as we know it.

In short, as Senior PR of the prestigious fashion label Moda, I'd be a very important person doing very important things.

Instead, I was here. At Happy Mummies Time. In a dirty school hall, surrounded by twenty badly dressed mums and their snotty-nosed kids, as we all pretended to be having the time of our lives. Oh, hang on, that was just me: everyone else, it seemed, really was having the time of their lives.

'And now for the Sing Song!' announced our self-appointed leader, Nikki, a brusque Mama Superior type in no-nonsense hiking sandals and a dog-hair-covered fleece.

A cacophony of delighted yelps and whoops filled the air, and before I knew it they were all plonking themselves down cross-legged on the floor with the fluid ease of lifelong yogis.

I hesitated. Being forced into close contact with the questionable hygiene of an assembly-hall floor was a bitter childhood memory I'd managed to suppress until now. And this time the lack of hygiene wasn't even in question: only moments before, we'd all seen little Crystabella demonstrate how she could yank up her dressing-up frock, pull off her dirty nappy and slide butt-naked across the floor. And the real kicker? Her mother had found the whole thing so completely adorable, she'd made her do it all over again so she could catch it on her iPhone.

If God could have granted me superpowers beyond surviving on three hours sleep I'd have rewound eighteen months and shown my flat-bellied, pre-baby self a snapshot of this. *So this is what you want to swap your fancy job and your gorgeous clothes and your monthly magazine allowance for? Really? Is it?!*

For a second I thought about grabbing Coco and making a run for it. But then I looked down at my excited baby girl, covered eyebrow-to-chin with the remnants of Mama Superior's 100 per cent free-range, sugar-free chocolate crackle, and realised that one of us was very happy indeed.

Sing Song, here we come.

I eased myself down awkwardly onto the floor in my still-two-sizes-too-small Sass & Bide jeans, and artfully positioned Coco on my lap so that no-one would be forced to see my gut spilling out of my pants if they suddenly gave out.

'How would our new mummy like to lead the Sing Song?' asked Smug Mummy, Mama Superior's eagle-eyed wingman and another fan of the Velcro-strapped hiking sandal.

I glanced around the circle to see who this clever Sing Song–singing new mummy was.

Oh shit, she was looking at me.

I thought about her question for a moment. Hmmm, let's see. In terms of desired activities, leading Sing Song would sit somewhere between stabbing hot forks into my eyeballs and reliving the second stage of labour. In slow motion.

'Sure,' I beamed. 'I'd love to!'

'Great. Shall we start with "Fruit Salad"? We've got props!' Mama Superior pulled a hemp bag labelled 'Fun Time' from the jaws of one of the drippy-nosed twins, and presented the room with an armload of musty-smelling old junk that might once, a very long time ago and by an extremely generous stretch of the imagination, have resembled apples and bananas.

As Snotty Twin One wailed and the assembled mothers oohed and aahed as though they'd just been presented with the secret to everlasting youth, it occurred to me that there must be an app out there for calculating how long it would take – in seconds – until Coco turned eighteen and I would finally, mercifully, be free of all this.

'Perfect,' I said. 'Now, remind me how it goes.'

Cue much laughter and tut-tutting from around the circle.

'Are you kidding me?' asked Smug Mummy. 'It's a Wiggles song. Surely you know The Wiggles?'

'Of course I know The Wiggles. As a matter of fact I've *met* the Wiggles. The original line-up.' I let that sink in, looking around to see who was impressed. Not a sausage. 'Coco and I just, you know, prefer our music a little more current.'

'Do you have a suggestion?' asked Mama Superior, pointedly stuffing the knitted fruit back in its hempy hideaway.

'What about that Nicki Minaj song?'

'Nicki Minaj,' she repeated, throwing me a hefty dose of side eye.

'Yes, Nicki Minaj. You do know Nicki Minaj, right? "Anaconda" is actually an incredibly empowering song. Which you'd all know, if you weren't so busy listening to "Fruit Bloody Salad".'

Silence. They all looked at me aghast, as if I were some foul-mouthed bogan crack whore who'd taken a wrong turn off Parramatta Road and accidentally landed in their hallowed midst.

Ugh. Where's a grande soy latte when you need one? This was going to be a long morning.

*

So why, you might ask, were we even there? For the answer, we'll need to backtrack a couple of weeks to an early morning appointment with my GP, Dr Krudnic.

I'd only gone in to grab a repeat for my eczema cream (burning, scaly skin of the sort most commonly seen on a blue-tongued skink being yet another unfortunate side effect of the stress and interminable boredom of child-rearing that nobody bothers to warn you about). But once I got there, she'd started peppering me with all sorts of questions about how I was finding motherhood and whether Matt and I were still having sex.

'Oh, it's great,' I said, bouncing Coco maniacally up and down on my knee, as if I'd suddenly developed Tourette's. 'Having Coco has given me a deeper understanding of what love really is. Just looking at her fills my heart with joy, and I thank Matt every day for the precious gift we've created together.' I couldn't remember the *exact* words Drew Barrymore had used in her *People* magazine interview about the birth of her second child, but I figured it was something along those lines.

Twenty seconds later, Dr Krudnic was holding the baby and I was a blubbering mess, literally sprawled across her examination room floor.

'Have you considered the possibility that you might be depressed?' she said.

I stared up at her, dumbfounded. No offence to anyone suffering from mental health problems, but in my family's vernacular 'depression' was just a polite way of saying 'complete and utter loser'. Perfectly fine in other people, of course, but we Humphries were supposed to be above such things. In this regard, my family was a little bit like the Royal Family. It didn't matter how crap you felt about all the horsey-looking ex-girlfriends your husband had secretly tucked away on his country estate, or how many times your wife was photographed sucking on other people's toes; keeping that stiff upper lip firmly in place was all that really mattered.

'I'm not depressed,' I said. 'I'm just fat and bored, and the thought that I've got to do this for, like, forever makes me want to slit my wrists.'

She gave me one of those heavy, pensive looks doctors do so well, while Coco gently gnawed away at the stethoscope around her neck. *Hmm, how do I deal with one so stubborn?* I could see her thinking.

'I'd really like to prescribe you a short course of anti-depressants,' she said at last.

No. Just no.

'There's got to be something else,' I pleaded. 'Some sort of juice cleanse or tai-chi exercises or something?'

'Well, do you get out much? Mix with other mums?'

And just how on earth did she expect me to find the time for that? As it was, looking after Coco left me with barely enough time to do my internet shopping, check Instagram and catch up on daytime TV. I was supposed to fit socialising in there too?

'There's a very nice playgroup near you – Happy Mummies. They're a very supportive social group.' She tore a slip of paper off a pad on her desk and scrawled the details across it. 'I'd like you to give it a try, just for a few weeks. Then come back and see me and we'll assess how things are going.'

She held Coco and the slip out towards me, and I took them both gingerly from her hands.

'You never know. You might actually enjoy it,' she said with a half smile. 'You two might make some friends.'

Well, duh, that part was a given: we could make friends in a heartbeat. What wasn't there to love about us?

2

#FashMumfail
#justgivemethepills

As I staggered back to the car with Coco, I tried to process everything that had just happened at Happy Mummies. One thing was for sure: I didn't care how many pills Dr Krudnic had to stuff me full of – I was never, ever going through that again.

Sing Song had been a complete disaster. I should have just kept my mouth shut and stuck with 'Fruit Salad'. My little lesson in feminist pop culture had quickly descended into an ear-splitting shouting contest, and earned me the dubious honour of being the first person in Happy Mummies' proud fifty-year history to piss off the school administration. Just as little Gypsy-Blu was hitting high notes I never even knew existed, the headmistress, an ominously named Ms Pricklethwaite, had burst through the doors to tell us off for disturbing a Year 3 spelling test. 'I just don't understand it. I've never had any problems with you lot before.' Twenty pairs of eyes had swung accusingly in my direction, making me feel like I was right back at school again (which, in a way, I guess I was).

I had then done my best to distract the little buggers by giving them a quick twerking lesson, which they took to with great gusto.

Unfortunately they weren't the only ones. The sight of Smug Mummy thumping her beefy behind into a super-sized stuffed version of Dorothy the Dinosaur was not something any of us were likely to forget in a hurry.

Next up was a back-breaking tidy-up session where every bit of plastic rubbish the kids had played with that morning had to not only be tidied away, but also *sterilised* so as not to contaminate the children coming in after us. Then there was a whole lot of standing around, listening to all the scintillating activities everyone had lined up for the afternoon ('kindergym', 'shopping for snowflakes for my daughter's *Frozen* party', 'taking the dog to his therapist'). My *God*, didn't these people have anything more interesting or important to do?

Then, just as I had one foot out the door, I got hauled back in for the Happy Mummies' goodbye routine, which involved all of us holding hands in a circle and sharing something we were thankful for. A beautiful lesson in gratitude for the kids, apparently. I didn't think my honest response – 'that this hell is nearly over' – would quite cut it, so I took my cue from the mum standing next to me and mumbled something about new friends and wonderful beginnings. I could actually feel the bile rising up from the pit of my stomach and burning the back of my throat as the words came out, but from the sugary smiles and moist eyes all around me, I think they pretty much bought it.

Back in my car, I had the overwhelming urge to vent to someone, anyone. I couldn't call Matt, of course, as I knew he'd only be interested in hearing the edited version of this morning's events and – it being 11:45 on a Tuesday – anyone else I could have called would be busy doing things of actual consequence. At the very least, they'd be en route to a champagne lunch at some divine little restaurant overlooking the harbour. Probably Catalina, I thought with a sigh. My favourite.

But there was no point moping. The one tiny silver lining in all this was that I could put it behind me now. I never had to see any of those ridiculous women again. I took a few deep, calmative breaths – inhale to a count of three through the nose, exhale to a count of four through the mouth, just as Guru Atma, my yoga instructor, had taught me – and reached into my pocket for my phone.

Seventeen missed calls. All from Lola.

I wondered what this morning's drama was. Had she forgotten the number of our courier company? Pissed off the editor of *Cosmo*? Lost the chai teabags again?

The thing about maternity leave is that you don't want someone actually competent doing your job while you're away. I'd been careful to pick a complete loser: it would make everyone in the workplace pathetically grateful when I decided to grace them with my presence again. I had handpicked Lola, with her perfect blend of ditziness and typically 22-year-old sense of over-entitlement, with more care and attention, to be completely honest, than I'd paid to our last three press campaigns.

But my sterling recruitment efforts had come back to bite me. Lola's real issue, it turned out, was personal boundaries. In that she had none. And apparently her sense of self-importance didn't come with an ability to make decisions on her own.

As if that wasn't enough, the girl also had an uncanny sense of timing. The minute Coco's eyes would finally – after two hours of non-stop rocking / singing / cuddling / tearing my hair out – take on that druggy look that signalled sleep was imminent and we were millimetres from a mattress touchdown – *bleep!* – that would be Lola. Or Matt and I would wake up and realise, sweet Jesus, the baby was still asleep, giving us exactly three minutes and forty-five seconds to cram in some mummy and daddy time. *Bleep!* Yep, you know who.

But for now, Lola would have to wait. There was someone far more important waiting for my call.

Matt picked up on the first ring. 'Hey, it's me,' I purred in my best you-may-have-seen-me-poop-on-the-table-giving-birth-but-I'm-still-the-woman-you-desire voice.

'Did you go?' he asked, all anxious and snippy and not at all picking up on my flirty undertones.

Three little words: enough to make my heart ache. He so badly wanted this to work – Coco, us, the whole becoming-a-family thing. I just wished he wouldn't make me feel like such a complete failure every time we went anywhere near the subject. Sometimes it felt like he thought Coco would be in better hands with anyone other than me. It was there in everything he said – and didn't say. 'What did you two do today? Did you leave the house?' or 'Do you think Coco's bored? Does she need a little friend?' When I'd told him yesterday that we'd be going to playgroup today, I thought he'd literally explode with excitement.

The fact is, I had wanted this whole thing to work too, maybe just not the same way he did.

Matt had seen Coco's arrival as his chance to create the perfect little unit he never had growing up – the Hallmark-card family: the ones who never fight, always listen, and share funny little in-jokes no-one else understands. Matt's dad died when Matt was still in uni, so I'd never got a chance to meet him, but from all accounts he'd been a bit of an arsehole – aloof, judgemental, master of the cutting put-down, that sort of thing. Matt was determined not to be like him, a fact he reminded me of constantly.

I, on the other hand, had thought Coco's arrival would be a chance to get off the hamster wheel for a while, relax, catch up on my reading (hah!) and laze around in all the great new cafés I'd been hearing about. I thought I might even crank out a couple of Gwyneth Paltrow–style cookbooks, if I found the time. Style-wise, I'd decided to fashion myself after my two favourite celeb mummies, Heidi Klum and Angelina Jolie, and had visions of afternoons spent sprinting up hillsides with Coco in her special edition Missoni-print Bugaboo and evenings wafting along red carpets in ethereal silk gowns with Coco tucked under my arm in a matching sling. I would be the type of yummy mummy *real* mothers could relate to, and had even coined the perfect hashtag for my Instagram feed – #FashMum. Then, at the end of a leisurely year, I would hand Coco over to a marvellously efficient nanny and dive straight back into my old life fully recharged and ready to kick some proverbial butt.

So maybe we'd both been a little deluded going into this, and were both a little disappointed with the outcome. But had Matt forgotten who he was dealing with here? Failure was not in the Ally Bloom (nee Humphries) vocabulary. Mark my words – not only would we be the happiest goddamn family in the history of families, but some day others would look to us to guide them through the murky waters of parenthood towards the utopia known as Having It All.

Hell, we might even score our own reality TV show.

'Yep, we went,' I said. 'And I think it's safe to say that me and my little co-pilot made quite the impression at Saddo Losers Mummy Morning.'

'So you had a good time? You made some friends?' *Ugh. Here we go again.*

'We will.' *With that group? When hell freezes over, maybe.*

'I'm so proud of you. Both of you. My two girls hitting the suburban mummy circuit. Who would have thought it, huh?'

Who indeed. I thought of Mama Superior sitting cross-legged on the floor with her hairy cankles peeping out the bottom of her culottes, and the Organic Spelt Mamas who had spent the entire morning with their four-year-olds (four-year-olds!) attached to their boobs while they debated whether the glass of red wine one of them had drunk two weeks ago would affect her little genius's chances of winning a Rhodes Scholarship or at the very least scoring a spot at a decent university – and thought just how bang-on-the-money Matt's words were.

I'd read all the books (well, bought them at least), and while my natural instinct had been to outsource all the boring stuff (weaning, sleep training and – in an ideal world – childbirth too), I knew that giving Coco a full twelve months of undiluted, one-on-one Mummy time was a pain worth suffering. This investment would yield results some sixteen or so years down the track when she'd probably be the only kid in her class not to come home with a nasty drug habit, a string of bad boyfriends, a baby or a weight problem.

But after this morning, I wasn't sure I had it in me. Would it really be such a big deal if I jumped ship a little earlier than planned? From what I'd read on mumsnet.com, Coco was already at least two, maybe three, months ahead of the game. Perhaps my work here was already done.

Plus, let's face it, the chances of me suddenly morphing into an Earth Mother were pretty much slim to none. For one, no matter how many articles my mother-in-law insisted on sending me about all the wonderful benefits of breastfeeding, I couldn't get Coco onto formula fast enough. Hell, that shop had shut the minute we'd come home from hospital. As for body hair, I'd been waging a one-woman war against it since I was fifteen, when Marta Lollback had compared my legs to a funnel-web spider's in front of our entire Year 10 home economics class, and I wasn't about to let a saggy post-birth belly and limited windows of time for grooming stop me now. My waxologist (an official title, btw), Flora, was such a close friend she'd helped choose my wedding dress. My house was a mess, my version of sterilising Coco's bottles was running them a couple of seconds under a lukewarm tap, and in a few years time I had every intention of allowing her to eat McDonald's on a semi-regular basis if it meant I could put my feet up with a glass of wine rather than cook dinner.

If the Mummy Mafia knew the real me, I'd probably have child protection services knocking on the door.

As we pulled into our driveway, my mind was still spinning with the million and one very good reasons to leave this SAHM malarkey behind me and run back to the office as fast as my Isabel Marant wedge sneakers could carry me. But the one very good reason *not* to was snoring gently behind me in her car seat and, of course, she trumped them all.

Having parked, I twisted around in my seat so I could inhale the sight of Coco sleeping, for a few indulgent moments. This whole sleep-watching thing was my embarrassing little secret – a pathetic motherly cliché I hated but could never quite seem to shake off. But how could I put a stop to it when Coco was so completely adorable? Every day there was something new: the delicate O shape she made with her mouth, as though she was having the most surprising of dreams; the pool of dribble that gathered stubbornly on her collar no matter when or where she slept; or today's delight – the way her tired little head squished into her body like Play-Doh, making her look like one those funny neck-less dolls you see in gift shops.

A busy morning of playing and socialising and chocolate crackle–eating had really taken it out of her, and she was down for the count. I thought about starting the engine back up and spending the next hour or so driving around aimlessly while she slept. With my weekly inner-city ashtanga yoga classes now a distant memory, burning through tanks of petrol by driving around the nearby 'burbs had become my precious new 'me time'. But then it occurred to me that I might bump into one of the Mummy Mafia. Or bump one of them over. Hardly ideal, either way.

So we headed inside instead. I lifted Coco gingerly onto my shoulder and attempted to navigate my way across our pebbled front path in my wedges without a) waking her up, b) falling on my arse, c) breaking an ankle, or d) doing all three at once. *Why, oh why*, I wondered, not for the first time, *did I insist on the zen bloody landscaping?*

I'd nearly made it to the front door when my foot got caught on the fat Breeze Buddha with the condescending smirk that I'd had specially shipped in from Kazakhstan or Laos or one of those other places I couldn't pronounce. At the time, I'd known in my heart of hearts – or, rather, that place of temporary insanity you reach in the midst of a late-night internet-shopping frenzy – that our 'oriental'-themed front garden wouldn't be complete without him. But now, every time I saw the cocky bastard I just wanted to dropkick him straight into the tranquillity water feature. And never more so than right now.

Using every bit of abdominal strength I could still muster, I fought to regain my balance without waking Coco up or dropping her on the kamikaze pathway. I'd just managed to stabilise myself when – *bleep!* – my pocket began to shrill.

Coco's eyes sprang open and her mouth curled into an angry arc. The sleeping angel had officially left the building and we both knew what was coming next.

I jammed a finger into my left ear before Coco had a chance to get going, and put the phone to my right. 'Lola – I can't talk now. I'll call you back,' I hissed.

'It's an emergency. I've called you, like, a hundred times. Where have you been?' Lola screeched back.

By now Coco was beginning to hit her stride, her vocal cords stretching down the road, round the corner and somewhere deep into the next suburb. Really, there was only one thing for it. I held the phone up to Coco's mouth for a couple of seconds. Then a couple more, just for good measure.

'Where do you think?' I said sweetly, returning the phone to my ear.

'Don't ever do that again. Jesus Christ, can't you give her something?'

'What, like a Xanax?' I snapped back.

'I'm serious. I think you just pierced my eardrum.'

'Actually, I'm doing you a favour,' I said. 'Think of this conversation five years from now when your ovaries start throbbing every time you watch a Huggies commercial and you're convinced beyond doubt that your biological clock is about to give up and die.'

As if on cue, Coco made a grab for the phone and hurled it towards the ground.

'Trust me, you'll thank me for this some day!' I shouted as I scrabbled awkwardly to pick it up.

'Ugh! Whatever the hell you two are doing over there, I'm begging you, please stop!' Lola's repulsion dripped through the phone.

'Ok, fine, hang on a minute.'

I reached deep into the bowels of my handbag in search of my secret stash: a pile of pink plastic dummies. God knows what this would cost us in orthodontic treatments ten years from now, but desperate times called for desperate measures.

I frantically scrabbled around the bottom of my bag, while the muffled sound of Lola's screeching continued from the phone stuck under my armpit . . . Eureka! I blew off the clumps of dried formula and crusted muesli flakes that were stuck to its lurid pink teat and jammed the dummy into Coco's mouth. She started sucking hard, like an addict getting her daily fix – and beautiful, blissful silence reigned.

I retrieved the phone from my armpit. 'So what's the emergency?' I asked calmly.

Lola let out a dramatic sigh. 'Trish from *LookSee* magazine won't give back the Taylor bag. I've called her, like, three thousand times, and now she's pissed.' She paused for a moment before lowering her voice. 'She says you two have a "special arrangement".'

Ah, yes, the special arrangement. The one where she photographs one of our handbags for the 'Too Hot to Handle' pages of her magazine, and I pretend not to notice when she accidentally keeps it. Not an arrangement I particularly wanted broadcast to the wider world.

'Maybe she's lost it,' I suggested.

'Celeste said she saw her wearing it at Groucho last night.'

Argh. 'Look, Lola, who really cares? It's just a bag. You need to learn to chill.'

'I can't chill. It's our only sample! You know I'm gonna have to tell Alejandro.'

Alejandro – pronounced with the full, guttural, rolling 'hhhh' sound like you're trying to hack up a hefty gob of phlegm from the back of your throat – formerly Alan from Campsie, now owner and head designer of Moda, and my boss.

Someone who most definitely did *not* need to know about all the dirty little shenanigans that went on behind the scenes to ensure the glossies showcased his latest designs over the competition's.

Not if I ever hoped to return to my job, that is.

'Leave it with me. I'll sort it,' I said at last.

'Thanks, doll, you're a lifesaver,' Lola trilled, all anger instantly forgotten.

Yeah, a lifesaver who'd just bought herself a six-hundred-dollar bag that was somehow going to have to sneak itself back into the Moda press cupboard. Matt was going to kill me. There was no way he was going to fall for the old 'nappies were on special so I bulk-bought' line again. Oh, for simpler times when credit-card statements came in envelopes that could just be stuffed behind the fridge.

'There was one other thing . . . it's a little awkward,' said Lola.

'What is it?'

'We were all just wondering when you're going to come in. You know, so we can see the baby and all.'

'Soon,' I said.

'It's been, like, forever. You can't still be fat. And there's this rumour going round that maybe there's something wrong with the baby. She's not, like, ugly, or anything is she?'

Excuse me?! Every hair on my body – including the ones I'd only discovered I had since I stopped my fortnightly visits to Flora and her magical waxing wand – raised itself in silent, startled defence of my beautiful baby girl.

For the record, I was not one of those mothers so blinded by love they can't tell they've spawned a baby Godzilla: Coco was – objectively – a stunner. It was an indisputable fact. And the thought that those scrawny bitches were going around the office spreading lies about her made me want to scratch their eyes out.

The truth was: it was me who'd been putting off facing everyone.

Every morning I'd wake up hoping that today was the day I'd have miraculously morphed into the yummy mummy I knew I was meant to be: flat-stomached, relaxed, in control. Happy even. And yet every morning, staring back at me in the mirror, was the same puffy-faced, frizzy-haired stranger who'd looked back at me yesterday. You know: the one with the saggy boobs, the bags under her eyes, and the remnants of last night's takeaway stuck to the front of her tracksuit (Stella McCartney, but still). On paper I was only 31, but I looked and felt more like 101.

I flung my phone and keys onto the console table in the hall and glanced in the mirror. My God, was that a hair growing out of my chin? I shoved Coco onto the floor so I could get a closer look. I gave it a yank. Firm and unyielding – less of a hair, more of a whisker. I knew baby hormones were meant to do strange things to a woman's body, but come on! Seriously?!

I slumped back against the wall. How had my life come to this? Only eighteen months earlier I'd stood barefoot on a private beach in Bali – the same beach where Jennifer fucking Hawkins had tied the knot – wearing vintage Galliano and swearing my eternal love to Matt in front of fifty of our closest and most beloved friends. This had been followed by ten blissful days sailing around the islands in a private yacht, just the two of us. We'd fed each other freshly-caught mahi mahi wrapped in banana leaves and swum naked with a school of dolphins. It had been the perfect start to our perfect fairytale life together. What had happened to that life? We'd had a six-page spread in *Modern Bride* magazine, for fuck's sake.

Coco began madly wrestling with the leg of the console table at my feet and sent my phone crashing to the floor. I hoiked her up and felt the tell-tale squelch of a very full nappy spread across the crook of my arm. Time for a change. I dragged us both upstairs to the bedroom.

And that's when I saw them.

Lying right there on the floor on my side of the bed. Brown, caked-on and sunny-side up, with absolutely no attempt made to conceal them: Matt's skiddies underpants.

Coco wriggling impatiently in my arms, I stook there staring at them for what felt like forever, as though waiting for them to stand up and explain themselves. But really, what was the point? Their very existence said it all.

I wasn't close enough to know how they smelt, but for argument's sake let's assume they did: wretchedly. In their cankerous, chocolatey brown way they said everything that Matt and I hadn't been able to say to each other these last few months. We'd lost sight of each other, and most frighteningly of all, we didn't even care. *Modern Bride* had called us 'Sydney's most lovalicious power couple' – a fact I was reminded of every single day when I passed the open magazine sitting casually on the coffee table for the benefit of anyone who happened to walk by. I wondered how 'lovalicious' they'd find us now.

If ever I was looking for a sign, this was it. I knew exactly what I had to do.

I grabbed my phone again and messaged Lola before I had a chance to change my mind.

Get the girls set for Friday. Coco and I will be with you at 10.

It was time to pull on the double Spanx, do something about that whisker, and get my life back.

3

#FashMumrecovery
#bringbacktheromance #lovesurprises

For the first time in forever, I felt like I was on a mission. A familiar buzz coursed through my veins, making me realise just how dead I'd been feeling for the last nine months.

I had exactly 70 hours and 14 minutes to get my shit together before D-day. Surely that was enough time?

I thought back to the hallway mirror and grabbed the phone again.

Let's make it 11 am. Lunch is on me. xxoo

Did people still text each other hugs and kisses? I wasn't entirely sure, but establishing that little note of affection seemed like the right thing to do at this point. Chances were I'd need all the support I could get come Friday.

Later that evening, Matt came home to find Coco sitting in the middle of our bed, happily munching on the label of a very nice Christopher Kane peplum dress I'd forgotten I even owned, and me collapsed in a heap on the floor, surrounded by a sea of discarded clothes, clad in my maternity bra – the only one that still fit – and two pairs of Spanx.

For the record, saggy belly overhang is another perfect example of the motherhood conspiracy. Had anyone warned me about it? No, they had not. Had I expected it to still be there nine months after Coco exited my body, in place of the washboard stomach I'd busted my balls for in the gym (when I still had time to go to the gym)? No, I had not. Had anyone cared to mention that sticking to Tracy Anderson's Dynamic Eating Plan, aka complete fucking starvation, for two solid weeks would be a total waste of time that wouldn't make a scrap of difference or get me even one millimetre closer to looking like Gwyneth Paltrow? That would be a no, too. Apparently the only way to get rid of the damn thing was with an old-fashioned girdle of the type our grandmothers used to wear, which you're supposed to strap on right there in the delivery room and leave untouched for the next six months – a memo I hadn't received until Coco was a good two months old, at which point the damage was done, the overhang was permanent, and the only solution was either surgery or Spanx. And, quite frankly, at this point, I'd be more enthusiastic about strapping on a pair of the Happy Mummies' beloved hiking sandals than stepping foot inside a hospital again.

The skundies, meanwhile, were now artfully positioned on top of Matt's pillow. I wondered how long it would take him to notice.

'It's no use,' I sniffed as I flung yet another Saba jacket I could barely squeeze my arms into across the room. 'Nothing fits.'

'That's not true. What about these?' said Matt, pulling something black out from under his feet.

'They're pyjamas, Matt. It's official, I am now a fully fledged member of the elasticated pant brigade,' I wailed.

'Nothing wrong with a bit of elastic,' he said, stretching the waistband out so far it would probably have been roomy on a baby hippopotamus. 'It's practical. You always complained about those tight skirts and stilettos. Now you'll be really comfortable.'

'Comfortable? Nobody in fashion wants to be comfortable! The whole point is to be as un-bloody-comfortable as you possibly can. Pain, lack of circulation – these things are a badge of honour. Jesus, Matt, don't you get it?'

'I'm trying to,' he said, gently prising the soggy remains of the Christopher Kane label from Coco's mouth.

'Do you think if I'm really good and only eat protein for the next two days I'll fit into something? They say you can lose up to three kilos in a couple of days that way, which means I'll only have another . . . nine to lose after that.' Big, fat tears began to obscure my vision, and before I knew it Matt was on the floor with his arms around me.

'You're beautiful. And you made a baby. A beautiful baby, just for you and me,' he whispered into my neck. 'And let's face it – no-one's going to be looking at you when you wheel that little bundle into the room.'

Oh. My. God. 'So you're saying I'm invisible now?'

He took a deep breath and did that thing with his face that he does when he's trying not to get angry or frustrated or start a fight. 'Okay, you know what Ally? We need a change of scene. Let's go downstairs, have some dinner, and we can spend the whole night watching re-runs of *The Real Housewives of Albuquerque*, *Hoarders*, *Dance Moms*, whatever you like. Peace?' He held up his stupid peace sign and I couldn't help but smile.

'For the record, it's Atlanta, not Albuquerque,' I said. 'You really should learn these things if we're going to stay married.'

And no. He still hadn't noticed them.

I went downstairs with Coco, leaving Matt to get changed.

Ten minutes later, we stood in the kitchen surveying the contents of the open freezer. 'What do you feel like? Spinach and cauliflower?' I asked. 'Liver and lentils? Or maybe something with a bit of a Caribbean vibe . . . banana and avocado perhaps?'

'Is there anything in there that's not puréed?' he asked.

'As a matter of fact, yes. I can offer you two frozen pitta breads and a bag of minted peas, but I'm afraid I can't attest to the freshness of either.'

We looked at each other. 'Pizza?'

While Matt opened the wine and I kicked back on the sofa, flicking through the hundred or so episodes of *Hoarders* I'd recorded but never gotten around to watching, he delivered the corker he'd obviously been waiting to unleash all night.

'Ally, I've organised a surprise for you,' he said.

Thank God. Thank *God*. He must have seen the skundies after all and got my message loud and clear.

'A surprise? Tell me what it is!'

'I can't tell you. Then it wouldn't be a surprise.'

'Is it the box set of *Game of Thrones*? That necklace I've been eyeing off in Tiffany? Those red shoes? Surely not the . . .' I didn't dare say the word, not wanting to recall the one bleak moment of our perfect honeymoon.

On our wedding night, Flora had presented us with the most wonderful gift – a hand-carved wooden Ganesh she'd had specially blessed by some Hindu priest she'd found wandering along the beach. He had said it would guarantee us long lives filled with good luck, fine foods, wealth and luxury – my wishlist for life, in a nutshell. I had wept at the sight of it, unable to imagine a better friend or a more perfect gift, and promised to treasure Ganesh forever.

When it had come time to head home after our honeymoon, I'd assumed we would just pop Ganesh in my suitcase between the sarongs and shell necklaces and breeze through Customs like I'd done a thousand times before, but Matt was all 'we need to declare it! I don't want the rubber glove treatment!' In an effort to demonstrate that I was all about marital compromise, I'd given in, and of course the miserable old cow at Customs had confiscated Ganesh on sight and sent him straight to the furnace. 'God knows what revolting things it might be riddled with,' she'd said, rubbing her fat rubber-gloved hands together with glee.

Even thinking about it now brought a tear to my eye, and of course I'd never dared tell Flora. I was pretty sure our failure to protect Ganesh properly had set off some kind of anti-blessing that was the root of all our current problems. Matt had promised to get me another one, but months had gone by, and, well . . . pigs might fly one day too. And of course, he could hardly have organised Ganesh in the ten minutes between seeing the skundies and organising take-out. Then again, there were plenty of other things he could surprise me with . . . I put thoughts of a smouldering Ganesh out of my mind.

'I can't wait! Will I love it?'

'I hope so,' he said with a tight little smile.

'When's it coming?'

'Tomorrow.'

'You are too sweet. But why did you get me a surprise? It's not even my birthday.' *Come on, say it. Just say you saw them.*

He took my hand in his. 'Because I'm not blind, Al. I can see what's happening here and I want you to know I'm going to do whatever it takes.'

I beamed back at him.

'I really hope you like it.' Come to think of it, he actually looked a little nervous about the whole thing. How could you get stressed about a present? Even if it wasn't Ganesh, I didn't care. Right now, just knowing we were back on the same page and both committed to keeping the romance alive was enough for me.

'You're the best husband in the world and if you carry on like this I'll have to take you back to Bali and marry you all over again,' I said, covering his face with kisses and vowing that I would never again put a dirty pair of undies on the spot where he laid his head at night. I ran upstairs to whip them off his pillow and into the wash.

Only one more sleep and my big surprise would be here!

*

Pitch-blackness outside, Coco mumbling gently in her sleep beside me in her cot . . . and sharp rapping on the front door. Huh? Why was there rapping? Then it dawned on me – my surprise! So typical of Matt to choose a courier service so efficient they delivered before the day had even begun.

I leapt out of bed, Matt scrambling after me.

Giggling with excitement, I pulled open the front door.

And came face-to-face with my worst living nightmare.

My mother-in-law, Judy, stood on the doorstep, wearing the same pissed-off expression that Coco wore whenever I removed something fun (scissors, meat cleaver, industrial-strength nail gun) from her grasp. She had a suitcase by her side. A very large suitcase.

'I've been knocking for ages,' she said, thrusting the aforementioned suitcase between Matt and I, so she could wrestle her way into the hall. 'God only knows what you two were doing up there. I hope this isn't how you treat my granddaughter when she wakes up in the night.'

Matt looked at me, his eyes still crusty with sleep. 'Surprise!'

I opened my mouth to speak. Nothing came out. Not a peep. But, let me assure you, inside my head there was plenty going on.

4

#hatesurprises
#whatdodivorcelawyerschargethesedays?

First things first, I made a cup of tea. Because what else do you do when your evil witch of a mother-in-law turns up on your doorstep in the middle of the night and your quite clearly deranged husband thinks this is something you'd actually be happy about?

We sat together on the sofa, sipping Earl Grey (them) and a Diet Coke (me), discussing the various disappointments that had made up Judy's week so far: namely, the national rail network (crowded, filthy, hopelessly inefficient), the state of her neighbour's front lawn (really, so inconsiderate), and the poor quality of the loafers she'd picked up on the bargain rack in Target, which had already caused two very painful blisters (not much of a bargain, it turned out).

Meanwhile, I mentally tallied up the various ways I would make Matt pay for this for the rest of our married lives. The list was long and Judy's monologue exhausting, so it was something of a relief to hear Coco's piercing cries come through the baby monitor.

'Oh, let me go to her,' said Judy, looking around for a coaster on which to place her mug and, finding none, settling for a well-thumbed copy of the July issue of American *Vogue* instead. Despite this added disappointment to her day, she actually cracked a smile. This made me laugh. We'd see who was smiling twelve hours from now. Had I mentioned Coco was teething?

With Judy upstairs with Coco, spewing forth the sort of sugar-laced baby-talk that makes me want to scratch my own skin off, Matt and I sat side by side on the sofa, sipping our pre-dawn drinks like a couple of complete strangers. I couldn't look at him and he didn't dare look at me. He was obviously doing his best to ignore the toxic waves of fury emanating from every pore of my body. What the hell had he been thinking?

I thought of the vows we'd made on the beach in Bali. In sickness and in health, sure, but there had been nothing in there about your spouse losing his mind and in one deftly aimed curveball destroying life as you knew it. Or maybe there had, and I just hadn't been listening.

Judy came downstairs with a very cranky and confused-looking Coco in her arms. 'I think someone needs a nappy change,' she said, crinkling up her nose.

'I'll do it,' said Matt, leaping up from the sofa.

Funny, I'd never seen him so enthusiastic to change Coco's nappy before. Usually it was more of a Mexican stand-off, with both of us pretending we hadn't noticed the evil smells emanating from our beloved girl's behind until the nappy contents threatened to leak all over the furniture and one of us finally caved in. I wasn't buying this whole Perfect Dad act for a second, but from the look on Judy's face I could see she'd bought, paid and ticked the home-delivery option.

'Don't forget the powder,' I said to his retreating back, upending my Diet Coke so I could slurp down the dregs.

'You're very lucky, you know,' said Judy. 'I had four children and Matthew's father never changed a single nappy.'

A guffaw might have escaped from me at this point. 'And here I was thinking Matt was the lucky one.'

Judy shot me one of her withering I-always-knew-he-was-too-good-for-you looks, and picked up her tea.

Well, you know what, Judy? With the way things are going, you're perfectly welcome to have him back.

In truth, I knew she'd never really forgiven me. Not for the neon-pink bra and see-through tank-top combo I'd worn to her house the first time we met (to be fair, I hadn't actually realised it was a 'meet the mother' moment, as we'd only popped round to pick up a cordless vacuum cleaner, and I'd been hoping to stay in the car: plus, I'd been in the midst of a full-blown '90s flashback Carrie Bradshaw phase at the time). Nor for the time I'd accidentally-on-purpose sprinkled the wrong type of paprika into her goulash and ruined Sunday lunch (seriously, how could smoked and sweet be all that different?). Nor for my refusal to give in to her pleas to have the wedding in an ugly little church in Balmain where Matt had been baptised as a baby.

We'd flown Judy out to Bali for the wedding – business class. You'd have thought she'd be bloody grateful. But no.

'True love doesn't need all these bells and whistles,' she'd sniffily when she saw the hundreds of candles lining the petal-strewn path to our wedding arbour and the trio of little Balinese schoolchildren in traditional costume out on the water, preparing to launch into a bridal serenade. 'Yes, but *Modern Bride* does,' I'd snapped back. 'It's not as though they can do a six-page spread of us trying to dodge traffic along Darling Street, now, can they?' She'd pfft-pfft'd in response, before stomping off across the sand as best she could in her orthotic pumps and refusing to utter another word to me the entire rest of the trip, only going to prove I'd been right all along: we should have put her in economy.

A few agonising minutes later, Matt reappeared with a clean and sweet-smelling Coco. He popped her down on her playmat with a bottle, and then it was back to small talk.

God, I hated small talk.

'So, how long are you planning to stay, Judy?'

'As long as it takes,' she replied curtly.

'As long as what takes?' Was there an actual plan here? If so, no-one had been good enough to share it with me.

'As long as it takes to get you lot settled. Matt tells me you've been in a terrible state. He's been dreadfully worried.'

'He has, has he?' I said, directing my best dagger eyes at Matt, who suddenly took a passionate interest in the herringbone repeat on our new Coco Republic throw cushions.

'Well, it takes two to tango, and I don't blame you entirely, Alexis.' Just ninety-nine-point-nine-nine-nine per cent, presumably.

So my husband, who barely had time to exchange more than two sentences with his wife during the day, what with preparing shareholder presentations and rushing between life-or-death meetings to discuss KPIs or financial waterfalls or some such crap, had managed to find the time to bare his soul – and all the details of his immensely disappointing marriage – to his mother.

Who was this man? And what had he done with the Matt I'd married?

'It's still early. Why don't you two go back to bed for a bit and I'll sort Coco out,' said Judy. We looked at her, doubtful. 'I have done this before, you know.'

Since I'd never been one to look a gift horse in the mouth, even if the horse was a cantankerous old mule like Judy, we did as we were told.

As Matt and I climbed back under the duvet, I noticed the sun was starting to peep through the break in the curtains, a clear sign that it was time to get up, not go back to sleep. Everything about today was wrong so far: why did this little detail trouble me so much?

I had my back deliberately turned to Matt. I felt his hand on my shoulder, hesitant. 'I know it's not from Tiffany and it's not the red shoes, but I figured once you got used to the idea you'd be pleased. My grandmother stayed for months after each of my brothers and my sister were born. She's here to help, you'll see.'

I closed my eyes.

After a couple of seconds he nudged me. 'Ally, say something.'

Do you remember what you said when Coco was born? 'We're the Three Amigos now.' Where did those Three Amigos go? And how will we ever find our way back to them?

'Even the box set would have been a better surprise than this,' I said, before shifting my body as far as possible away from his.

*

It was too bright. I'd slept in. I woke up with that stomach-churning feeling you get when something awful has happened but you can't for the life of you remember what it is. Then I heard the muffled sounds of talking and laughing downstairs, and it all came flooding back.

Judy. The suitcase. As long as it takes.

I came downstairs to find Matt sitting at the breakfast table, mopping up the remains of a plate of scrambled eggs with a corner of toast. Seeing as we'd never actually eaten at the breakfast table before, this immediately struck me as odd. There hadn't been room among the mountains of bills, take-out menus and various crap that had found its way into the house and then stayed exactly where it landed for the next year and a half.

Other things in this picture were out of sync, too. Where were the plates piled up in the sink? The lumps of Coco's rejected Weet-Bix trailing down the wall? And why were my tea towels hanging in neat rows on a rack I never even knew I owned?

Shit, what was the time? Wasn't Matt going to miss his train?

Nope, apparently it had all been arranged. He was going in to work a couple of hours late today, to see Judy 'settle in'. Everyone had been in on this clever plan, it seemed, even Coco. How wonderfully organised of them all.

My gorgeous girl reached out her arms for a cuddle. At least someone here understood the meaning of loyalty. Bending down to breathe her in, I couldn't help but notice she was washed, dressed and smelt completely divine.

'I tried to find those sweet little smocked dresses I bought her at the Widows of Waverley Craft Fair,' said Judy, attacking an invisible stain on the windowsill with my retro (read: decorative, not intended for actual use) Pottery Barn scrubber. 'You know, the ones with the little ducks riding tricycles. Where are they?'

Um, probably warming the back of some poor little bugger out west, whose mum picked them up at the local Salvo's where I left them. 'Hmm, not sure. In the laundry, maybe.'

'No, they're not there. I've been through all that.'

Ah, yes, so she had. The laundry hamper that normally resembled the pointy tip of Mount Fuji was now a great vacuous hole, its contents laid out in neat piles, washed and ironed, on the dining table. My God, how long had I been asleep, a year?

'So what do your days look like, Alexis?'

God, I wished she wouldn't call me that. No-one called me that, except for my mother, a woman who to this day saw nothing wrong with having named her only child after the most famous bitch on '80s television. This had been one of an avalanche of good reasons I'd had to put as much distance as possible between myself and my family the minute I hit eighteen – even half a country didn't always feel far enough.

Judy was still looking at me expectantly. Oh right, our days. Eat. Sleep. A little online shopping. Bit of *Ellen*. Instagram a few shots of Coco doing interesting things like eating, sleeping and watching *Ellen*. Maybe the café down the road if we were feeling adventurous. Then do it all again. And again. And again. Until Coco headed off for uni.

'It depends what we're in the mood for. We don't like being tied down by a schedule.'

'Are you telling me you don't have her in any kind of a routine?' she spluttered, looking at me as though I'd just told her I'd signed Coco and I up for Mummy N' Me pole-dancing classes. 'How on earth do you get anything done? Washing, housework, shopping, that sort of thing?'

Quite frankly, I didn't think Judy had any idea about the kind of pressure modern mothers were under. Sure, she might have had to cook and clean for four kids day in, day out for twenty years with no dishwasher and nothing but a fondue set to fall back on. But was she expected to be bikini-ready half an hour after giving birth? Or take urgent calls from her boss in the maternity ward while a sour-faced nurse squeezed the bejesus out of her left breast in an effort to extract two pathetic droplets of colustrum? Or hold down a high-powered job while co-ordinating the entire family's complicated schedule of playdates, doctor's appointments, and sports, recreational and social activities? And then come home at night and seduce her husband with the energy and enthusiasm of a 22-year-old gymnast? All the while showing the world how effortlessly she does it all approximately seventy-five times a day on Facebook? Somehow, I thought not.

I tried to explain it to her in a way she'd understand. 'Life is a little more complicated than it was back in your day, Judy. And domestic drudgery's not really my thing. I'm a professional. This whole thing is temporary – I'll be going back to work soon.'

'And what about Coco? Where will she go?'

'We're still figuring that out, but I think we'll probably get a nanny,' I said.

I may have sounded blasé about the whole thing, but in truth I had done some research into the topic. My search for a jolly-hockey-sticks Mary-Poppins-type nanny had led me to Au-Pairs-Online, where I'd spent a thoroughly depressing night scrolling through a global procession of perky early-twenty-somethings leering into the camera with expressions that screamed 'I want to steal your husband' while bursting out of their low-cut tops. I'd actually had to double-check I hadn't accidentally logged in to Tinder. I didn't care how much they loved kids or how many times they'd babysat their cousins when they were growing up; the thought of one of them parading bra-less through the house at six o'clock in the morning had been enough to make me scotch the whole idea on the spot.

But I wasn't overly worried. Around the same time, I'd also stumbled upon the website Asktheuniverse.net. All I had to do was pop in my request to find an alternative childcare solution for Coco and then sit back and wait for the universe to answer. A couple of weeks had passed already, but I figured the universe was pretty tied up with other things – terrorism, famine, natural disasters – so it was probably best not to nag.

'What do the other mums say? Can they suggest anyone suitable?' asked Judy.

'Don't know. Haven't asked them.' Was it just me, or was this beginning to feel like a police interrogation?

'And what about your friends? Do you see much of them?'

Friends. Hmm, now that was a tricky one. I had over five hundred journalists, bloggers and editors on my contacts list. I sent them flowers on their birthdays; I knew which ones couldn't start the day without a line of coke or a cuddle with their childhood teddy; I'd gotten pissed, danced on tables and shed tears with others over the breakdown of any number of shitty relationships; in my pre-Matt days, I'd even slept with a couple of them. But could I actually call them my friends? Once the flowers had turned to stink and the cards of congratulations had been stuffed in the recycling bin, I hadn't seen or heard from a single one of them. Not even Flora.

But I didn't want to think about any of that right now. Before I could muster up a response to Judy's Spanish-Inquisition-dressed-as-friendly-chitchat, Matt jumped in: 'She's joined a playgroup!'

'Well, that's a start. When's the next session? I'll go with you.'

'I'm not actually sure we'll be going back,' I said, glaring in Matt's direction.

His face fell, puppy-dog style.

'That's fine. I'm sure you and I can keep ourselves busy at home, just the two of us,' Judy beamed.

Right. It was settled. Happy Mummies next Tuesday it was. Even another session with the moronic mummies would be better than spending twenty-four hours a day alone with the monster-in-law.

I'd thought things couldn't possibly get worse but they did: it rained all day. Fortunately, Judy, Coco and I had plenty to keep us busy. First up: clearing out the cupboard in the spare room so Judy would have somewhere to hang upside down and sleep.

'Goodness, look at all this exercise gear,' she said, eyeballing the shiny free weights and state-of-the-art squat cage, still in their original packaging, that I'd insisted on buying in the days leading up to Coco's birth. (This had been about the same time as I'd splashed out on birthing crystals, a relaxing ylang-ylang spritz, and a CD of dolphins singing along to wind chimes, which collectively had promised to deliver me a 'serene and harmonious birthing experience'. Sometimes I didn't know whether to hug my woefully optimistic former self or punch her in the face.) 'It's not even been opened. When did you get it?' she asked.

'A few weeks ago.' Give or take nine or ten months.

Once the bed was made and the gym gear shoved into the bottom of the cupboard, I made an excuse about checking my emails and left Judy to it.

I popped Coco in her highchair with a pile of Play-Doh and a fistful of Cheerios and checked my phone. Nothing. Not even a peep from Lola. We hadn't even made it to lunchtime. What the hell was I supposed to do for the rest of the day? My two favourite pastimes, surfing the web and watching TV, were clearly out of the question in Judy's presence – she'd probably report me for neglectful parenting.

For a fleeting moment, I wondered whether Lola's uncharacteristic silence was cause for concern. Then again, why complain? Particularly when I had far more important matters to attend to right now, namely proving to Judy that Matt was entirely wrong – we weren't adrift here. I had this ship well and truly under control. So, really, she and her cheap Target loafers may as well hit the road.

First order of business: play the part of the perfect housewife Judy had always imagined for her son. I glanced around the kitchen for something suitably domestic to busy myself with, and my eyes fell on the bulging fridge: it hadn't seen a bottle of Jif since Miley Cyrus still wore clothes. Perfect. Big project, highly visible.

Coco watched in amusement as I squeezed my eyes shut and plunged my hands deep into the bowels of the fridge, pulling out each frond of soggy roquette, every round of mouldy Camembert and every half-drunk can of Diet Coke. I then filled a bucket with warm soapy water and set about scrubbing the insides. Racks were soaked, unidentifiable goo was mopped up. Hell, I even ran down the door seals with a Q-tip.

How, how, *how* was I expected to survive this? I asked myself, as I just about sliced my finger off with a steak knife while wrestling with an ice mass the size of the *Titanic* at the back of the freezer. All I could think about was the suitcase: its girth, the straining seams. Clearly it contained enough clothes and budget footwear to last Judy well into summer. That was five months away. Coco would practically have her drivers licence by then, and I'd probably be decorating my cell at the local loony bin.

Then I had an epiphany. The black and grey of the day suddenly transformed into beautiful, blinding technicolour.

The universe had finally answered.

It was time to go back to work.

Why hadn't I thought of this before? If Judy was here to stay for as long as it looked like, I may as well take full advantage of her.

Ah, work. Even thinking about it brought a smile to my face. Moda. That happy place where everyone praised me just for turning up in a nice outfit and cranking out a few press releases. Where invisible hands were paid to do God-awful things like clean out the inside of the fridge, so I didn't have to. And if there wasn't an invisible pair of hands in sight? No problem, I could just palm it off onto the workie and dress it up as a character-building exercise. And, of course, having Judy look after her would be wonderful for Coco. It was about time she got to know her extended family, beyond Ellen and Dr. Phil.

Just then, Judy came in, interrupting my reverie.

'Do you know that every tap in this house drips?' she asked. 'How either of you manages to get any sleep is beyond me. It'd drive me bananas. You'll really have to get onto that, Alexis.'

I stared at her. Why exactly was that *my* problem? Wasn't her generation all about gender-based division of labour? Surely plumbing issues fell squarely into the prodigal son's domain. Oh no, hang on, he was too busy making his squillions: the modern-day version of spearing wildebeest. Clearly, in Judy's world, leaky taps and thankless domestic chores = women's work. Further evidence of why it paid to be born male in the Bloom household.

Judy was scribbling away at something at the kitchen table. I wondered whether now was the right time to unveil my glorious back-to-work plan. I tried to catch her eye and share an indulgent smile over Coco's determined efforts to stuff as many of her carefully crafted Cheerio-and-Play-Doh patties into her mouth as she could at the one time. Nothing. She was too busy to notice either Coco's adorable antics or my seething desperation.

'Ta da! All finished,' she said at last, holding up a bunch of cards covered with letters and drawings. 'All my children could read before they went to school. No need for private schools and fancy tutors. All children need to get a leg-up with their education is a bit of time and imagination.'

Ugh. Clearly another one of Judy's how-to-be-a-perfect-parent sermons was coming on.

Taking a deep breath and remembering that I wanted her to look after my child eight hours a day for the next four years or so, give or take, I resisted the urge to point out that her supposedly marvellous parenting skills hadn't exactly paid off with her own kids. Sure, Matt was the CEO of the hip marketing communications group Milkfed Media, but he was the only one of the lot who had made anything of himself. Her other children were all either unemployed, pot-smoking hippies or unemployed-pot-smoking hippies.

'I thought that was what school was for, Judy. You don't want her to be bored. She'll probably end up getting sucked into an early-initiative drug ring or something.'

'Aim a little higher, my dear. At least running the drug ring,' she said with a wry smile, shoving the 'A for apple' card under Coco's nose, and then Coco proceeded to spit up her Play-Doh on it.

Ah, she was a firecracker that mother-in-law of mine. And here I'd been thinking Coco got it from me.

*

In the days that followed, Judy launched into a one-woman mission to prove just how useless and inept I was at absolutely everything home-related (not hard, but still).

Before she'd even had a chance to unpack, she was reorganising drawers, clearing out cupboards and casting her silent judgement on every aspect of my life with her old-school and supposedly far superior way of doing things. It started with the vinegar ('all natural – and cheap!'). She used it for everything from cleaning the front windows to nuking the pesky ants that kept crawling up the kitchen drain. Now the whole house reeked like the inside of a fish and chip shop.

The message was loud and clear: she was infinitely better than me at everything. What made it worse was that my beloved husband seemed to agree with her.

Case in point, some time towards the middle of her first week with us, I was on kitchen tidy-up duty, having been forced to plough through yet another of Judy's famously tasteless shepherd's pies for dinner (apparently Matt's favourite – who knew?). The season finale of *Keeping Up With The Kardashians* was due to start in fifteen minutes. I was shoving cling film on the remnants of the pie, mashed potatoes and minted peas as fast as humanly possible, when Judy wandered in. She watched my speed routine for a few seconds – bung cling, bung fridge; bung cling, bung fridge – and I thought she was about to compliment me on my super-efficiency when suddenly, like a woman possessed, she snatched the box of cling film from my hands.

'Not like that! It's called "cling" for a reason – you don't just lay it over the top, you need it to cling! CLING!' she hollered. 'And you're using twice as much as you actually need.' She then proceeded to demonstrate.

Yes, folks, a lesson in the proper way to cling one's film.

Matt came in, his interest obviously piqued by the maniacal screeching coming from the kitchen.

I spun towards him: *Do you see what you've done? What I'm dealing with here?*

'Well,' he said. 'Mum has got a point. We'd probably save a lot on cling film.'

That night, alone in my room, I watched Khloe split from Lamar, on my laptop.

5

#D-Day
#chinesewatertorture
#whoateallthekale? #goinginsane

How was it that I'd spent eighteen months living in a house with dripping taps in practically every room and not noticed a thing? Now it was all I could hear! As I tossed and turned beside Matt, doing everything in my power to ensure that not one single part of my body touched his – a challenging task when you're stuck in a poxy queen-sized bed and your generously padded husband favours sleeping like a starfish – my mind refused to stop its minute-by-minute countdown to D-Day.

Currently: 11 hours, 42 minutes.

The protein-only plan hadn't been a success, something I blamed Judy and Matt for entirely. They'd spent so much of the week fussing over where to find a good plumber (nobody had said it out loud, but clearly the consensus was that I was too scatty and irresponsible for a job of this magnitude – forget the fact that I'd spent the last six years putting on thousand-strong fashion shows and balancing the egos of journalists from sixteen different countries), that we'd ended up having takeaway nearly every night. I'd probably gained another two kilos in tandoori stress weight. This was hardly ideal when I needed every-thing – battle armour included – to be perfect tomorrow.

My mind raced through every possible scenario that might unfold when I got to the office. What if Alejandro wanted me to start back straight away? Would Judy kick up a stink about having to look after Coco? And what about Lola – was she going to slink away without a fuss when I made my big announcement? Or would she stalk me on Facebook for the rest of my life as punishment for kicking her out of a job three months early? Most worryingly of all, how the hell was I going to squeeze my new fat feet, now so accustomed to padding around the house in slouchy Havianas, into a pair of proper working-person's heels?

As I lay there wrestling with these life-or-death problems to the sound of Matt's irritating, adenoidal snoring, I wondered whether it was too late to place an emergency Net-A-Porter order. And were there any health dangers associated with layering up a triple Spanx number?

Ugh. Why was God punishing me so? Surely tonight had been bad enough to be more than enough payback for whatever awful things I'd done in my previous life?

It had all started with *Q&A*. While Judy and Matt debated the pros and cons of a proposed new childcare system put forward my Mr Something-or-other from the Too-dull-to-remember party, I'd sat bored to death beside them, watching Tanya Plibersek, with her bank manager's haircut, make all sorts of salient points about the importance of helping women get back into the workplace, while parading around in yet another boring plum-coloured suit that made it hard to tell where she ended and the studio backdrop began. Seriously, these people wanted our votes, did they not? I really didn't think enlisting the services of a decent stylist was too much to ask.

I glanced over at Matt and Judy, who were too busy tearing up the proposed legislation to be aware of the fashion crime being played out right before their eyes. For the first time, I noticed just how similar they were: funny little earlobes, shadowy monobrow . . . and the way they both ran both hands through their hair when they got frustrated and gave their opponents a bug-eyed stare whenever they dared contradict them. The two of them were in perfect sync.

And then a very scary thought occurred to me: was my husband turning into his mother? Instead of marrying a hot, successful marketing executive who indulged my penchant for bad '80s movies and brought me Bloody Marys and peanut-butter toast in bed when I had a hangover, had I actually married Judy in men's clothing?

Scarier still: was Coco going to inherit that monobrow?

All these thoughts, combined with my ongoing dread at revealing to my colleagues a body that wasn't much smaller than the version they'd seen the day I'd left to go on maternity leave, made sleep impossible. Then two words came crashing through my mind like a bolt of lightning: Optical illusion.

Fuck the protein-only diet. If one of those dresses with the snazzy panels down the sides could make Victoria Beckham practically disappear, surely it would at least give me the appearance of being back to my old self by tomorrow?

Giddy with the joy of finding a perfect solution that required absolutely no physical effort whatsoever, I crept out of bed and logged on to Net-a-Porter. There they were, in all colours of the rainbow: optical illusion dresses. I slid Matt's credit card out of his wallet, clicked on the black (natch), double-clicked the super-duper, express, get-it-to-me-so-fast-it-actually-got-here-yesterday shipping option – costing three times as much as the actual dress – and fell into a wondrous deep sleep.

With a bit of luck, maybe – just maybe – this was all going to work out.

*

As if the pressure of returning to Moda wasn't already enough, I woke up to news of a global crisis. It was official: there was a worldwide kale shortage and in less time than it takes to whip up a Vitamin-Enhanced Energiser Shot we were going to run out completely. Seriously, how could the kale farmers be so dumb? Surely they'd had some inkling that kale was about to become the next big thing after goji berries and the Werewolf Diet?

I tried to impress upon Matt the gravity of the situation – thrusting my iPad under his nose to show him the horrifying pictures of kale fields laid bare, while he adjusted his tie in the wardrobe mirror. But he was more concerned that he was about to miss the express train into work and might have to stand up for the entire journey than that his insides might never be clean and green again.

'But hey, good luck today,' he said, grazing my forehead with the lightest of pecks as he reached for his briefcase. At least he'd remembered.

Downstairs, I found that Judy had reorganised the entire contents of the pantry into neat Tupperware containers. Where the hell were my activated almonds?!

'Look under A,' said Judy. 'Top shelf.'

Oh, right – alphabetised to boot.

I spent the next hour pottering around the living room, fluffing up cushions and rearranging the coffee-table books, waiting for the miracle dress to arrive, worrying about the kale, and trying to push aside fantasies about concealing Judy's dismembered body beneath our tranquillity water feature. I also spent a considerable amount of time examining Coco's forehead for evidence of hair sprouting in places it shouldn't be, while she banged away at her Dora the Explorer laptop. I even pulled on Judy's magnifying Menu Mates specs to get a closer look, but save for a few stray strands in the middle of her forehead, it seemed that so far we were in the clear.

At one point, Coco set Dora aside and peered back at me through the glass, her inky-lashed eyes magnified to super-size. *Have you lost your mind again, Mama?* they seemed to ask.

Maybe I have, my love. Maybe I have.

By nine-thirty the dress still hadn't arrived and I was antsy. I distracted myself by waxing my upper lip and choosing a show-stopping outfit for Coco.

I was in the middle of wrestling her very unaccommodating legs into a divine Collette Dinnigan pantsuit, when I heard Judy shriek from downstairs.

'There's a man at the door who says he has an urgent delivery for you! What is it? What's so important?'

Eureka!

I'd just about managed to get Coco's right leg through the pants hole, but for the life of me I couldn't locate the left. As I searched madly for the missing limb, Coco giggled away as though we were playing the funniest game in the world.

'Just sign for it, will you, Judy?' I shouted back with as much sweetness as my gritted teeth would allow. 'I'll be down in a minute.'

Today was all about exuding zen-like calm and good vibrations, the plan being that all that positive shit would come flooding back to me in approximately ninety-four minutes when I needed it most.

I came downstairs to find the package sitting in the middle of the kitchen table, Judy seated beside it, eyeing it as though it was a bomb about to go off.

'It's just a dress. For me to wear to the office today,' I said.

'But you've got a wardrobe full of clothes.'

I grabbed my miracle dress from under her nose and headed upstairs. 'Yes, but none of them actually fit me.'

After several minutes of Cirque du Soleil–style acrobatics, I managed to get the damn thing on. It held me in so tight I felt like a sausage about to burst out of its skin. As I reached for my hair straightener, I discovered that I couldn't actually move my arms. Or my knees, for that matter. Surely, Posh didn't suffer this hell in hers?

I hobbled geisha-style to the mirror to see if the torture dress was worth the pain. Okay, promising. With its two black faux-leather panels running down the sides, it was clear that if I were to stand in front of a black wall I'd magically lose about ten centimetres. Clever stuff. Except all the walls in our office were white. Oh God, did that mean it would work in reverse and I'd gain another 10 centimetres . . . per side? Suddenly the elasticated pyjama pants were looking like a very viable option.

Too late. 'Alexis, your taxi's here!'

Ah, yes, the taxi I'd ordered specifically so I could indulge in a few wines over lunch. A whole fifteen minutes early. When – *when* – was a cab ever early?

As Judy stood by, tut-tutting, I staggered outside to the cab, only to discover that there was no sign of the car seat I'd ordered and that the whole thing smelt like a wrestler's crotch. The driver lounged in the front seat, picking something out of his teeth with what looked like the nib of a pencil, while I hauled Coco's car seat out of our Audi and into the back of the cab. A ten-minute battle with the various seatbelts followed, as I struggled to get the damn thing strapped in followed. Despite the numerous cranky looks I threw his way, the driver didn't budge; clearly far too busy with his dental excavations to, you know, actually do his job.

Finally, with sweat bucketing down my face and pooling attractively on my newly hair-free upper lip, I managed to strap Coco in, deposit her buggy and 64-piece travel set in the boot, and fling myself down, exhausted but triumphant, beside her.

This was it. No going back.

The driver withdrew the pencil from his mouth and cautiously sniffed the air. 'What's that smell?'

Shit.

I half walked, half hopped back upstairs with Coco, only to discover that we had a Code-Red situation, with Number Threes leaking all the way up the back of the gorgeous Collette. Taking a deep breath and remembering my zen resolution, I refused to get stressy and even more sweaty about it. It was totally fine; we'd just go for more of a rock-chick vibe instead.

In one smooth move, I pulled the Collette off, grabbed Coco's boyfriend jeans, Guns N' Roses T-shirt and roadies' bandana from the cupboard, tossed the steaming nappy in the bin, and decked Coco out as a mini badass Axl Rose, all the while congratulating myself on my cool calmness under pressure.

I then glanced down – and realised the Number Threes had left their mark on more than just the Collette.

Shit, shit, *shit*.

'Hurry up, Alexis. Your taxi's on the meter!' Judy shouted up helpfully.

There was no time to change. In fact, I wasn't sure I could extricate myself from the torture dress even if I wanted to. I wiped the solids off as best I could with a fistful of baby wipes, and sprinkled baby powder and a hefty dose of Matt's Gucci Guilty Intense down the inside of the front of my dress. I was now a mix of sweat, baby pooh, powder and men's cologne: just the effect I was after.

'Have a lovely time, you two,' Judy cooed as I hobbled past her towards the taxi. 'How lovely for the ladies in your office to meet our little clownie Coco.'

'*Chanel!*' I shouted inches from her face. 'I've told you that a thousand times, Judy: it's Chanel! Should we take this as a sign of early-onset Alzheimer's? She's named after the Queen of Fashion, not Coco the bloody Clown!'

Next time, maybe.

For now, I simply muttered: 'Chanel, Judy. Google her.'

And with that we swept out.

In the taxi, I sweltered in the back seat, fanning myself with the only thing I could lay my hands on – a once-clean nappy that was now covered in all the Post-it notes, empty Tampax wrappers and clumps of dry baby formula that shared happy and harmonious digs in the bottom of my handbag.

'Can't you turn on the air conditioning?' I asked the driver.

'It's broken.'

Of course it was.

I looked across at Coco, who was gazing happily out the window at the shops and houses and dogs straining on leads going by, and realised this was her first ever taxi ride. What a momentous day in a girl's life! I laid my hand across her tiny lap, and she grabbed my fingers tight. *We can do this*, the grip said. *I've got your back.*

Ah, but you don't know what you're up against, my darling girl. These women aren't like the ones you've met before – they're unlikely to be swayed by a cute outfit and a disarming smile.

I should know. I had trained them that way.

6

#Moda #homesweethome #FashMumreturns

Helena, Celeste and Robbie. My three bitches, as I affectionately liked to call them. All lean, mean fighting machines who knew how to work a killer smile and a Target designer rip-off with equal finesse, and could rattle off sixteen different adjectives for 'beige' without breaking a sweat. Graduates of the Ally Bloom School of PR, they had the three pillars of any successful press campaign etched into their DNA:

1. Get the journalist so spectacularly drunk you can capture them in a compromising position on your phone camera.
2. Play the part of the trusted confidante so well the journalist forgets you're the enemy and reveals the sordid details of their relationship, which usually involves no sex, weird sex, or sex with the wrong person – i.e. not them.
3. If all else fails and the journo is a teetotaller or celibate or a complete and utter bore in some other way, ply them with free stuff. I'm yet to meet anyone, living or dead, who can resist a freebie.

As I'd explained to them time and time again, it didn't matter which of these routes you chose, at the end of the day it was all about results, which in our case meant guaranteed coverage for whatever shite Alejandro decided to put out that season, no principles of good taste raised, no questions asked.

My heart started hammering against my chest as all the familiar landmarks of my old life came into view: my favourite Italian coffee shop, where the cappuccinos were a tad on the watery side but the hunky little macchiatos serving them more than made up for it; the tree I'd thrown up under after the '09 resort-wear launch; and the dodgy bit of pavement, where I'd snapped off not one but two heels of a very expensive pair of stilettoed Miu Miu sandals. I still missed those sandals.

'You can stop here,' I said to the driver as we approached a double-fronted terrace painted an oh-so-subtle shade of Berocca orange (which, by pure synchronicity, was both the colour of the season and Alejandro's favourite hangover cure). 'This is it.'

And it was. I was finally home.

Moda's head office was located on a leafy inner-city street where all the offices looked more like houses. Which, of course, they once had been. It was the sort of house that – back in his Alan days, when he'd still thought a polyester zoot suit was a good look for a Saturday night – Alejandro had probably stood outside, drooling, thinking 'One day . . .'

Well, lucky for him, that day had come, and so here we all were.

The wholesale showroom and Alejandro's design studio took up the downstairs living areas of the house – glorious, light-filled spaces with arched doorways, etched panelling on the walls, and floor-to-ceiling windows framed with timber shutters.

The press office was located upstairs in three large, interconnecting bedrooms – less obviously grand, but perfectly suited to me and my bitches.

Journalists were swept up the grand staircase into the master bedroom – now the press showroom – where the key picks from Moda's latest fashion and accessories lines were laid out and lit to their best advantage. If an editor from one of the big four – *Vogue, Elle, Marie Claire* or *Harper's Bazaar* – was coming in, we might even hire a model to do a mini fashion-show up and down the hallway, before whisking them off for lunch. (The editors, that is, not the models. Not that the distinction mattered: neither ever ate.)

The bitches' desks occupied bedroom two, and my office was in the third.

Shoving the great orange front door open with one hand and balancing Coco's buggy precariously on the top step with the other, I looked into this world that was so familiar to me and yet suddenly seemed so foreign.

I stood in the entrance hall, listening to the sound of phones ringing and people chattering and barking instructions at each other. I remembered the way I used to storm through this hallway and run up those stairs, always on a mission, always right up against some seemingly life-or-death deadline. How was it I'd never noticed that the pictures lining the wall of a smiling Alejandro receiving his various fashion accolades were all just a little bit off-kilter? Or that the towering orchid on the console was, in fact, a nasty fake?

But now wasn't the time for introspection – I had a job to do. I hauled myself backwards up the stairs to the press office as best I could in my bondage dress, with Coco and her buggy in one hand and the stupid damn car seat in the other. Nobody even noticed when I landed arse over tit in the doorway; they were too busy playing out my former life in high definition, complete with very important phone calls and earth-shattering reports on the birth or death of stud detailing.

'Uguloo!' Coco screeched at the top of her voice, causing Helena, Celeste and Robbie to drop what they were doing and spin our way as though a couple of aliens had landed in their midst. From the looks on their faces, it was clear they'd completely forgotten we were coming in.

But they were nothing if not professional. Baffled looks were swiftly replaced by rapturous expressions of joy and affection, kisses and hugs.

'Oh my God, you look amaaaazing!' drawled Celeste. Eyeing my belly, she continued: 'You're not . . . you know, *again?*'

'God, no, just a big breakfast.' Damn that optical illusion dress and its false promises.

'You've gotta try Spanx, they're a lifesaver.' She turned her attention to Coco. 'Oh. My. God. Get off the bus. She's the most beautiful thing I've ever seen.' Love at first sight was swiftly replaced by confusion: 'But where's the nanny?' she asked, craning behind me as though I had the hired help cunningly tucked up the back of my dress (dear God, as if they would fit!).

'I don't believe in them,' I declared. 'I'm hands-on with Coco all the way, and I'm happier and more fulfilled than I've ever been in my entire life.' Because rule number four of any successful press campaign: reality is what you choose it to be.

There were sharp intakes of breath and startled gasps; and the word 'heroic' might even have been thrown my way.

Basking in the glow of my own fabulousness, I glanced around for my soon-to-be-out-of-a-job replacement. 'Where's Lola?' I poked my head through the door to my office. All the press clippings I'd lovingly collected over the past six years and pinned above my desk had been replaced by selfies of Lola on a bike, Lola on the beach, Lola sipping a mojito, and Lola on a bike on the beach sipping a mojito (which, as a mother, I have to say looked incredibly irresponsible), interspersed with a few torn-out recipes for gluten-free salads. Ugh. They'd be the first things to go.

'She's in with Alejandro,' said Robbie. 'They're usually a while.'

'Ah, I see,' I said, not seeing at all. Where in her job description had I put 'have lengthy meetings with the boss'?

Celeste grabbed my arm. 'Forget that, Ally. I desperately need your help.' Now this felt more like it. 'Alejandro wants to take Colin out tonight to celebrate their three-month anniversary. He wants us to book somewhere – quote, unquote – ridiculously hot and completely impossible to get into.'

I quickly rearranged my expression into one that suggested I knew who Colin was. When I'd left, Alejandro had been dating a gorgeous young dancer from the National Ballet, who'd recently hightailed it out of Ukraine. Marvellous calves. But then again, nine months is a long time in the life of a hot and happening fashion designer, and I guess that even enviable calf muscles aren't always enough to keep the romance alive forever. I racked my brain for the names of some of the fashionable restaurants I used to book for Alejandro and Konstantinos, but found it impossible to think beyond the only two food joints I'd visited recently: the Hog's Breath Cafe and Big Papa's Pizza.

Finally, it came to me. 'Basilico,' I said. 'It's perfect. There'll be no tables free until next June, of course, but Bobbi, the maître d', owes me a few favours. I'll give him a call –'

'Basilico? You must be joking!' Lola guffawed as she strutted into the room. I guess the meeting was over. 'The only people who go there are Z-listers from *Big Brother* and old people who don't know any better. I'll get him a reservation at Lupus.'

'Lupus. Isn't that a disease?' I said.

'It's the hottest new restaurant in Surry Hills.'

'And pretty much impossible to get into,' Robbie added.

'But I thought you'd know that, Ally,' said Lola, sweet as pie. 'You look great, by the way. I love that you're still doing optical illusions – they're almost vintage now, aren't they? And Coco's just the cutest. Is that a little monobrow I can see?'

Ouch.

What had happened to the blubbering waste of space who couldn't find her own nose to pick without fifteen phone calls to me? And had she just inferred I was old?

'I wish I could join you guys for lunch but I've got an appointment with Flora,' simpered Lola.

Flora. My Flora, who was more intimately acquainted with the internal workings of my body and mind – quite literally – than any other person on the face of the planet. (Well she used to be, at least. Before

I lost her precious wedding gift, that is, and then grew my very own hair forest and felt too embarrassed to face up to her. Even the closest of friends have their limitations.)

This was it. The time had come. Positioning myself in front of the nearest thing to a black wall I could find – a rack of navy-blue feather-trimmed poly-cotton kaftans – I raised myself up to my full five-foot-three inches and unleashed a corker of my own. 'Guess what? I'm coming back to work!'

Ha. 'Old people' that one, Lola.

'Really? That's wonderful! It's been hell without you! We need you!' Helena, Celeste and Robbie cried in unison.

There were hugs and kisses all round, even from Lola. Didn't she get it? This meant she was out of a job, out on the street. Man, this chick was dumber than I thought.

'So, have you told Alejandro?' asked Lola sweetly.

I leaned over my – sorry, *her* – desk, plucked a recipe for gluten-free almond biscotti off the pinboard and attempted to feign some sort of vague interest in it. 'Not yet, but I know he'll be thrilled.'

Alejandro loved me. He called me his 'little piranha', only, in his faux-Eurotrash accent, it sounded more like 'little pariah'. When I'd told him I was leaving to have a baby he'd cried real tears and tried to convince me to leave Coco in a mountain-top yurt to be raised by monks and then collect her again at eighteen. 'Because let's face it, before that they're not even interesting.'

Much as I loved and adored Coco, I couldn't deny that he had a fair point.

I popped Coco into Robbie's startled arms ('But what do I do with her?!' he cried: words reminiscent of ones I'd uttered myself in the moments after giving birth), and set off downstairs to Alejandro's studio.

I rapped on the door. No answer. I knocked again. Still nothing.

After a few minutes of standing there jiggling from side to side in an effort to get the blood flowing in my Lycra-strangulated thighs,

I opened the door a crack and peeped through. Alejandro, resplendent in what could best be described as a matador's outfit, all high-waisted leather breeches and skin-tight satin shirt, was waving his tailoring shears at his pattern cutter, Sally – better known around these parts as 'Poor Old Sally', the invisible mastermind behind all of Alejandro's best work, who got all the headaches and none of the glory. The shears were perilously close to the tip of Sally's nose but, to her credit, she didn't budge. Even to someone who hadn't set foot in an office for nine months, it was clear this meeting wasn't going well.

The object of Alejandro's fury hung before them on a tailor's dummy – a wisp of fuchsia silk held together at the shoulder with an oversized safety pin. I couldn't help but be reminded of the dress-up outfit I'd seen little Crystabella prance around in at Happy Mummies.

I crept in and the heavy door shut behind me with a bang. Alejandro turned my way, and Sally threw me a grateful smile, before taking the opportunity to make a run for it.

In a flash, all anger was forgotten. Alejandro took me warmly in his arms and spun me around like Cinderella at the grand ball. 'Look at you, beautiful mama!'

After all the air kisses and exclamations about how fabulous I looked were out of the way, he got serious. 'You have to tell me what it's like.'

'What's what like?'

'Parenthood. Colin wants to try for a baby,' he said.

'It's great,' I lied. 'Particularly the way you'd do it, with the yurt and the monks and all.'

'Oh, that. I'd never do any of that,' he said, waving the thought away with a flick of a well-manicured hand. 'I'd want the spawn of my loins to be by my side at all times. Well, not when I'm working or socialising or on holiday or anything. But you know what I mean.'

'I do.'

He reached under his desk to the little bar fridge that housed his emergency stash of champagne – kept on permanent standby for moments of stress, boredom, excessive heat or occasionally, as in this case, happiness – and handed me a chilled glass. He popped open a bottle with expert ease. The wonderfully familiar sound of it was like music to my ears.

'Please tell me you don't love playing the hausfrau too much though,' he said. 'The girls are floundering without you. We all are. We need you far more than that little baby could ever need you. When, when, when are you coming back?'

'As soon as you want me,' I replied.

'Are you serious?' he gasped, accompanied by a full theatrical hand-on-heart backwards stagger as though he'd just been told he'd won the lottery.

'Yep, I think it's time.'

'A toast then,' he said, raising his glass. 'To the return of my little pariah!'

We clinked glasses, and it all felt completely fabulous. I was officially back where I belonged. Soon Judy and the skundies and those horrible, hairy Happy Mummies would be nothing more than a distant memory.

'Of course there've been a few changes while you've been away.'

Not quite so fabulous. 'What kind of changes?'

'Well, we've jigged things around a bit. The digital division now oversees press. It just makes more sense, what with most of our coverage now being in the online space. Bloggers the new rock-stars and all that.' He sniggered at his own finger-on-the-pulse-ness.

'What digital division?'

'The one that handles our website, online ordering, that sort of thing,' he said casually.

'And who runs that?'

'Lola.'

A little bit of champagne may have squirted out my nose at that point.

'Please tell me you're joking.'

'I'm deadly serious,' he replied. 'The girl's a genius; you were such a superstar to find her. She's set up our Twitter account, Facebook, Instagram, the whole works . . . and I even do a weekly blog – you really should check it out, it's hilarious. I write the whole thing under the guise of Enzo – Lola's idea of course. It's a hoot, already has quite the following.'

Digital division? Facebook? Alejandro writing a blog as his *spoodle*? Where the fuck had all of that been in Lola's job description?

'So you're telling me if I come back to work Lola will be my boss?' I stammered.

At least he had the good grace to squirm a bit. 'In a manner of speaking.'

'But she's a complete imbecile!' I spat out before I had time to think. 'That's the whole point of her!'

'No darling,' he purred. 'She's a digital specialist.'

'Isn't that the same thing?'

'Look, sweetie, you and I are of a different generation. None of these things even existed in our day. Twittering, tweeting, twooting . . . how could we possibly expect to keep up? But you can learn an awful lot from Lola.'

On the inside, I hollered, cursed, stood my ground and told Alejandro and Lola to shove their digital love affair up their arses.

On the outside, I stood dumbstruck, like a weak, pathetic rabbit gazing into the headlights of an oncoming car and waiting to be splattered all over the road.

How was this even happening? I thought of the countless nights I'd spent on my hands and knees in this very room, stuffing press releases and jewel-encrusted handcuffs (don't ask) into hundreds of press packs till two in the morning. I thought of the hours of agonising small talk I'd had to make with journalists too strung out to even look me in the eye, and the kidney I'm pretty sure I promised to an editor just for putting Alejandro's hideous neon quilted clutch bag circa 2011 on the front cover of her magazine. And now I was being cast aside for a 22-year-old who couldn't even spell *Vogue*, let alone secure coverage in it?

I took a glug of champagne. It felt warm and flat in my mouth. I set it down on Alejandro's antique mahogany desk, deliberately ignoring the coaster he pushed my way.

'I can't.' The words were so quiet even I could barely make them out.

'What's that?' Alejandro asked.

'You're going to have to find yourself a new pariah. Looks like you already have.'

He opened his mouth to speak and then closed it again. He wasn't even going to try to stop me. I hated myself for it, but I still gave him a beat to try.

Nada.

I began to hobble out of the room. Then it occurred to me – no, it didn't have to be like this.

I turned back to Alejandro's desk and grabbed the gigantic scissors. They were heavy in my hand, and the gold on the huge blades glinted in the sunlight that streamed through the floor-to-ceiling windows. The colour drained from Alejandro's face, and for a second I saw what he would actually look like if half of it wasn't pinned back somewhere behind his ears.

I carefully separated the blades, bent over, and cut a six-inch slit from the hem of my dress to mid-thigh.

The relief was instant. Fat oozed out of unmentionable places, cellulite sprang back to its rightful position, and the tiny part of me that wasn't metaphorically lying prostrate on the floor in a pool of blood and guts felt liberated.

Alejandro stared back at me, mouth open, champagne glass poised in mid-air, a look of repulsion mixed with relief on his face.

It was time to go.

Taking two steps at a time, I stormed back upstairs where Helena, Celeste and Robbie were all gathered around Coco.

'I love it – no thigh gap anxiety here. This chick will consume anything in sight – cold coffee, last night's leftover sushi – here, check it out!' trilled Robbie as he dangled something over Coco's head. My God, was that bubble wrap? Coco gazed up at him silently. 'Well she was chowing down on the whole lot a second ago,' he said sulkily before flinging the bubble wrap into the bin.

I said nothing, but scooped up Coco, the buggy, the car seat and her coterie of luggage as quickly as I could before I erupted into a flood of tears. The slit in my dress was taking on a life of its own, and was now up somewhere near my undies. The Moda team eyeballed it in collective horror, but no-one said a word.

So this is it, I thought. *This is how life officially ends for one half of Sydney's most lovalicious power couple. The most important half at that.*

All the while, Lola smirked away at me from behind her/my desk. 'So how did it go?'

As if she didn't already know. 'I want my press clippings back,' I said.

She pulled open the bottom drawer of the desk, and thrust a pile of tattered sheets into my hands. 'All that old stuff was just cluttering up the office anyway.'

Yep, I could see that now.

I stood before her, legs defiantly apart, double Spanx no doubt on full display, racking my mind for something cutting to say, words so powerful she'd remember them as she took her last breath.

Nothing.

'Before you go, did you get the Taylor bag back from Trish like you promised? Or did you let her go with a "special arrangement"?' she asked with a snigger.

I thought of the countless fools I'd put neatly back into their places over the years with perfect, biting retorts. The satisfying feeling of knowing you've cut some little shit right back down to where they belong. Of all the times in my life, why were my words failing me now?

And then, just like that, Coco projectile-vomited tuna sashimi all over Lola's desk. Lola took on the glassy-eyed look of someone about to faint.

That's my girl. Frida Kahlo she may be, but at least she had my back.

7

#fuckthenipplecovers
#lifeofficiallyover #where'smyPlanB?

Had what I thought just happened actually happened?

After twenty minutes on the kerb outside Moda, we finally hailed a cab and I slumped despondently in my seat. Coco spent the entire journey expressing every emotion I was feeling – she was a hysterical, squalling mess who made her misery known all the way across the Harbour Bridge, along the highway and through the suburban backstreets to our front door. The taxi driver snatched a hefty tip from my hand, executed the fastest three-point turn known to man, and sped off.

Before I'd even made it to the front door, my phone pinged.

Emergency. Can't find the nipple covers. Any ideas? xx Lola

I hit delete.

Today was meant to be my return to glory. How the hell had it come to this? And more importantly, what the hell was I supposed to do with the rest of my life now?

I dumped all the travelling gear in a heap in the hallway and dragged Coco into the living room.

We found Judy on a ladder, attacking the top of our roman blinds.

'You've got no idea what I've discovered up here – there's a whole permaculture growing right above your heads,' she said, flushed with the thrill of it. 'Oh and I almost forgot,' she added, beginning to make a wobbly descent. 'You had a call today – some lady named Nikki. Apparently it's a bit of a tradition that every new mum hosts an at-home coffee morning. She said they've put you down for the twenty-first.'

'Huh?' Who on earth was Nikki?

Oh God, doggy-smelling Jumper, Velcro sandals, nauseating, bossy field-marshal voice. Happy Mummies – Mother Superior. That Nikki.

'What, here?!' I spluttered, looking around my gorgeous living room, with its chic, pared-back lines and sumptuous velvet upholstery. I pictured it overrun with hordes of screaming children and women who wouldn't know the difference between Charles Eames and Mies van der Rohe if they both turned up and smacked them in the face.

'She said catering for the core group of six, plus an extra four or so drop-ins, should be fine, not including the kids. And don't forget that Archie has a tree-nut allergy and on no account should Bree be offered carbs – apparently they do dreadful things to her.'

So, there you had it. This was my life now.

I popped a grizzly Coco on her playmat and forced myself to look around for something to settle her. Ten minutes later, I was all out of ideas. She'd pushed away the slices of fruit and cheese cut paper-thin just the way she liked them and the stash of choc-coated Tiny Teddys I kept on hand for emergency moments like these. Not even Dora and Boots and the fabulous multitasking purple backpack on TV could weave their magic today. I jiggled her around on my hip, trying to distract her with anything I could lay my hands on, when all I really wanted was to curl up in a ball and see out the remainder of my living days under my duvet.

Judy, watching this pathetic display of motherly incompetence, came and took Coco from my arms.

I didn't even bother trying to resist.

'Did you have a lovely time? Go somewhere nice for lunch?' she asked, as though I'd been whipping up frosted cupcakes at a girl scouts' meeting and not finding out my whole career had been hacked to pieces by an evil little ho.

'Nowhere special,' I replied, heading back in to the kitchen to find some food. This morning's bloodbath hadn't, unfortunately, done much to quell my appetite. I concocted a squishy tomato, a couple of slices of stale bread and a wedge of cheddar into a toastie, while trying to ignore the fact that Coco seemed considerably chirpier in Judy's arms than she had been in mine a few moments ago.

Judy eyed me and the tomato quizzically while Coco happily pulled at one of her dangly earrings.

'Are you okay with her for a bit?' I asked.

Judy nodded and I headed upstairs.

I peeled the remains of the disaster dress from my body like soggy bits of cling film and then sat on the edge of the bed in my bra and Spanx, watching myself in the mirror opposite as I munched on the toastie. The words 'pig' and 'trough' came to mind.

God, if this is what I looked like eating, no wonder they were so keen to replace me.

Unemployed.

Unemployable.

Old.

Me and Coco – and, let's face it, since I was so damn incompetent, probably Judy too – at home together, all day every day, for the next eighteen years.

One hot, fat tear followed by another sploshed down onto my empty plate. Judy was right; they were all right. Who was I kidding? I couldn't do it all. I couldn't do even one teeny tiny crumb of it all. I'd passed my sell-by date at work, couldn't settle my own child, and didn't even know what to talk to my own husband about over dinner. I was crap at this whole motherhood thing and always would be.

Worst of all, now all I had left was Happy Mummies.

But then as I sat there, eye to eye with this broken, bloated version of myself, something shifted.

Well, fuck it. If that was how things stood, I'd do what I'd always done at Moda: make the most of whatever shit sandwich was served up to me. Okay, fine. Plan A: Return to Work might not have been a success. It was time to make a Plan B – and I would make damn sure this one kicked arse.

I would stay at home with Coco and become a fully signed-up member of the permanent SAHM brigade. I would commit to being the perfect wife and mother, and do whatever it took to find the Ally that Matt had fallen in love with – because under all the flab and resentment and food-stained tracksuits, I was pretty sure she was still in there somewhere. And in the process I would help Matt see his way back to being the man I'd fallen in love with too.

Rather than fleeing the skundies, it was time to face them head-on.

*

I decided to tell Matt everything later that evening when he got home from work. It was a delicate operation that required careful handling; above all, it was vital to get him to see the positives in the situation. (Okay, fine, we might have suddenly morphed into a single-income household with three mouths to feed, but really, we weren't likely to starve or be forced to read by candlelight or wash our clothes in the river. And just think of all the money we'd save on shoes!) I had it all planned: Coco would be asleep, Judy would be off somewhere watching one of the trashy Harlequin made-for-TV movies she loved so much, a delicious dinner would be bubbling away on the stove, and I would soften the blow with the very nice bottle of merlot I'd picked up this afternoon.

Great plan, in theory. In reality, when Matt walked in Judy was still faffing around the kitchen, rifling through every drawer in sight in search of the sewing kit she was convinced we owned because apparently 'every house has a sewing kit' and she point-blank refused to hear otherwise; Coco was grizzly and clinging to my leg like a limpet; and a delicious dinner had not been made.

'Why is the fridge full of kale?' Matt asked, reaching into its depths for a beer and releasing a mini-avalanche of leafy greens. He stepped back to a safe distance, holding the door open with his fingertips as though the vegies were about to jump right out and attack him.

God, did no-one in this house ever listen to a word I said? 'Because there's a worldwide crisis going on, and soon there will be none left.'

He looked unconvinced. 'But we never eat kale.'

'Yes, but it's very good for you. We don't want to be deprived of the option, do we, should we suddenly decide we want it?' I sighed. 'You really should watch more news and less footy if you want to keep up.'

'Ally, I couldn't keep up with you if I tried,' he said, kissing the top of my head.

I gazed up at him mournfully. 'I had great intentions of cooking you a wonderful meal tonight, Matt, but plans came unstuck somewhere along the way. So what do you feel like? Pretty sure I've got some fish fingers back there somewhere.'

'I think I'd rather eat the kale. Take-out?'

'Fine, just as long as it's not another tikka masala,' I said.

'Roger that. Let's go Thai.'

Judy piped up. 'Oh no, not Thai. It gives me the most awful constipation. Comes out like those little hard raisins you find in French recipes sometimes.'

'Craisins,' said Matt, helpfully. And just like that my appetite for pad thai vanished – now and forever more.

In the end, we settled for a slightly fuzzy round of camembert and some kalamata olives we found languishing behind the kale. We ate them around the kitchen table, me bouncing Coco on my knee, and Judy single-handedly working her way through the $42-dollar bottle of merlot I'd been planning to enjoy with Matt.

'A top up, dear?' she asked, tipping her empty glass towards Matt. 'I don't know what this is, but it goes down a treat.'

Yep, so I'd heard.

After the bottle had been emptied and the camembert demolished, I took Coco back upstairs and had another crack at getting her off to sleep.

Matt popped his head in several times. 'Let me have a shot – you go back down.'

No way. The new me would stand on my own two feet with this child if it killed me.

I rocked, I read to her, I cuddled . . . hell, I even sang . . . but every time my poor girl lay her head down to sleep, a nanosecond later she was up again, screaming.

Eventually, after an hour and a half of me lying on the floor beside her cot and rubbing her belly through the bars, she gave in to her exhaustion.

I dragged my now half-dead arm back downstairs and found Matt and Judy curled up asleep together on the sofa while some wretched documentary about a wife attacking her husband with a hedge trimmer (she had a new baby – go figure) played out on the TV.

I had to tell him – it was now or never. I switched off the television and gave his shoulder a shake. 'Wake up, I need to talk to you.'

'What? Is it Coco?' he asked, a look of panic flashing across his face.

I knew exactly what he'd say: 'We've got bills to pay and a mortgage; we need two jobs. Besides, you wouldn't be happy staying at home every day; it's not you.' Translation: 'You haven't got what it takes.'

Matt was still looking at me, waiting for me to tell him whatever it was that was so important. My mouth was dry. God, why was this so hard?

'It's nothing,' I said. 'Let's just go to bed – we'll talk about it tomorrow.'

According to my phone, it was 2.32 in the morning. Coco was scream-ing blue murder in her cot, and any second now I fully expected the police or DoCS – or, at the very least, the nasty neighbours with the overgrown lawn – to start hammering on the door. Matt and I rushed to her side – a well-trained team when the shit hit the fan – to find our baby girl scarlet in the face and drenched in sweat. She looked terrified. I didn't have to reach for the thermometer; I knew she was burning up.

We squirted a hefty dose of Panadol into her mouth and took turns cuddling her while we waited for it to kick in.

Fifteen minutes later, she was still hot and hysterical. Time for the back-up plan. Matt ran a tepid bath and I got in, laying Coco's slippery little body across my belly, just like I'd done when she was a fractious newborn. Matt perched beside us on the tiles, dribbling cool water onto her back with a face cloth.

After a few minutes the crying grew softer.

'Do you think it's her ears again?' whispered Matt.

'I quit my job.'

'You what?' he said, a little louder this time.

'Well, I didn't exactly quit. It's probably more accurate to say the situation at work became untenable and we decided to part ways by mutual consent.'

'You *quit your job?*'

'Untenable.'

'God, Ally, this is not the time to be looking for another job. What with the economic climate –'

'I didn't say I wanted to look for another one.'

He took a moment to digest my words. 'But what will you do? You hate being stuck here at home.'

'I'm going to do what generations of women have done before me,' I said. 'I'm going to be a mother. And a wife. And I'm going to do both jobs extremely well –' He cocked an eyebrow. 'I know what you're thinking, but you're wrong. Look at Coco tonight – it's pretty clear she needs her mother at home, not stuck in the office until ten o'clock every night.'

'We haven't even talked about this,' he said.

'We're talking about it now.'

'But you've already quit. It's a bit late to start a conversation. For God's sake, Ally, we've got a mortgage . . . a certain lifestyle. Not to mention a very expensive Balinese wedding to pay off –'

'Then we'll have to change our lifestyle and, my *God*, don't you just love reminding me at every single opportunity how much the wedding cost? We'll be there in the old people's home, rolling down the halls on our Zimmer frames, and you'll still be banging on about it. Well, let me remind you, mister – you were there too!'

He was doing that thing with his face he does when he tries not to get riled up, only this time it didn't seem to be working too well for him. His next words came out cool as ice. 'You hate other mothers, you hate mothers' group, you hate *my* mother. What on earth makes you think you'd enjoy being a stay-at-home mum?'

'Now that's unfair. I never said I hated your mother. Not in actual words.'

Blah, blah, words, words.

He droned on and on, and I zoned out somewhere around 'ever-increasing insurance premiums'.

Fine, in theory this whole thing might seem a little impulsive, stupid even, but I wasn't going into it half-arsed. I had a plan, for God's sake – in my head at least – and I was fairly confident that if I stuck to it diligently not only would I have the other mums eating out of my hand, but pretty soon Matt and I would be well on our way to marital harmony: something I would have been happy to explain if he'd let me get a word in edgeways.

I pulled Coco's slippery, dozing body in closer to mine and watched Matt as if from a distance as he reeled off the million and one very rational reasons why this was a completely bonkers idea.

I stroked the tufty little curls on the back of Coco's head and breathed in her irresistible baby scent.

Couldn't he see it wasn't just Coco who needed this, but *us* too? This might be our one and only shot to make things right.

8

#HappyMummies #MasterPlan #PerfectMother

If I was going to do this thing, I'd give it the same killer focus I gave every one of Moda's advertising campaigns. So I wrote my master plan down, in black and white, to keep me firmly on track.

1. **Behave like a proper mother:** Talk, read, sing to Coco, or just generally interact with her. Minimum 15 minutes per day.

2. **Adopt the Happy Mummies uniform:** nothing black, nothing tight, nothing current season – or even last season – preferably homespun or second-hand (not vintage: they are quite different things).

3. **Embrace inner earth mama:** Weave, bake, plant fragrant herb path or veggie patch, and Insta everything as I go along. Use tag #soblessed at least once per day.

4. **Social media:** Replace current style apps with links to popular mummy blogs from around the world for 24/7 feed of badly dressed mums grappling with life-or-death decisions like 'buckwheat bagel or brioche?' and 'what's the fat

count in a skinny macchiato?' While I'm at it, join the stupid Facebook group the Happy Mummies are all so excited about (group name: Happy Mummies Rock! Need I say more?).

5. **Learn to cook:** Buy multi cooker, yogurt maker and one of those dehydrating thingamajigs (also perfect opportunity to use up bountiful produce resulting from point 3 above).

6. **Invest in appropriate SAHM bling:** in-car basket to hold assortment of educational toys and books so Coco can boost her learning potential while we're at the traffic lights; baby backpack for weekends of hearty mountain-hiking; and some of those annoying stickers for the back of the car that show every member of the family as stick people (dread to think what my stick person would look like – Mummy lying prostrate on the floor with an empty wine glass in hand?).

7. **Family PR campaign:** Organise one of those tacky family photo shoots and line every wall of the house with super-sized canvases of Matt, Coco and I in Photoshopped perfection, cuddling/laughing/having the time of our lives. Turn self-same pictures into nifty mugs, key rings and tea towels, and give them to our friends and families as Christmas presents. Vom.

8. **Develop unhealthy fixation with Coco's future:** Track down Sanskrit, advanced computer programming and tai chi classes for toddlers. And enrol Coco in the most expensive private school I can find. The fact she'll never actually go is a moot point – the $1500 deposit for the opportunity to brag over coffee is a bargain.

9. **Tupperware parties:** Accept that they still exist and that people still hold random gatherings with the express purpose of making you fork out money for things you know you'll never want or use. Commit to going at least once.

10. **Health kick:**

~~Caffeine~~ → dandelion tea

~~Full-fat straight-from-the-cow's udder milk~~ → soy milk

~~Sweet chilli chips and onion dip~~ → edamame

~~Cheese toastie~~ → quinoa

As Sun Tzu – or was it Chairman Mao? – said: every battle is won long before it's fought.

9

#SAHMDay1
#HappyMummies #chickenpoxparties
#fistfights #whatnow?

This was it. The first official day of my new life as a permanent SAHM.

So far, so good. Matt had gone off to work with only a minimum amount of grumbling about rising living costs and the impossibility of surviving on a single salary in one of the most expensive cities in the world. Judy, meanwhile, had signed herself up to do an internet training course for the blue-rinse brigade, up at the local community centre. 'Might as well make the most of my time while I'm here,' she'd said, loading up her David Jones shopper with pens, paper and a fistful of Earl Grey tea bags. 'But don't worry, I'll still be coming to playgroup tomorrow!' Yippee.

Which just left me and Coco.

I logged on to Facebook to see where the Happy Mummies would be meeting today. From a quick scroll through their posts last night I had gleaned their schedule: playgroup on Tuesdays, coffee shop on Mondays and Wednesdays, park on Thursdays or an indoor play-centre if it rained. On Fridays, you were released from this tortuous regime to get on with your shopping and domestic duties in preparation for a picture-perfect family weekend. It was enough to make me want to shove my shiny new Birkenstock sandals down my throat.

Reading between the sugar-laced comments about what fun they'd had at the local petting zoo and the snapshots of toddlers making milk moustaches with the froth of their babycinos, the message was loud and clear: break ranks and fly solo on your 'group days' – barring a very good reason such as a doctor's / hair / personal training appointment – was akin to desertion and ran the risk of exclusion from the group forever.

To the (large) non-joiner part of me, permanent exclusion sounded perfectly fine. Better than fine, actually. But, I forced myself to remember the bigger picture here: my lack of gainful employment and general purpose in life. Happy Mummies it was.

Today they were meeting at Pecorinos, a coffee shop in Turramurra I'd never heard of, but which was apparently famed for its fat-free oat-bran muffins and tolerance for large and destructive groups of under-fives.

As with everything the Happy Mummies did, the plan had been arranged with military precision. They'd meet at nine twenty-five – just after the older ones had been dropped off at school – and then finish at eleven, in time for the little ones to have lunch and go down for their afternoon nap. Everyone was to pitch in ten dollars to cover the cost of lattes, oat-bran muffins and a little something for the kids. Just the thought of it made me want to cut loose and order a full-scale builder's breakfast with a side of full-fat muffins. I wondered if Mama Superior et al. would post pics of that on their stupid Facebook page?

Parking was a nightmare, as I should have known it would be, every spot occupied by gigantic four-wheel drives with 'Slow Down! Baby on Board!' signs splashed across the windows.

By the time Coco and I had found a spot and reached Pecorinos, it was pushing ten.

As a group, the Happy Mummies were hard to miss, swallowing up the entire back half of the café, where they'd pushed together several tables for two and four to create one huge long table for about twenty-five.

Kids were crawling under chairs and abseiling off walls. All the while, their mothers ignored them with the ease of seasoned professionals and carried on chatting calmly to each other over their hot drinks. I couldn't help but notice that every table in the immediate perimeter around the Happy Mummies was empty. It was as if they were radiating some sort of lethal gamma rays: anyone who valued their life, or at the very least their sanity, was keeping a very safe distance.

'Ally, I didn't know you'd be joining us today. How lovely!' said Nikki, when she spotted me, looking like it was anything but lovely.

'Well, I've given up my job, so I've got a little more time on my hands.' Why did I feel the need to give her an explanation? Tolerance and openness were supposed to be the mantra of the Happy Mummies, or so their Facebook header proudly proclaimed.

But the response to my admission made it worth it. I felt a subtle shift in the atmosphere, like the doors of some inner sanctum were being cranked open a few inches, just wide enough to let me squeeze through.

There was much gushing about what a wonderful decision I'd made, how Coco would thank me for it when she was a rich, famous and completely emotionally centred heart surgeon / industry leader / saviour of the world, and how disgusting it was that so few working mothers put their children's needs before their own.

'Devoting yourself to Coco at this very precious time in her life – don't you just feel so blessed?' gushed Organic Spelt Mama One (Harriet), all drippy condescension. Ugh.

Smug Mummy (Lisa) gave me the once-over from across the table, taking in my daggy elasticated pants and zip-up hoodie. 'You even look different,' she said.

'Yep, I decided if I'm doing the SAHM thing on a full-time basis, I better do a little shopping,' I replied. She nodded approvingly. Yes, sirree, never underestimate the power of a good uniform.

Lycra Mum (Bree) pulled a chair from the next table over for me with about as much enthusiasm as she'd have if I were here to pull her wisdom teeth. She shifted her own chair aside a couple of millimetres so I could squeeze half a thigh into the gap. She then pulled out a packet of antibacterial wipes and proceeded to wipe down every surface, implement, man, woman and child in the near vicinity. By the looks of it, no-one else found this odd.

The waitress took my coffee order, as Nikki leaned across the table and pointed out a Happy Mummy I hadn't met yet. 'This is Sharon. She's just come back from overseas.'

'We've been trekking Machu Picchu,' she informed me. 'You can read all about it on my blog.' Hmmm. 'Well, it's nice to meet you, Sharon,' I said.

'Sharron. It rhymes with "bomb",' she corrected sweetly, telling me absolutely everything I needed to know about her.

This being very much a reconnaissance mission, I didn't say much for a while, just let myself sit back and take it all in. No-one seemed to mind: they carried on talking like I wasn't even there. They spoke a secret language all their own, these women, peppered with mind-boggling jargon and abbreviations artfully designed to keep any interlopers like me from understanding – 'Ashleigh's got her NAPLANs coming up in two weeks'; 'Did you hear the Foster boy made it into the OC?'; 'Has anyone got the name of a good ENT I can take Freddy to?'; 'Are you all coming to my PDP next week?'

After a while I couldn't take it anymore and decided it was time to introduce some abbreviations of my own and ask the question every self-respecting SAHM fears. 'So, what did you lot do before you had kids?' Ah yes, the dreaded 'LBK' question.

Talk of head lice and who kept shirking their responsibilities at canteen duty ground to a halt, and I felt an audible chill sweep up the table. Shit. Maybe I'd gone too far.

At first, they were reluctant to spill the beans. They seemed to be wary about saying anything that might suggest their lives pre-children had held any actual discernible value. But, like any discussion among women about money or weight loss or nice clothes, it soon warmed up into a very polite game of one-upmanship.

Organic Spelt Mama Two (Jenna) had been a big-shot entertainment lawyer and spent six years working from a huge corner office in the city overlooking the Harbour Bridge. She'd actually seen Kate and Wills sailing down the harbour at the start of their last Royal Visit, while she'd been at her desk nutting out the finer details of next season's *X Factor* contract. Harriet had been a sports physio for the Socceroos, Lisa published glossy coffee-table books on drop-dead gorgeous homes from around the world, and Bree had once been fat (was that an actual job now?) before she discovered the beauty of the Five and Two Diet. 'On Mondays and Thursdays I fill up on nothing but air.'

Nikki was the quietest of the lot, and it soon became clear why. Turned out she was still working part-time in the same finance role she'd had since before the twins were born, and from the sounds of it, not very happily so.

'Part-time is an absolute joke,' she said. 'Real translation, you work fifty hours a week and get paid for twenty-five.' She gazed into the depths of her empty mug as if it held the answer to everything. 'But one day maybe I'll jack it all in. Once Cameron's photography business is properly up and running, that is.'

I was just about to ask more about this mysterious camera-wielding Cameron when what felt like a hundred hungry, hot-tempered mouths descended on our table. Ah, snack time. Plastic tubs and bibs were duly dug out from bags under the table and little people were popped and strapped into position. Thankfully I'd come prepared. I whipped a shiny pouch of Farmer Joey's Organic Chickin Lickin' Chicken Casserole from my handbag and twenty startled eyes swung in my direction as though I'd just pulled out a bong.

As Sharron forced some sort of lumpy, evil-smelling green goo into the mouth of her lazy-eyed daughter opposite me, I cast around for the waitress to see if she could give Coco's snack a quick zap in the microwave. I grabbed her arm as she walked past: 'Sixty seconds, thirty if your microwave's really zooped-up.'

Nobody said a word, but all eyes were on me. God, why didn't they just come out and say it? 'Not only are you poisoning your child with that over-processed, shop-bought crap (and did we mention the packaging? For the love of God, the polluted environment she'll be left to inherit!), but you're planning to serve it to her freshly nuked from the microwave?!' I may as well have been spoon-feeding her crack from the gutter, judging by their faces. Then again, was I really surprised? These were, after all, the sort of women who minced their own meat because they didn't fully trust the butcher ('When he says one hundred per cent organic, what does that mean exactly? Where's the authentication, hmm?').

I made a mental note: next time decant the damn stuff into biodegradable pawpaw leaves glued together with my own saliva, and roll the whole lot around on the back lawn for a bit of earthy authenticity before serving it up.

As Coco gobbled up every last bit of her Chickin Lickin' Casserole while her peers got busy decorating the floor and walls with their lovingly homemade gunk, as the conversation turned to one of my favourite topics – botox.

'Archie's Little League coach, Marjorie, said she had it done for a –' insert pause for dramatic eyebrow raise designed to cast firm shadow of doubt over Marjorie's credibility – 'sweating problem,' said Harriet.

They all looked suitably aghast.

'Wouldn't have helped anyway,' I offered up. 'She really should have tried Xeomin. Dysport, at a push. Those newer versions are far more effective than traditional, old-school botox.'

There was silence around the table, which I took as my cue to go on. 'I know the absolute best place to go, if any of you are interested. All the news presenters from Seven and Ten go there.'

'You can't be serious,' spluttered Sharron through her latte.

'Well, how else do you think they look so line-free and perfect at six o'clock in the morning?' I asked.

'No, she means the botox. You haven't, have you?' asked Jenna.

Only about five hundred times. Hell, I used to pop into the clinic in my lunch hour and still manage to squeeze in a quick trip to the David Jones shoe department. I explained this, in not quite so many words.

'But what about Coco?' asked Sharron, incredulous.

'I think she's probably still a little young.'

'No, her development,' she said. 'Aren't you worried that if your face can't move she won't be able to read your emotions? However will she learn empathy?'

God, empathy. Was I supposed to be teaching her that too?

I stole a quick glance under the table at Coco to get some clue as to whether her inner emotional life was suffering because of all the shit I'd pumped into my face over the years, and found her upending a box of apple and blackcurrant juice onto the head of one of the snotty-nosed twins, completely oblivious to the fact he was sobbing his nasally challenged little heart out. Oh, shit. It was official. My daughter was The Tin Man.

Then again, was the alternative any better? Surely being forced to look at my wrinkles and furrowed brow day in, day out would result in its own brand of psychological damage?

Nikki ordered a round of oat-bran muffins – a treat for the kids now that they'd finished their healthy morning tea. This confused me. On what planet was oat-bran considered a treat? Nevertheless, Coco took her cue from all the other kids, and dug into her muffin as though it was the first chocolate egg of Easter.

Once hers was gone, Coco tried to pry the muffin from the child next to her (Tin Man, anyone?), who loudly voiced her protest.

This ruckus made it near impossible to eavesdrop on what Nikki and Jenna were saying across the table. I leaned in closer.

'To top it all off, Ashleigh's got chicken pox,' I heard Nikki say with a sigh.

Sharron was all breathy excitement. 'Ooh, can I bring the kids round?'

I'm sorry, was I missing something here?

Lisa caught sight of my confused expression. 'Sharron doesn't vaccinate,' she said, as though that explained everything. My blank look must have told her I was going to need a little more than that. 'Viruses are viewed as a gift in her house – she tries to get them all in as early as possible in order to build up her children's immune systems.'

Wonderful. So no worries about all the pregnant women and tiny babies who could drop dead like flies at any moment from the bug your kid passes on because he's busy building up his immunity the good ol' natural way?

'Sure, come by any time,' said Nikki to Sharron. 'Ashleigh's just lying around the house feeling sorry for herself, trying not to scratch at her spots and ruin her chances of winning *Australia's Next Top Model*. Yep, we're all about aiming high.'

Sharron looked fit to burst. 'Perfect,' she trilled. 'We'll be there straight after school pick-up. I'll bring a poppyseed cake.' Now there's a fair exchange if ever I heard one – one homemade poppyseed cake for a faceful of pox. 'Anyway, must dash. Ruby's got a speech therapy appointment in Gordon this morning.'

'Still the lisp?' asked Jenna.

Sharron shook her head. 'She just can't manage the tones on her Pinyin syllables,' she said with a pained sigh. 'Her Mandarin tutor says it's becoming a real problem.'

Shoot me now. Ruby was still in nappies.

And with that, Sharron dropped ten dollars in coins on the table, threw us a backwards wave and was off.

'Phew, I thought she'd never leave,' said Jenna. 'Now I can tell you all about the party I'm planning. Saturday week. You all have to come. Even you, Ally.'

Gee, thanks. But more importantly, why they hell couldn't Sharron know about it?

'Because of The Incident, of course,' explained Jenna in a hushed tone, before stealing a quick glance at Harriet, who was racing around the room after Archie, pleading with him to return her iPhone. 'There's no way Sharron's husband, Ian, can be in the same room as Harriet's Toby again.'

They all nodded sagely, apparently understanding the potential ramifications of such a thing completely.

I, of course, understood nothing. 'What incident?' I whispered back. At this point I would have offered up Coco's first teeth to know more.

Jenna shifted her chair closer towards me. 'It happened early one Saturday morning in the Woolworths car park –'

'The timing couldn't have been worse,' Lisa threw in with a half-whisper. 'Half the suburb was up there doing their weekend shop. And the story had already spread to the other half by the time we'd reached the front of the checkout queue,' she said, clearly thrilling at the memory.

'And what was "it"? What was The Incident?' Christ alive, this was juicier than the TMZ Twitter feed.

'Fisticuffs,' spat Jenna, all tight-lipped disapproval. 'Ian was parked right next to Toby: such rotten luck. They were both loading up their cars when Ian just threw down his shopping bags and punched Toby clean in the face. What Ian didn't know, of course, was that Toby had been doing Father and Son taekwondo classes with Alexander on Friday nights at the community centre, so he flattened him with a Jumping Axe Kick. It was just awful.'

'Awful,' agreed Lisa, while Bree tut-tutted beside her and attacked the underside of the table with yet another antibacterial wipe.

'But why?' I spluttered. 'Why would they do that?'

'Well, it all started with cupcakes. And the terrible heartburn Sharron suffered throughout her pregnancy with Ruby,' said Jenna.

Cupcakes?

She went on: 'See, Sharron and Harriet had been friends since their Orgasmic Birthing classes, but more recently they'd struggled to find a common ground. They'd tried blogging, Tupperware-ing . . . but none of it took. But Sharron makes these amazing frosted cupcakes, see – peanut butter, fudge, strawberries and cream, you name it, she makes them – and they had this brilliant idea to start selling them to local businesses, all emblazoned with logos and the like. They decided to share the baking duties and go fifty-fifty on the profits. It was a perfect arrangement.'

'Perfect,' said Lisa.

'Problem was, Sharron would never let Harriet near her precious secret recipes. She'd just present her with a bowlful of batter and they'd work from that. Which was fine, until Sharron was laid up with heartburn –'

'Which really was awful,' interjected Lisa.

'Harriet was desperate, left to make five hundred cupcakes a week all by herself. She did the only thing she could think of.' Dramatic pause. 'Boxed kits.' Even the memory of it was enough to make the other mums shudder, evidently. 'She was a practising vegan Buddhist by this point, so the whole thing was naturally very stressful for her.'

Naturally.

'Anyway, to cut a long story short the cupcake business soon dried up, and Sharron accused Harriet of destroying her brand,' said Jenna.

'And Harriet accused Sharron of being a fat lazy cow,' added Lisa. 'Which was hardly very Buddhist. Or particularly vegan, now I come to think of it.'

Jenna continued. 'They stopped speaking. It went on for months. After a while, they agreed to a state of peaceful coexistence. Had to, really. They were in a carpooling arrangement for kindergym and the whole not-speaking thing was proving to be a logistical nightmare. So, we all thought it was water under the bridge and sort of forgot about it. How wrong we were, as we realised that fateful Saturday morning in the Woolies car park.' Man, this woman sure knew how to string out a story. I was on the edge of my seat. 'Worse still, Alexander was in the back of the car and saw the whole thing. He regaled his entire Year 4 class with the story at "News" the following week. It made him a hero at school, of course, but poor Harriet never got over the humiliation.'

'But we never speak of it,' said Jenna.

'Never,' repeated Smug Mummy. And with that, they clamped their lips shut like the true and loyal friends they were.

But there was still a piece missing. 'So . . . the orgasmic births?'

'Didn't happen,' said Jenna, licking Hamish's plastic spoon and fork clean with her tongue and popping them in a zip-lock bag. 'Sharron ended up having a caesarean and Harriet almost carked it in the birthing suite. But they were both beautiful births, nevertheless.'

By now the kids had moved on to a huge stack of menus on the counter, and were shooting them across the floor at the other customers' ankles. The café owner began throwing us dirty looks.

'Come on, guys, time to pay up and push on,' ordered drill sergeant Nikki.

The fun game of 'Break An Old Person's Ankle' was officially called to an end, crotchety toddlers were rounded up, and a few token attempts were made to tidy up the carnage they'd left in their wake.

Just as I was about to head off, Lisa grabbed my arm. 'Tell me you can make it to my PDP next week. Thursday at eleven.'

God, what was it with these women and their abbreviations?

'Yep, sure, PDP,' I said, nodding away like I knew what the hell she was talking about. I racked my brain for clues and suddenly remembered some boring talk around the table about a sales – Tupperware? – party at her place and how we all had to be there. We could bring the kids; she had a sitter. Fine, whatever. 'A girl can never have too much plastic in her pantry, huh?' I said with a cheery wink. 'Consider me in.'

She gave me a funny look. 'Okay, great.'

Multilingual toddlers, fist fights in the supermarket car park, an underground virus trade, and an invite to my first proper grown-up mums and dads dinner party. Not bad for my first day!

10

#perfectmother(not) #hotdaddy #Judyenvy #neversawthatonecoming

In the spirit of my newfound motherly self-sacrifice, I decided to spend the afternoon doing some serious floor time with Coco. I switched off the TV, laptop and iPhone, lined up the My Little Ponies, and artfully arranged the wooden blocks on the shagpile to resemble the sort of cosy and inviting stable our trusty flock of plastic steeds might appreciate. Coco was in simultaneous arm- and leg-jiggling ecstasy.

After approximately three and a half minutes of galloping ponies across the plains of the Ikea rug, feeding them soggy bits of spinach I'd found in the bottom of the fridge, and putting them to nigh-nighs in their stable, I had the overwhelming urge to start tearing every hair on my body out strand by strand. This was swiftly followed by equally overwhelming remorse that I evidently had the staying power of a gnat.

Poor Coco. *What had she done to deserve such a horribly selfish mother?*, I wondered as I packed the ponies and blocks away, switched my phone back on, and popped her in front of a DVD. Surely, I'd hit my stride once she reached a more interesting phase and started getting into clothes and boys and who was banging who on *Rich Kids of Beverly Hills?*

Perhaps I'd be better off demonstrating my unconditional love for Coco in the kitchen.

*

'What's all this?' asked Matt later that evening, as he took in the tantalising aromas of paprika, cream and crushed cardamom pods wafting about the kitchen.

Judy was busy on the laptop at the dining table, trying out all the snazzy new skills she'd picked up at her internet course and showing Coco how she could upload home movies and set up video conferences – all marvellous skills no OAP should be without, clearly.

'It's a sort of Thai beef stroganoff thing,' I said with more than a hint of pride. 'We are now the official owners of a slow cooker.'

'I have absolutely no idea what that is, but it sure smells good.'

'And that's not all,' I said, pulling open the door of the freezer like a game-show hostess to reveal row upon row of neat plastic boxes containing equally tempting treats for the nights ahead. Slow-pulled Sardinian lamb, spaghetti meatballs, chicken a la King . . . you name it, we had it. Who said I couldn't crack this SAHM malarkey?

But now for my pièce de résistance.

'So, one of the Happy Mummies has invited us to dinner on Saturday night,' I announced, brimming with the smugness that comes from social acceptance by one's peers.

Matt's shoulders sagged. 'We don't really have to go, do we?'

'Of course we do. Welcome to the brave new world of the stay-at-home mum. We'll be friendly, socialise with our neighbours –'

'Two words for you, Ally,' he interjected. 'Controlled crying. Our neighbours can't stand us.'

'Okay fine, maybe not those neighbours. But the women at playgroup. You will meet them and their husbands at Jenna's party, and you will play nice.'

'And since when did *you* ever play nice?' he teased. 'It's one of the things I love about you.' He wrapped his arms around me and nuzzled his face into my neck, the smell of paprika and cream mingling between us.

It was the first even remotely flirtatious moment we'd had in what felt like forever. And yet, still I found myself pushing him away. The memory of the skundies burnt too bright.

*

I learnt a lot of things on my third visit to Happy Mummies Time.

I learnt that no matter how many mothers you're hoping to impress with your thrifty ways, Spandex skinny jeans are not something you should buy in a cut-price store unless you're willing to spend the entire morning hoiking them up from somewhere around your ankles. Fifteen per cent Spandex, my arse.

I learnt that Lisa had a recipe for gluten-free flapjacks that was the envy of the entire group but she kept it close to her chest.

I learnt that the Organic Spelt Mamas were planning to wean their children in the next few months, before they started school – a plan that was causing them considerable anguish, but one that would surely come as something of a relief to their children's teacher.

I learnt that telling off someone else's child for throwing sand in your little girl's face was not the done thing.

And – most importantly of all – I learnt that you should never take your witch of a mother-in-law to Happy Mummies Time, or chances are everyone will like her far more than they did you.

The thing was, Judy could speak their language.

'I just can't get Milly to take her medicine. I've tried everything – mixing it with milk, bribing her with one of those atrocious Beanie Boos. Nothing works,' whined Lisa.

Despite not being part of the conversation, Judy didn't hesitate to jump right in: 'Well, have you tried squirting it into a marshmallow?

I know it was a long time ago, but when my kids were small that always worked.'

'Marshmallows – genius!' they cried. Oohs and ahhs all round. You'd think she'd invented the bloody things.

How did she remember this stuff? I couldn't even remember what I'd had for dinner last night. And, more importantly, were there crib notes I could buy?

But perhaps the biggest lesson I learnt today was that you should never judge a book – or a cheap pair of sandals housing a hideously calloused pair of feet – by its cover. Because sometimes even the drabbest book most desperately in need of a pedicure can harbour the most surprising of treats.

Standing idly by the coffee-and-tea table, trying to look like I belonged, I cast around for our glorious leader, Mama Superior. Seeing as this was very much her gig, I was surprised to find her nowhere in sight. Suddenly a little shiver of activity ran through the room. What was going on here? Did I just spot Lisa grabbing the last of her famous flapjacks right from Bree's jaws? Did Harriet just inch her nursing bra down a little further so we could all catch a glimpse of her tasty blue-veined boob?

I turned towards the door and it all suddenly made sense. Hot Daddy had arrived.

And my, what a beauty he was. Even the snotty-nosed twins looked significantly more appealing cradled in his lean, sculpted arms. What was it about men with kids, puppies or anything vaguely vulnerable that makes them look so achingly, unbelievably . . .

Coco yanked on the hem of my harem pants and pointed at the bowl of popcorn she'd just upended on the floor, only stopping when I gently shooed her away with the pointy bit of my shoe.

Oh God, was that a hint of a tattoo I spied peeking out from the sleeve of his perfectly distressed polo shirt?

He was my every teenage dream come true; he was Dylan McKay all grown up. (An addiction to cheesy soaps is the one thing I'll admit to inheriting from my mother. I spent the entire summer of Year 9 holed up in my bedroom watching ten years' worth of episodes of *Beverly Hills, 90210* and dreaming about being torn between my ridiculously rich and handsome quarterback boyfriend and the emotionally messed-up, motorcycle-riding badass I really wanted.)

In a flash, Lisa and her flapjack were by my side, snatching at the paper plates and napkins, while Bree simmered in the corner.

'Who's that?' I asked Lisa nonchalantly, nodding in Hot Daddy's direction.

'Cameron. Nikki's husband,' she said.

Mama Superior? Culottes. Hairy cankles. Callouses sharp enough to cut through the sexual tension in this room like a knife. This was her photographer husband with the failing business? How. The. Bloody. Hell. 'Wow, he's a little, erm, unexpected.'

'He works freelance,' she rabbited on. 'They split the parenting duties straight down the middle –'

'Of course they do.' The last thing I was interested in was a blow-by-blow account of Mama Superior's – sorry, Nikki's – gender-equal parenting principles.

'Cameron's here every fortnight, pitching in. They figure it's a far healthier example for the twins –'

Seriously, did this woman not get it? 'Yeah, yeah. So he's here every two weeks?'

'That's normally what it means: fortnightly,' she said wryly before taking her offering over to the godly one.

I watched from a distance as the mums swarmed around him like flies on a fresh carcass. Really, for a bunch of married women, their behaviour was nothing short of pitiful. I turned back to making myself a cup of vomit-flavoured herbal tea (oolong – apparently marvellous not just for the sinuses, but also for developing the perfect, pristine skin of a newborn).

'You're new,' said a deep male voice beside me, making me almost leap out of my skin.

I turned around and sank into a pair of sparkling blue eyes, crinkled around the corners from a life of laughing, award-winning picture-taking and earth-shattering sex.

Something flipped in my stomach that hadn't been flipped in a very long time.

Get a grip! Matt. Husband. Home. Love.

Judy.

I stood frozen, staring into those eyes for what seemed like forever. 'I am,' I stammered at last. I grabbed Coco and wrenched the empty popcorn bowl off her head. 'We both are. This is Coco, I'm her mum. Matt's her dad, my husband.' God, I sounded ridiculous.

'Welcome – Coco and her mum, whose name I don't know, and her invisible husband, Matt. I hope everyone's been making you feel at home.'

'That's one way of describing it,' I said, holding my cup of green vomit towards him.

He laughed and reached out a hand to touch my hair. It was the last thing I expected, and I let out a gasp, just a tiny one, but loud enough for him to hear. He pulled a piece of popcorn out from somewhere above my left ear and held it towards me. 'Occupational hazard,' he said with a cheeky grin.

Oh God, sexy married men were most definitely not what I needed right now. Nowhere did they feature in my carefully crafted ten-point master plan.

Bree appeared, saving me from further humiliation. 'Cam, can I borrow your muscles for a minute?' she purred, touching his arm lightly. 'I'm having nightmares erecting the sandpit slide.'

Yeah, I bet she was.

Later, after the Sing Song had been sung, the tea drunk, and Hot Daddy released from the fawning grip of twenty underdressed and oversexed mums to take the twins home for their midday nap, Judy helped me bustle Coco and her truckloads of popsicle paintings into the car.

'Well that was an interesting morning,' she said, rolling up Coco's works of art and shoving them under the passenger seat.

For once I had to agree with her.

11

#notimeformemorylane
#OperationBaby-Proofing

That morning's unexpected stomach flip got me thinking about Matt. Hard as it was to believe now, but not so long ago he had been the only man on the face of the planet who'd ever had an effect like that on me.

Sprawled on the sofa with a Diet Coke and a toasted ham-and-cheese croissant (quinoa, I'd promised myself, was definitely top of the menu tomorrow), I thought about the first time we met – five years ago. I was at the after-party for the Zimmermann Autumn/Winter launch at The Ivy, having been dragged there by a sleazy freelancer from *Who* magazine, who had subsequently abandoned me in the corner with a bunch of boring city suits so he could chat up some underage bimbo in a crop-top at the bar.

At first, the suits blended into one mildly irritating blur as they peppered me with drunken questions about where I lived and how it was humanly possible to walk on heels so high. But then, so slowly I didn't even notice it happening, one of them came into pin-sharp focus – the one at the back who didn't say much, who didn't sound like he had a ping-pong ball stuck in the corner of his mouth, and who didn't try to drag me onto the dance floor to cut a rug to bad '90s Europop.

He had a lopsided smile, big bear arms that suggested the cosiest cuddles, and a cheeky, knowing glint in his eye that seemed to say 'Funny, isn't it, that this is how we should meet?' Most definitely not my usual type. But something in the pit of my stomach, in that place where ugly and beautiful truths sit side by side, looked past the unfortunate polo neck and sports jacket combo and the slightly portly middle and responded. I knew, in that way you just do sometimes, that after more disappointing boyfriends and horrific first dates than I dared count, I'd finally met The One.

And for a very long time after, I had actually believed that.

'Where's Coco?' asked Judy, jamming the brakes on my little trip down memory lane.

'She's right there,' I said, nodding towards the playmat.

Only, she wasn't.

I leapt to my feet, my heart lurching, and stared at the lurid green and red and yellow of the playmat, as though by staring hard enough Coco would suddenly reappear.

She'd been there just a second ago, I was sure of it. Hadn't she? My mind spun back through the various places I might possibly have left her between this morning and now. The trolley in the Westfield car park? The changing mat at playgroup? Please God, not the car. I really did not want to be one of those mothers who had their face plastered across the evening news because they'd been dumb enough to leave their kid strapped in the car while they went merrily about their day. How would I ever get over the embarrassment?

There was a loud crash, followed by peals of laughter.

Judy and I ran to the kitchen to find Coco knee-deep and pretty damn pleased with herself, beneath a pile of clean bottles and an overturned tub of formula. The formula was now spread around her chubby knees like freshly fallen snow.

In all my obsessing over Hot Daddy and his sinewy, tattooed arms, I'd failed to notice that my baby had become a world-class speed crawler.

'Just like Matt,' said Judy proudly. 'Straight from sitting to racing across the room, none of that in-between rolling around on the floor rubbish.'

Yeah great, only 'that rolling around the floor rubbish' would have given me time to think, to plan. Holding Coco as tight as her newly racing-fast body would allow, I looked around our cosy living room and saw it for what it actually was – a death trap.

The towering steel and glass floor lamp I'd waited six months for from Space Furniture – one mighty pull and it'd all be over for Coco. The open wall socket where Matt zapped his iPad every night? An electric shock strong enough to blast her from here into the next suburb. The razor-sharp edges of my replica Eames coffee table? Nice knowing you, eyeballs.

And with that, Operation Baby-Proofing began.

*

Four-and-a-half hours and $1400 later, I could finally exhale. Thanks to the very nice man at our local Mothercraft branch who understood my concerns completely and didn't think I was being at all over-zealous in my attempt to protect my daughter from the dangers lurking in every corner of her own home, every open socket was now plugged, every window sealed, every cord removed, and every drawer, cupboard and toilet locked shut. Coco was now happily exploring the confines of her new four-by-four prison cell, aka her FunTime playpen. Judy and I were exhausted.

Of course it would take a little getting used to for us too. The new layout meant we now only had room for one sofa, which had been shoved into the centre of the living room just a centimetre or two from the television (currently sitting on the floor while we awaited delivery of the two state-of-the-art steel rods that would bracket it securely to the wall). The rest of the furniture – the second sofa, Matt's armchair, the coffee table, the DVD cabinet and my beloved floor lamp – had been relegated to the back deck, awaiting disposal on eBay.

'I like it,' I said to Judy, nudging away the corner of Coco's playpen where it was digging into my left calf. 'It's cosy.'

I heard Matt's key turning in the lock, followed by a crash as he fell headfirst over the new safety gate.

'Guess what? Coco's learnt to crawl,' I shouted out to him. 'Don't worry about the gate – it's toddler-proof. Just press the button and lift the latch.'

'Just lift the what and press the what?' he cried back. He jiggled the gate, shoving and cursing.

Why is it men think if they jiggle about and swear at things hard enough they'll magically work?

'The damn thing's broken!' he cried. More jiggling, more swearing.

'The button – press the button. It's toddler-proof,' I said.

'Bullshit – it's more than that. You need an aeronautical degree to get this thing open.'

Finally, he cracked it. I heard him traipse up the stairs.

'What the hell, Ally?' Oh yeah. I forgot to tell him about the lock on the toilet seat. 'How am I meant to take a crap? Or did you want me to start wearing nappies too?' Matt yelled.

'Please tell me we've got a few years before we have to start having that conversation,' I muttered before hopping over the safety gate into the kitchen to pour myself another glass of wine.

Ten minutes later, Matt was back downstairs and beside me on the sofa, contorting his body in such a way that he could watch the news headlines on the screen at his feet.

Coco found the whole thing highly amusing. 'Don't laugh,' he grumbled at her. 'This is all your fault, clever clogs.'

Then it was my turn. 'Ally, don't you think this is all a little excessive? Seriously, you've turned the place into Fort Knox.'

I sighed. 'The question really should be: how much value do you place on your child's safety?' I asked. 'Do you want her to drink Draino? Slice her finger off in a drawer? Drown in the toilet?'

'Come on, when is the last time you heard of a child drowning in a toilet?'

'According to bubzone.com.au, two-thirds of the average nine-month-old's body weight is in their head – top heavy, see? One little peek into the toilet bowl to admire the results of their latest effort and, boom, that's it. Straight down the sewer.'

'You're morbid. And I've had a shit day, and I really don't want to hear about kids being sucked into sewers.'

He shifted uncomfortably and rolled his head back on the seat of the sofa – and straight onto the remote control for our new dummy locator (who even thinks of these things?), which started shrilling and creating a startling strobe-lighting effect inside Coco's mouth. Matt reached behind him, grabbed the remote, and tossed it across the room.

I bet Cameron didn't complain about taking measures to protect the twins. In fact, I bet he insisted on doing all the baby-proofing himself. Probably naked and smeared top to toe in olive oil.

Aghhhhhh! What was happening to me?

I immediately googled 'sick fantasies about olive oil' on my phone. It seems I wasn't alone on this one – a quick search revealed thousands of people who enjoyed doing far more sinister things with olive oil than baby-proofing their living rooms.

Judy plonked herself down next to me. 'So, what are we watching?'

'The Syrians are at it again,' said Matt from my other side.

As I sat there squished between the two of them, smelling the Vegemite toast and Earl Grey tea Judy had consumed for lunch every time she exhaled, I remembered something else Matt had said in the early days of our relationship, in the back of a cab coming home from the premiere of *The September Issue*. It was a time when he still happily joined me at things like that, when I still only had two stamps in my passport and was impressionable enough to believe every word he said. 'Ally, the world is our oyster and I want to show you all of it – every single little part,' he'd whispered into my ear.

Surely, *surely*, this hadn't been what he'd had in mind?

12

#HappyMummies #coffeemorning #soNOTfuckingblessed

I had exactly five days left to get my arse into gear for the dreaded at-home coffee morning.

I pushed aside my feelings of rage and resentment at having this event thrust upon me in such a scurrilous fashion and instead chose to view it for what it actually was: my chance to shine. A once-in-a-lifetime (God willing) opportunity to show the Happy Mummies I could play this mothering part to perfection, and maybe even give them a couple of pointers on how to lift their own games in the process. I mentally rolled up my sleeves as if I was on countdown for one of Alejandro's big fashion shows and threw myself into full-scale prep mode.

First order of business: find out what an at-home coffee morning actually entailed. Was I expected to have a theme? Provide entertainment?

A quick google revealed the perfect person to enlighten me: Rosie Jones, the blogger's equivalent of Martha Stewart, who authored a vom-worthy parenting blog called Scribbles & Honey where she dispensed advice on everything from how to safely remove a small pet rodent from the DVD player to folding the perfect napkin swan. As it turned out, hosting coffee mornings was one of Rosie's favourite pastimes, and she had plenty to say on the subject. The most important being, it seemed, that you must always smile and carry on graciously, even in the face of some little fucker drawing swastikas across your walls. She also indicated it was vitally important to arm yourself with sufficient quantities of paper towels (for dealing with all those little accidents like spilt cups of tea, as well as providing impromptu craft opportunities). Reading between the lines, I guessed that meant 'yes' to both the theming and the entertainment.

I spent Day One ordering all sorts of lovely things online – proper patterned teacups and matching cake plates, a linen tablecloth, a cake stand, and pretty little flags to pin along the table. I couldn't resist the urge to buy Coco and I matching outfits for the day – tongue-in-cheek 1950s tea dresses in a gorgeous pink and white posy print. Hell, if I was going to play the role of perfect housewife, I may as well look the part. All up, my bill came to $727.98, which I figured was a bargain in the scheme of things.

Day Two was all about the food. Taking my cue from Rosie, I resisted the urge to outsource any of it to the local catering company. I would do everything myself, like a proper housewife. I pored over *How to Be a Domestic Goddess*, which had been sitting unopened on the bookshelf since time began, marvelling at Nigella Lawson's teeny-tiny waist and ability to make the frumpiest cardigan look sexy. Carefully tagging the pages with Post-it notes, I learnt all about chocolate macarons and butterfly cakes and gooseberry cream crumble. Who said this couldn't be fun!

Our house wasn't exactly designed for large numbers, particularly now we were down to just the one sofa, so I decided to open up the back doors so everyone could spill out onto the back deck and into the garden. To encourage them to do so, Rosie suggested creating a focal point outside that would draw the eye and encourage natural migration. To achieve this, I hung brightly coloured paper lanterns (ten dollars for five at the local two-dollar shop – who knew!) along the trellis on the back deck and dotted through the trees, and then spent the next hour admiring the sheer beauty of it all.

Rosie had been quite firm on the subject of scheduling; it was important to be clear about what would happen when (food, colouring in, chit-chat, leave-taking, etc) and not let things wander off track. I wasn't quite sure what sort of hell this wandering off track would unleash, but I really didn't want to find out. So I wrote up a timetable of events, printed it off on the computer and stuck it on the front of the pantry door, where I could easily refer to it between dishing up savouries and pouring mango iced teas.

During all this, I made sure to take plenty of 'before' shots for my Instagram feed, and cleared enough space on my phone so I could capture all the fun of the day: Coco and I sprinkling icing sugar onto the butterfly cakes, her mingling adorably with her friends, the two of us wafting around in our matching frocks and generally being glorious.

All the while my thoughts flipped back constantly to Cameron. I wondered whether he'd come along to my coffee morning and, if he did, what it would feel like to have him here in my actual home. I removed all the snapshots of me, proud and pregnant and waddling down Palm Beach in a bikini from the fridge door, just in case.

By Day Four, things started coming ever so slightly unstuck. The stupid supermarket delivery guy forgot to bring both the desiccated coconut and the caster sugar for the coconut macaroons, and then informed me that mangoes were out of season, so in the end Matt had to do a late-night dash up to the shops to stock up on mango-flavoured cordial and whatever cut-price baked goods they still had left on the shelves. Oh, Rosie, will you ever be able to forgive me?

Early on the morning of the big day, while I was still racing around in my tracky dacks and unwashed hair, there was a knock on the door. Pulling it open, I came face to face with Cameron, standing there looking ridiculously gorgeous with a stack of folding chairs in his arms.

'I'm told you might be in need of extra seating,' he said.

'Oh great, thanks,' I said, attempting to take the chairs from him while simultaneously concealing as much of myself as possible behind the front door. 'So, uh, will you be coming along too today?' I asked casually.

He shook his head. 'Can't, unfortunately. I've got a meeting with an ad agency in the city this morning.'

'Oh well,' I said nonchalantly, while my heart sunk somewhere near the rubber soles of my ugg boots. There went about 90 per cent of today's fun.

He turned to go, then threw me a cheeky over-the-shoulder smile. 'But I'll be thinking of you.'

What the . . .? He'd be thinking of me? He would be Thinking. Of. Me. Did that mean what I thought it meant? Then again, he hadn't said he'd be thinking *about* me. That was different. Or was it?

My mind was still spinning with these thoughts forty-five minutes later, when the Happy Mummies arrived en masse. Within moments, my serene, peaceful home was transformed into a cesspit of noise, hysteria, abandoned sneakers and spilt cordial, with me in the middle of it, frantically running around with the paper towels (thank God for Rosie!).

Nobody followed the agenda or participated in the colouring in I'd set out in the corner, and not one single person naturally migrated outside. All of them squished onto the sofa, the floor – even the staircase in the hall – balancing their teacups and saucers on their knees. It was more hostile takeover than delightful morning tea.

'But where's Judy?' they all asked, looking genuinely disappointed that she wasn't there.

'Yeah, sorry, she's at her computer course, learning how to hack into the national security system, this morning,' I replied, feeling like some idiot who'd put on a circus and forgotten to bring the clown.

It was all downhill from there. Lisa did nothing as Milly clambered all over my beautiful sofa in her muddy sneakers. I wanted to grab the little fool by the ankle and cry, 'Silk velvet mix! One bit of damage and

I need to have the *whole thing* reupholstered!' Instead, I was very Rosie-esque about the whole thing and smiled graciously and didn't utter a single word.

Coco cried every time a child so much as looked at one of her toys and I wasn't having much luck with the mums either. Just like at our café outing, they all carried on chattering as if I wasn't there – they just grabbed a stale pastry from the plate I offered round like I was the hired help. At least I now understood what at-home coffee mornings were really about; they were just another excuse to carry on yesterday's conversation with the person next to you, only with different food and in a new location.

Finally, one of them turned to me. 'I think there's something wrong with your upstairs toilet,' Jenna announced breezily as she helped herself to a butterscotch.

What the? I pushed past the sixteen mums occupying the stairwell and raced into my ensuite – to find a scene of bloody carnage: every bit of makeup I owned was sprawled across the vanity and floor, red lipstick was scrawled on the wall, and the toilet was overflowing.

I spent the next half an hour on my hands and knees trying to fish my beloved Lancôme mascara out of the toilet bowl while listening to the muffled sounds of laughter and chatter coming up from downstairs.

At last, I got the damn thing out. I wiped it off as best I could on a Missoni handtowel, then forced myself to go back downstairs.

'Oh my God, are there nuts in this?' screeched Harriet, clutching a soggy lump of biscuit in one hand and a fast-ballooning Archie in the other.

I took a closer look at the biscuit. 'Uh, not sure,' I said. 'Are there actual nuts in almond biscotti?'

With that, my glorious entrée into the SAHM social circle ended with an emergency dash to the ER.

Safe to say, it was, quite possibly, the worst coffee morning in the history of coffee mornings. To top it all off, not one single moment of it had been worthy of my Instagram feed.

Okay, so Plan A (return to work) hadn't worked out. Now Plan B (become ultimate SAHM) wasn't looking too promising either. Maybe it was time to move on to Plan C.

If only I could think of one.

13

#dinnerparty
#propergrown-ups

Truth was, I didn't have a Plan C, which meant Plan B had to work, whether I liked it or not.

Actually, the mums had all been pretty cool about the Archie anaphylaxis episode. I had apologised profusely, and Harriet had even dropped over a lemongrass-scented candle to show she bore no hard feelings. I decided to put thoughts of the coffee morning failure behind me and focus fully on the next thing on the agenda – Jenna's dinner party. Here was a chance for social redemption served up on a platter, and I was determined not to screw it up.

As Matt and I began to get ready for our big night out, I couldn't help feeling a little buzz of excitement. Tonight we would officially take our place on the grown-up suburban dinner-party circuit. And I would not, under any circumstances, allow myself to be distracted by any sexy, flirtatious husbands married to other people in the room (even if they were thinking about me, hah!).

I didn't expect it to be the most scintillating of evenings, but thinking back to all the horrendous work dinners I'd had to suffer through, with journalists sitting across from me picking their noses or declaring that foie gras really wasn't what they were in the mood for that evening, how bad could it really be?

Plus, there was always the debrief to look forward to when we got home: Matt and I curled up together on the sofa, him rubbing my feet and me nursing a glass of wine, while we dissected the evening – who among the guests had bored our pants off and which couple had 'impending divorce' written all over them. I could already picture it.

Matt was dragging his feet getting dressed, still pissed off that I was making him go. I studiously ignored him, fully focused on primping myself to perfection. I'd plucked, I'd buffed, I'd waxed, I'd shaved – standard procedure before a night out in my old life, but one that now left me feeling like something of the Christmas turkey, trussed up and ready to be presented to the table for a carving.

I tried to convince myself that the push-up bra I'd dug out from the depths of my underwear drawer was for Matt's benefit: making an effort to be the attractive wife he'd married and all that. But seeing as I hadn't put it on since he'd knocked me up, I'm not sure either of us was buying that one. Nevertheless, with my bust threatening to erupt out of my Carla Zampatti wrap-dress, I was ready to take on the mummy mafia for all their worth.

I turned side-on to the full-length mirror to see whether sucking in my stomach made any difference to the lumpy tyre bulging over the waistband of my Spanx.

Matt was watching me in the glass. 'You look beautiful,' he said.

The kindness of his words was an unexpected sting, like touching the metal handle of a drawer and getting a tiny electric shock. I looked back at him in the mirror, squeezed reluctantly into his best Country Road jeans and the cashmere V-neck I'd bought him for his birthday. He looked good too.

But it was all so achingly different to how it used to be. Hard as I tried not to let myself think about it, the memories forced their way in. There was a time when we used to be late for every party because getting our clothes on invariably led to taking them off. And then later, separated either by design or accident across a crowded room, I had still felt tethered to him by an invisible thread. I was always aware of exactly where he was and who he was with, and felt part of every conversation he was having, no matter how far apart we stood. And I knew he felt it too, because whenever I happened to glance up, his eyes would spring straight to mine with a look that said 'Not long now'.

But now we could be lying right beside each other, skin against skin, and we may as well have been on different continents. I had thought staying at home with Coco would change all that and bring us closer together, but watching us as we skirted politely around each other to slip on socks and stockings and fasten our shoes, lost in our own thoughts and barely exchanging a word, I wasn't so sure. The duvet and console table and the rattan baskets under the bed might have looked the same as they had in our happier days, but they felt entirely different now – like a warm, snuggly jumper that suddenly, when the weather warms up, feels all scratchy and wrong.

But I was determined to move to the next phase – the better, grown-up phase – and I would take Matt with me whether he liked it or not. I couldn't shake the feeling, though, that I was standing on the edge of a precipice. Step one way and it's a lovely gentle stroll down a well-worn mountain path, step the other and go crashing 100 metres to earth.

Finally, when we looked as good as we could, we headed downstairs. I touched up my lipstick in the hallway mirror while Matt put the wine in a cooler bag.

Judy came out with Coco in her arms. 'Don't Mummy and Daddy look nice,' she cooed.

Coco reached out a chubby little paw to pull at the Tiffany chain around my neck that Matt had given me for our third anniversary. Thoughts of snuggling up in bed bedside her, cosy and warm as we read her favourite pages of *Goodnight Moon*, flashed through my mind before I shoved them firmly aside.

'Thanks for looking after her tonight, Mum,' said Matt.

'That's what I'm here for.'

Was it? I wondered. I looked at her closely to see whether her words were loaded with any other meaning, but she'd moved on and was busy licking her finger and rubbing at something behind Coco's ear. There was no time to worry about Judy's double entendres now anyway; we were already late.

*

Jenna's house at 62 Rossdale Place was exactly what I'd expected it to be. The perfectly manicured front lawn was punctuated with a tyre swing swaying idly in the breeze. Trees heavy with fruit lined the perimeter. A shiny Range Rover was parked in the driveway. Hell, I thought I even spied a chicken coop in the distance. It looked like a *Country Life* magazine spread.

We parked on the road outside. I glanced over at Matt in the driver's seat beside me, thinking we might share a giggle about the chicken coop, but he was too busy checking something on his phone to notice. Once upon a time, he would have found it funny. Oh well, I reasoned, maybe he was just nervous, not having met the Happy Mummies gang yet and having heard so many horror stories about them. I reached over and gave his hand a squeeze and he looked up from his phone, startled.

As we walked up the front path, I took the opportunity to have a stickybeak through the front windows. From what I could tell, the chicken run was only the start of it – far worse was to come inside. Ugly bits of craft were lined up like museum showpieces along the front windowsills – darling creations the kids had no doubt made on fun afternoons with mum, while the rest of us were lying prostrate on our sofas nursing warm Bacardi Breezers and dipping stale chips into tubs of cheese-and-onion dip. And just in case anyone was in any doubt about where we were, large swirly letters spelled out 'Home' above the front door.

Before we'd even had a chance to press the bell, Jenna was at the door showering us with hugs and kisses, like we were her oldest, dearest friends. A cute grey-haired schnauzer leapt up at us in greeting, then abruptly plonked his bum down on the mat.

'Wow, he's well-trained,' I observed.

'Nope, just zapped him,' Jenna replied, holding up a shiny red remote control. 'Twenty-two volts: not enough to kill him, just enough to stop him jumping up or getting on the Aubussons. Marvellous little gadget. Only wish I could get one for the kids.'

'Nice top,' said Matt, unable to tear his eyes away from the hideous crocheted tunic Jenna was sporting.

'I made it myself,' she said, proudly.

Really? I would never have guessed, I thought sarcastically. *I thought all tunics came with a conveniently placed chest-flap so you can whip out a boob at a moment's notice if your youngest gets a little thirsty in between blasting people on his Xbox and belting the neighbours with his Nerf gun.*

But Matt nodded and smiled, and I wondered whether he really did think it was nice.

We then met Elliot, Jenna's husband, a great hulk of a man who told us in not so many words that he had a very important job at a very important law firm in the city. He had apparently helped Nikki sort out an icky divorce from her first husband, Reuben (yes, like the sandwich). But tonight Elliot was in off-duty mode – in a pastel Sportscraft polo shirt and perfectly ironed chinos, he delivered warm double-handed handshakes all round.

He ruffled his boys' hair as they ran out to the garden. 'Where are you lot off to in such a hurry?' he chortled.

They looked back at him in wide-eyed confusion, as though he was some random stranger who'd just wandered in from the street.

'So, what do you do?' he asked, turning to me and sounding actually, genuinely interested.

Hmm, how to respond? Did 'stay-at-home mum' sound too pathetic? Should I tell him that I used to have a real job that paid me in actual money, not in migraines and dirty dishes? 'I'm in PR,' I said finally.

'Ah, PR. I've always wondered what PR actually is,' he said thought-fully, before turning on his heel and walking off.

Matt looked at me and shrugged. Guess I should have gone with the SAHM option.

Nikki and Cameron arrived, Nikki bearing a bouquet of tatty flow-ers and wearing some sort of crumpled sack she'd probably plucked from the floor of her people-mover on the way over. Cameron, mean-while, was mouthwateringly delicious in faded jeans and had on the most adorable little polka-dot bow-tie. He was Hugh to her Deborra-Lee, Matthew Broderick to her SJP. The two of them just didn't make sense. Then again, I thought, glancing over at Matt, who was absent-mindedly tucking his sweater into the waistband of his jeans, what would other people's take on the two of us be?

There followed a horribly awkward moment as my husband and the father of my child shook hands with the object of my lustful, olive-oil-coated fantasies. I squirmed and fidgeted like a spotty-faced schoolgirl and waited for the ground to swallow me whole.

I was saved from the hellishness of it all by the arrival of more party guests: Harriet and Jumping Axe Kick Toby, Lisa and her de facto partner, Gideon; Bree and her sleazy-looking husband, Egor, who sported a hipster beard and slicked-back man bun, and a couple of faceless suburbanites whose names I couldn't be bothered to remember.

'Looks like the gang's all here!' trilled Jenna, and with that we were ushered towards the dining room to eat.

It had just gone six-thirty.

As we all headed in, Cameron put his hand on my arm to draw me back. 'I was hoping you'd be here tonight. These things are always bor-ing as fuck,' he whispered in my ear. 'You look great, by the way.'

I stammered something incomprehensible in reply, agonisingly aware of his eyes on my face, my hair, my breasts that were pushed up so high they could quite conceivably take someone's eye out. *Good God, was he actually flirting with me?*

Matt, walking a few steps ahead of me, glanced back. I lowered my gaze to floor-level and stumbled blindly to the table.

Dining at Jenna and Elliot's was the very grown-up affair I knew it would be, all fine bone china and solid silver cutlery that felt like dead weights in your hand – precious heirlooms passed down from Elliot's dead grandmother, natch. I couldn't shake the feeling that we were all just playing at being grown-ups and any minute now dead Granny would walk through the door and tell us off for touching her good dinnerware. Jenna had written little place cards telling us where to sit. Cameron, much to my disappointment, was down the other end of the table, preventing me from indulging in any sort of light-hearted flirtation over the hors d'oeuvres. Instead, I had leery Egor opposite me, asking my cleavage a series of deceptively polite questions about where I lived and how long I'd known the Drummonds.

Before Elliot took his place at the head of the table, he circled the room pouring cheap white plonk into everyone's wine glasses, the two very nice bottles of wine that Matt and I had given him presumably being kept aside for another far more special occasion.

Jenna toyed with the glass in her hand. 'I really shouldn't,' she said, even though no-one had actually suggested she should. 'Oh, go on then, Elliot, just a splash,' she said with a wicked giggle.

The tiny thimbleful he poured out was downed in one delicate sip. Oh well, I thought, there goes her dream of little Hamish winning that coveted Rhodes scholarship when he's older.

The very civilised (read: boring) talk soon turned to the one thing we all had in common: playgroup.

'I'm not sure if you realise, Ally, but a lot of us actually went to Happy Mummies when we were little,' said Jenna. 'In fact, it's where Harriet and I first met.'

Harriet simpered away happily at the memory, while the rest of us oohed and aahed at the sweetness of it all. But I swear to God I saw Bree take the opportunity to whip out a couple of antibacterial wipes and give her cutlery a quick going-over under the table.

I wondered if Happy Mummies was the only tradition Jenna and Harriet were carrying on. Had their own mothers subjected their peers to the horrific sight of them breastfeeding school-age versions of Jenna and Harriet?

Despite this, a small part of me had to admit the tradition was sort of nice, and I realised that I wanted this for Coco too: a safe and steady continuity. Or at least the option of it, if she so chose.

'Your entrée tonight is something very special,' announced Jenna solemnly, bringing out a heavy platter of fritters with a side of creamy dipping sauce.

What was it about the SAHM brigade that made them talk about food like it was high-class art? They were just fritters, for fuck's sake. Whatever. I was at least glad to see there were a lot of them – I was starving, having been unable to eat a thing all day at the thought of seeing Cameron here tonight.

Jenna carried on. 'They're made with eggs laid only this morning by Topsy and Dame Margot.' Ah yes, the chickens. 'And a little something extra I hope you'll all appreciate.' She held the plate out towards me first, and I naturally reached for the biggest fritter in sight.

Hmm, it was chewy and it had a taste I couldn't quite identify: possibly game.

'I have been saving the placenta from the birth of my beloved twins to share with my oldest and dearest friends,' Jenna nodded sagely in my direction, as she continued to proffer the platter, 'and my new ones.'

Hang on a minute, did she just say *placenta*?

I spat what remained in my mouth straight into the napkin in my lap.

'Beef jerky, that's what it reminds me of,' announced Toby triumphantly. Nikki, to her credit, was looking a little green around the gills, while Matt, staring at me like a frightened rabbit in headlights, held his fork mid-air, fritter quivering plaintively on the end.

Harriet touched Jenna's arm, great soulful tears swelling in her eyes. 'Thank you for this gift,' she said, before chomping through the jerky-ish placenta in one humongous mouthful and reaching out for seconds.

No, just no.

'Excuse me a moment,' I said, and hotfooted it to the guest bathroom under the stairs.

I turned on the tap to full blast and made myself retch into the toilet in a way I hadn't since high school. Thankfully, old habits die hard and I was able to get most of it out on the first gag. Then I sat down on the toilet and tried to process what had just happened.

After a while, I heard Matt's voice at the door. 'You'd better come out now, it's getting embarrassing.'

I opened the door a crack. 'We have to leave.'

'What, *now?*'

'Right now,' I spat. 'Just grab my handbag from the living room and I'll meet you out front. Run!'

And so we did.

*

We drove home in silence. Then, just as we were pulling into the drive, Matt erupted: 'What the hell are you doing, Ally? You drag me there, then you drag me out. You're acting like a completely spoilt and demented child. You *are* aware of that, right?'

'She fed us her *placenta*, Matt. Surely I did you a favour getting you out of there.'

'I had to tell her you had the runs, that it was uncontrollable. I had to lie to a whole table full of complete strangers.'

'Yeah, well, I'll drop her over a bottle of Jif tomorrow,' I said sulkily.

Matt was silent for a beat. Then, without warning, he banged both hands on the steering wheel with an anger I'd never seen in him before. I jumped back in my seat. 'Every single person stayed put at that table, we all did the right thing, every single one of us. Why was it you, only *you*, who had to make a run for it like some candy-coated princess who can't stand not getting her own way?'

My natural instinct was to make a joke of it or hurl the words right back in his face, but for some reason I couldn't bring myself to do either. For once in our married life I was all out of comebacks. 'Because I'm not like them,' I said quietly. 'I'm trying really, really hard, Matt . . . but I'm just not.'

By the time we got in, the speaking to each other part of our evening was well and truly over. Matt didn't even look at me as he said a curt goodnight to Judy and disappeared up to bed. So much for the foot rub.

Why was this so hard? Things were meant to be getting better, not worse. I was still far from the yummy mummy extraordinaire I'd imagined and my visions of the two of us bound together in love and ready to face the world, or at the very least the local mummy mafia, were crumbling.

I went to the kitchen and poured myself a large vodka. I took a long glug and savoured the burn as it made its way down the back of my throat, imagining its wonderful disinfectant qualities erasing all trace of Jenna's innards from my body and, with a bit of luck, Matt's cruel words from my ears.

'Things don't always go to plan, you know,' said Judy, coming in to the kitchen behind me and reaching up for a glass. 'And that's alright.'

God, couldn't I just have a moment of peace to wallow in my misery by myself, for once? I turned away from her so I could stare out the kitchen window, hoping that would be enough of a hint. 'Please don't give me the Amsterdam story,' I muttered.

'The Amsterdam story?' She sounded confused.

'You know, the one where you think you're going on a luxury cruise around the Bahamas when what you're actually on is a ride round the Amsterdam canals on a cut-price barge with a bunch of Westies with poor personal hygiene.'

'Well it's a little bit like that, I suppose,' she said. I heard her drop the teensiest splash of vodka into her glass. 'You're trying to control something that has its own will.'

'Please, I'm not an idiot. I know perfectly well that Coco is her own person,' I said, knocking back the last of my vodka and turning to go.

'I'm talking about parenthood. The messy corners, the spilt milk, the bumpy patches where for a while you can't stand the sight of each other. But it's all part of the journey. Rather than trying to control it, just hold on tight and try to enjoy the ride,' she said.

Please God, let this little pep talk be almost over.

'Besides, you're a far better mother than you think, Alexis.'

The tears welled up in my eyes before I had the chance to stop them. I pushed past Judy as fast as I could so she wouldn't see.

God, I hated her. When, when, *when* was she going to leave?

14

**#Enzosfashionablelife
#wtf #goodtastestillmatters
#sextoys #nowords**

Okay, so I was prepared to admit it – things weren't exactly going to plan. First, there had been the disastrous coffee morning, complete with me almost killing one of my guests' children, and now Matt and I had attended a placenta dinner party.

For the life of me, I couldn't figure out where I was going wrong. I was dressed like a Happy Mummy. I'd stopped wearing deodorant. I'd even bought a stupid yogurt maker, for God's sake. I was following the plan to the letter – well, as best I could – so why, why, *why* wasn't it working?

I cringed every time I thought back to Matt's steering-wheel-banging episode last night. His horrible words about princesses and uncontrollable diarrhoea still rang in my ears. While I thought it was fair to say his delivery had been a tad over the top, I suppose he'd had a point. Why the hell hadn't I stayed put at that damn table and just smiled and swallowed like everyone else?

I distracted myself from these angsty thoughts by embarking on something I'd been putting off for the last two weeks – the ceremonial retirement of my old life. It was time to make way for my new one, whether I liked it or not.

I carefully laid every pretty dress, spindle-heeled shoe and designer handbag on the bed, stroking each one tenderly, farewelling my beloved old friends. I folded each item of clothing and placed it between sheets of acid-free tissue paper. Then I returned my beautiful heels to their original boxes, where they'd now live until they were once more called into duty.

'One day, you'll have the best vintage wardrobe of all of your friends,' I promised Coco solemnly. Just the thought of it brought a tear to my eye, but Coco was too busy seeing how many bits of tissue she could stack on top of her head to notice.

Judy barged in, shattering my sacred fashion funeral ceremony. 'You'll never have enough room in your wardrobe for all that lot,' she proclaimed at the sight of the artfully arranged mountain on the bed. 'Why don't you shove the whole lot in some of those whizzy space-saving bags?'

Er, excuse me, did the woman just say 'shove'?

'You just suck out the air with a vacuum cleaner, and voila! Mountains of clothes go down to the size of little bricks and you can stack them in a pile on the top shelf of your cupboard.'

I didn't even dignify that with a response. Did she not understand that what she was suggesting was akin to vacuuming the air out of my own children's lungs?

I pulled the beautiful fabrics – the leathers and slips of feather-light silk – protectively towards my chest. This, I thought to myself, was exactly why people with little taste and no money were not welcome in designer shops.

Thankfully, she'd be out of my hair soon, as she had another internet training session scheduled. Today, apparently, she'd be learning how to hack her way into other people's websites, which she'd then block and hold to ransom, charging the owners to visit them via a

PayPal account. Fabulous. My mother-in-law was now a cyber-terrorist.

Once I'd cleared out the majority of Matt's clothes from his side of the cupboard and relegated them to a couple of plastic roller bins under the bed so I could make way for my eminently more important archival collection, I felt I'd closed the door on the past and could focus on the here and now.

I took a deep breath and texted Lisa to find out whether my hasty exit last night meant Coco and I had been permanently exiled to the playgroup equivalent of Antarctica.

She messaged back straightaway:

Don't worry about last night. U still coming over Thurs?

Ah yes, the Tupperware party. The show did indeed go on.

In the meantime, there was just one more thing I'd been meaning to do . . . Timing was everything: I waited until Judy was safely out of the house and Coco was fast asleep, then logged in to my computer like a sicko getting his internet porn fix.

There it was – enzosfashionablelife.blogspot.com. A heartwarming picture of Enzo, the caramel-coloured, long-haired spoodle, lapping up coconut water from a Swarovski-encrusted bowl sprang up, followed by post after titillating post of Enzo's thoughts on everything from animal print to old-school tailoring. In one post, he bemoaned the inappropriateness of peek-a-boo panelling on anyone over the age of 23 or who could bend over without their rib poking out the eye of the person standing next to them. All of this was peppered with caustic comments on the latest celebrity fashion missteps.

If you double-clicked on a shot of Kim Kardashian wearing a rather unfortunate rear-enhancing leopard-print number, you unleashed an audible fart, accompanied by Alejandro's voice: 'That one's a stinker!'

Cute. Very cute. I could just picture Alejandro sniggering away at his own brilliance when he came up with that one.

But the real killer was the stream of gushing compliments that followed every post. 'Enzo's voice is so original!' 'Enzo is my new fashion hero!' 'I can't start the day without my daily dose of Enzo!' There was even an article on Popculture.com about how Enzo's canine fashion cred held more sway than the editors at *Elle*, *Vogue* and *Marie Claire* combined. Seriously, would the torture never end?

Well, it was high time to redress the balance.

I selected for myself the suitably erudite username of 'goodtaste-stillmatters' and set about posting my own views. 'Man, for a male dog, Enzo's sure showing his bitchy side'; 'Seriously, folks, taking fashion advice from someone who enjoys the taste of his own poop?'; 'Face it – Enzo's not even a pure-breed.'

'Well, it's official,' I announced with a flourish when Coco woke up from her nap. 'Your mother is now an internet troll.'

Only later that night, after everyone had gone to bed and I was alone on the sofa with my iPad, did I discover the stream of vitriol I'd unleashed. The whole internet, it seemed, was in love with Enzo and his hilarious musings, and goodtastestillmatters was now public enemy number one. Among top trending hashtags that day were: #goodtastestillmatterssucks and #whostherealdognowgoodtastestillmatters.

Ugh. Clearly these people had absolutely no sense of humour.

Still smarting from my very public internet fail, I limped on till Thursday. Mentally, physically and emotionally, the last thing I felt like doing was spending the morning at Lisa's Tupperware party, discussing the benefits of vented versus click-top lunchbox lids, and then being forced to hand over real money for them. But like the ~~dopey-eyed fool~~ eyes-on-the-prize professional I was, I blundered on.

Since parking was apparently non-existent in the streets around Lisa's place, the plan was that Coco and I would get a lift with Nikki and the twins. At 9.55 am on the dot, with me and Coco waiting outside on the pavement as instructed, Nikki bounced up in her rusty people mover and slid the rear door open so hard it was a miracle the thing didn't fly off into the neighbours' yard. 'If you don't go at it like you really mean it, the damn thing refuses to open and you have to winch yourself in via the back window,' she explained. Oh my God. 'There's a few extra booster seats in the back,' she said, nodding towards Coco. 'Just take your pick and strap her in.'

Holding Coco close, I stepped carefully inside. Wow, you could actually stand up in this thing – there was a veritable hallway big enough to amble up and down, plus enough seating for what looked like fifteen to twenty people. Really, Lisa should have thought about having her Tupperware party in here.

Once Coco was strapped into the back and I'd taken up position beside Nikki in the front, we set off towards Lisa's, jiggling and screeching through the streets on the people mover's dodgy suspension, the kids laughing themselves silly in the back and me trying to scoot as far down in my seat as humanly possible, so that nobody outside would recognise me. There might not be much of it left, granted, but I did have a reputation to uphold.

It was quite possibly the longest and most uncomfortable journey of my life. So much so that I missed all the obvious signs when we got to Lisa's. Looking back now, the weird light coming from the windows of her house should have been my first clue. It was like somebody had draped red fabric over all the lamps, giving the whole place a weird, moody haze.

No-one answered the doorbell, so Nikki and I let ourselves into a hall lined with hundreds of pictures of children at various stages of the life cycle: nursing, sleeping, Christmases, birthdays, riding bikes, dancing on stage, graduating high school. It was like a shrine to fertility, an advertisement for mass reproduction. My God, how many kids did the woman have? It was hard to tell as they'd all obviously come straight out of the womb with Lisa's frizzy brown hair and Gideon's weird clefted chin; it would have taken DNA testing to put an exact figure on it.

In the living room, the mums were all huddled together on a single corner of Lisa's easy-wipe, leather-look modular. They were giggly and fractious and there was an atmosphere of nervous excitement as the sound of Busta Rhymes pumped out of the stereo. Unusually for a group of women who never stopped espousing the benefits of attachment parenting, there wasn't a single child or sticky finger in the room.

A bouncy teenage girl appeared from nowhere in an alarmingly short crop-top and denim cut-offs that perfectly highlighted the razor-sharp crease of her butt cheeks (for the love of God, not an ounce of cellulite!), whipped Coco from my arms with a knowing smile and disappeared.

'Don't worry – that's Tessa, our neighbour's daughter,' said Lisa. 'Gideon and I use her all the time. The kids love her. She goes to Rangecliff.' Translation: she goes to a ridiculously expensive private school, which makes her eminently more capable than you of handling anything life throws at her, your own child included.

I could just make out Jenna through the red haze, busy admiring the gold cast of Lisa's pregnant belly, which stood like a fat, headless corpse on a spotlit plinth in the corner. I opened my mouth to speak to her, but she cut me off with a raised hand: 'I know what you're going to say, and I don't want to hear it. You're not to worry at all about the other night,' she said magnanimously. 'You're not there yet. But I know you will be.'

What the hell was that supposed to mean? For the record, I will never ever want to eat another woman's placenta. Or their appendix, or their spleen, or even the teensiest little corner of their small intestine. Really, she's lucky I didn't sue.

Still mulling over Jenna's high-handedness, it took me a moment to register that a mysterious stranger had swept into our midst: a stunning Dita Von Teese type with a black lace corset cinched in to inhuman proportions at the waist, a death-defying décolletage, and hooker heels that click-clacked across Lisa's spotted-gum floors. She paused in the centre of the living room, hand on shapely hip, like a succulent, well-tended bloom, as she looked out over the sea of brittle, half-dead hydrangeas in dog-hair-covered fleeces and thongs.

'Welcome, everyone, and thank you for coming to our Pleasure Dome Party,' she purred. 'Lisa and I are delighted that you've decided to spice things up in the bedroom with your significant others.'

Pleasure Dome? Spice things up in the bedroom? 'Wrong party!' I wanted to shout, casting around to see if everyone else was as confused as me.

Nope, they all looked pretty on top of things, pardon the pun.

A sex toy party? *This* was how Lisa was planning to boost the family coffers? I suddenly felt a fervent devotion to good old-fashioned Tupperware.

'As every woman knows, all marriages can do with a little fine-tuning from time to time.' There were sniggers of agreement around the room. 'And this morning Lisa and I will give you the essential tools to get you back on the road to passion and to drive your significant other wild.'

With that, Lisa whipped a slinky red velvet cloth off her folding picnic table to reveal an assortment of S&M gear kinky enough to make Christian Grey blush, and proceeded to give us a rundown on the uses of the various devices.

I could barely make myself look. God, oh, God, why was I such a prude?

The others trotted straight on up to the table for a proper look and feel. They switched them on, fired them up, and compared notes like they were road testing the latest snazzy new vacuum cleaners or hand-held mixers.

Someone passed round a tray of champagne glasses. I grabbed two, sculling the contents in quick succession.

Collectively, we analysed the contents of the Hanky Spanky Gift Set, and then launched into a lengthy debate over the pros and cons of an ornamental nipple trap, a painful-looking contraption that locked your nips in place with a pair of decorative steel bars.

'Gideon would go crazy for something like this,' said Lisa, coquettishly, turning it over in her hands.

I stared at her in astonishment. The woman wouldn't share her stupid flapjack recipe for love or money, but she was more than happy to reveal Gideon's penchant for a bit of fetish action?

The next hour felt like it would never end. The only moment of mild reprieve came when Nikki handed over her Mastercard details for a leather-studded ankle-to-wrist bed restraint. 'It'll be perfect for when Cameron's trying to hog the remote control,' she guffawed.

Hmm, really? So that was the kind of thing he was into, was it? My mind wandered off in all sorts of unhealthy directions, none of which featured a remote control.

Wowsers. This was all way too much to take in before we'd even had lunch.

For the record, the morning's shopping haul looked something like this:

- Seven-speed vibrating his n' hers nipple suckers that looked alarmingly like one of those suction devices you attach to milk a cow – purchased by Bree. According to Dita you just popped these ladies in position, flicked the switch, and prepared to get sent into orbit. I dreaded to think what might happen when you turned the dial up to a full seven – nipples fly right off across the room, perhaps? For an extra $39, you could purchase a matching device for your clit.
- A pink spanking paddle and an industrial-size tube of lube – to be enjoyed by Harriet and Jumping Axe Kick Toby.
- A feathery ball tickler – an early birthday present for Ian from Sharron.
- An inflatable anal plug – Jenna for Elliot. NO words. None.
- Wi-Vibe – a really rather impressive wi-fi-enabled ten-speed vibrator you could switch on with your iPhone. Why you'd want to do this, I'm not exactly sure, but once the third glass of champagne had kicked in I admit I was sorely tempted.

In the end, not wanting to look like a complete tight-fisted prude, I forked out $173 for the Seven-Piece Starter Bondage Kit, while sending up a silent prayer to the gods that the details wouldn't appear on our combined Visa card statement.

Lisa was pleased as punch with the morning's progress. As party host, she walked away with a tidy $83 profit and a complimentary pair of pink satin crotchless panties.

Once the bondage goodies and picnic table had been neatly packed away, and Dita had taken her hooker heels and intimidating bust-line back to Smutland, the mums got stuck into the remaining four bottles of champagne. It was like the better parts of high-school parties – after all the boring people had gone home and it was just the core crew left behind, lounging around in their PJs, talking and laughing about the disasters of the night: bad breath, braces locking together, bra straps that refused to come undone. Maybe it was the champagne or maybe it was my gratitude that the hideousness of this morning was over, but I felt myself start to relax.

In keeping with the theme of the day, the conversation soon turned to sex.

'I can never give Toby enough; he's constantly pawing at me,' said Harriet, tucking her bare feet under her on the sofa and taking a delicate sip of champagne.

'I know exactly what you mean,' said Jenna from her cosy spot beside the headless corpse. 'Sometimes I feel like I'm sharing a bed with a hormone-charged teenage boy, and if I ever say "no, I'm just too bloody tired", he spends the whole night sulking. Honest to God, he never lets up, not even when I'm about to give birth.'

There was much nodding and agreeing from around the room.

Suddenly I wasn't having so much fun anymore. I nodded along with everyone else, but inside I was squirming. Matt and I hadn't made love since Judy had moved in. And truthfully I couldn't remember the last time we'd done it *before* she'd moved in. In any case, now, what with the high cringe factor of having to scuttle across the creaky floorboards outside Judy's room to carry Coco back to her own bedroom and the fact that Matt and I were still barely on speaking terms, it was just easier not to even think about it.

'To be honest, I never feel sexier than when I'm pregnant,' said Lisa, shooting a look of yearning across the room towards her plaster-cast belly. 'I'm like a dog in heat. Gideon has to push me away.'

And quite frankly, who could blame him? Terrifying visions of Lisa, eight-and-a-half-months pregnant, in nothing but her pink crotchless panties, lunging at poor, defenceless Gideon like a great, fertile sow flooded my brain.

As I did my best to push these images away, Bree turned to me, her bare thighs squeaking on the plastic-y faux-leather of the sofa. 'What about you, Ally? Does Matt ever let you get a decent night's sleep?'

My God, the woman was like a trained sniffer dog, whiffing out an ounce of weakness and going straight for the jugular.

'Well, you know, new baby and all,' I muttered. 'I think a decent night's sleep is the only thing we're fantasising about.' Phew, got myself out of that one.

Or maybe not quite out of it. Six pairs of eyes bore into me, seeing right through my words, their pity almost palpable.

'What you need is a date night,' announced Lisa as though it were the most obvious thing in the world. 'Go somewhere really special, just the two of you, where you can reconnect and remind yourselves why you fell in love in the first place. And if that doesn't work, you've always got your new toys to fall back on.'

Was it just me, or did a decent night's sleep actually sound a whole lot more appealing than any of that?

'But there are rules,' chimed in Nikki. 'Absolutely no kid talk.' Firm nods of agreement from the other mums. 'Or bills or money or work.'

Geez, what the hell else was there?

A short while later, Bouncy Buttcheeks reappeared with her condescending smile – Haha! Sex toys not necessary when you're seventeen years old and cellulite-free! – and a gaggle of hungry, fractious toddlers.

We said our goodbyes and Nikki dropped Coco and I home.

'Remember – date night,' she said with a wink as I eased my bruised and aching body out of the front seat of the people mover.

I smiled wanly as she sped off, a cloud of black smoke spluttering in her wake.

15

#shoppingemergency #datenight

I tried to shake off the cringe-worthy memories of the sex-toy party by sifting through my hate comments. I'd got down as far as #183, but they were still coming through thick and fast, Enzo's legion of loyal fans refusing to let up without a fight.

Suddenly I heard the 'ping' of new email arriving. Oh God, they'd found me!

No, it was Sunnylove Family Photography.

We look forward to welcoming you and your beautiful family to our studio next Friday at eleven o'clock.

Shit! Point Seven of my plan of attack – the family photo shoot I'd arranged in the first flurry of Master Plan mania – had completely slipped my mind. The timing couldn't have been worse. Matt and I were still officially in the Cold War Zone (my suggestion that we book in a date night had gone down like a lead balloon), and Coco was nursing the tail end of a nasty bout of conjunctivitis, which meant every now and then I had to manually prise her eyelids open.

Happy picture-perfect family we were not!

I dug back through my previous email correspondence with the photographer, a woman who went by the intimidating name of Pascale-Augustine Beaulieu (when I'd first booked our session, I'd thought her Frenchness would lend us some sort of fabulously European flair) to find out what I was supposed to have organised over the past three weeks.

Hobbies, I was supposed to bring along a list of hobbies. Oh God, did late-night internet shopping and lusting over a friend's husband count as hobbies?

Plus, of course, there was the little matter of finding something suitably flattering/non-ageing/timeless for Coco and I to wear that wouldn't have either of us cringing with embarrassment five years from now. My own childhood memories haunted me to this day: I still shuddered at the thought of having to scuttle every boyfriend down the hall at breakneck speed past blown-up images of my mother sitting ramrod straight in her rattan peacock armchair, all Dynasty shoulder pads and poodle perm, Dad hand-on-shoulder in a powder-blue tux behind her, and me elegantly sprawled at their feet, gap-toothed and ridiculous in an oversized peter pan collar.

Obviously nothing I already owned would do, so I palmed Coco off to Judy and made a mad dash into the city.

Destination: David Jones. My fail-safe shopping destination for everything from the most mouth-watering crumbed lamb cutlets imaginable to the babygrows Coco wore home from hospital. Surely they would have the perfect dress to make me feel like a 23-year-old supermodel the minute I set foot in Pascale-Augustine's studio?!

Nooooo, I didn't have overblown expectations at all!

Ah, just inhaling the scent of the perfumes fighting for air space on the ground floor felt like coming home.

I took the escalator up to ladies' fashion on the first floor, a journey I could have made backwards with my eyes closed. I walked past willowy mannequins rocking 1970s-style geometric print dresses and tailored houndstooth pants, giving them the subtlest of nods like they were old friends, and only stopping once to greet a divine mint-green Fendi bodycon number that wrapped Teflon-like around the mannequin's teeny-tiny curves. Oh, to dream.

I ran my fingers along the racks of pretty dresses I knew I would never be able to afford or fit into ever again, and studiously bypassed the Moda concession, from where Alejandro's super-sized disapproving gaze followed me as I did the walk of shame towards the fat corner.

Here, in the Plus Size section, the lights weren't quite as flattering and the sales assistants not quite as pretty, but I knew I'd at least be able to find something that had a vague chance of doing up.

I pulled a couple of stretchy jersey things off the rail without even looking at them, and scuttled into the changing room.

The attendant from Lusty and Large followed me in. 'Are you all right in there? Need a bigger size?'

I hadn't even had time to get my own clothes off yet, let alone pull any of the jersey tents on.

I tried ignoring her, but she wouldn't let up. After several minutes of one-sided conversation I couldn't take it any more. I popped my head out of the cubicle in my maternity bra and control-topped pants to tell her in the nicest possible way to fuck the hell off.

And there – twirling in front of the communal mirror ('cause what's the point hiding in a changing room when you're a Size Negative Two?) in the Teflon Fendi number I'd seen earlier – was *Lola*.

Why, why, *why*?

I quickly slammed the cubicle door shut, but not fast enough.

'Ally, is that you?' Lola yanked the cubicle door open and gave an audible gasp at the sight of me. 'Wow, it really *is* you!' She grabbed the label of the jersey tent in my hand. 'Aeroplane. That's one of my granny's favourites.'

I chose to ignore that. 'So, how's it all going at work? Haven't seen much coverage lately,' I said, hoping to strike the perfect balance between casual interest among former colleagues and bitchy, pointed jab, as I stood there basically naked.

'Oh, we're focusing on the online space now,' she said, gaping unashamedly at the flabby baby apron hanging over the top of my undies (that will never happen to me! I will never let it! I could almost hear her screeching inside her head). 'You probably wouldn't have heard of any of the new online magazines we're targeting,' she said to my belly. 'They're very hip and young.'

There it was again – the *old* reference. For the record, 31 is not old. In Madonna years, it's positively pre-pubescent. But again, in the spirit of my newfound SAHM serenity, I chose not to take the bait.

'So, where are you off to in that pretty dress?' I asked her.

'We've got the Creative Excellence Awards coming up.'

'Alejandro's finally been nominated, huh? That's great. Give him my congratulations,' I said.

'It's me actually. In the PR category. PR Manager of the Year.'

Okay, *ouch*.

At this point, it's probably worth me mentioning that in my whole life I'd never been nominated for a single thing, let alone won anything. I didn't even make school library monitor, a wound I carry with me to this day.

'They talk about you, you know,' said Lola.

'Who does?'

'The girls in the office. And Alejandro, sometimes. I think they miss you.'

Well, give them a middle finger for me, a swift kick up the arse, a piece of Jenna's placenta pie. 'Give them my love.'

Two hours later, I slunk back home, laden down with fifteen bags of old granny clothes I knew I'd probably return in the next week or so, and a mightily bruised ego.

Creative Excellence Awards. PR Manager of the Year.

More like back-stabbing, job-stealing bitch of the year.

How, God, *how*?

Before God could answer, Judy grabbed my arm. 'I've been trying to call you. Something's happened.'

I checked my phone, which was set to silent so it wouldn't interrupt my very important shopping mission. Eleven missed calls. Idiot! 'What is it? Is she alright?' I screeched.

'Coco said her first word,' she gasped, hand to throat. 'Nana.'

'Nana,' I repeated, just to make sure I'd heard her right.

'She was playing with Zippo, her wind-up giraffe. You know – the one I got her at that educational toyshop up in Lindfield? And then she just looked up at me, clear as day, and said it: "Nana."'

'And you're sure it wasn't "Mama"?'

'Nana.'

I eyed Coco in her FunTime playpen. She was now trying to eat the aforementioned educational giraffe. Judy, meanwhile, couldn't wipe the stupid smug smile off her face for love nor money.

'With a bit of luck, she'll do it again in a minute. Anyway, I must dash. I'm meeting up with the internet gang for coffee in Gordon.'

Perfectly fine. A little time alone with Coco was exactly what I needed to deal with this 'Nana' situation before it got out of hand.

Once I was sure we were completely alone, I lifted Coco gently out of her playpen and carried her up to my bedroom. I sat her on my knee in front of the mirror and kissed her smooth little neck. It smelt like banana yogurt.

'Mama,' I said, calm as custard, smiling at her reflection in the glass. Nothing. 'Mama,' a little less custard-like. Again, nothing. She craned around to look me in the eye.

Then, suddenly, with no warning at all, her face changed. Something was going on, I could see it. It was right there on the tip of her tongue. Her mouth opened, forming that darling little 'O' shape I love so much . . . here it was . . . it was coming, I just knew it . . .

'Nana.'

Shit. Fuckety shit. The woman had to go.

*

I was chucking things around the living room when Matt came in.

'What's going on?' he asked, dodging Zippo the fucking educational giraffe as he flew through the air like an Exocet missile towards the toy box.

'Why don't you ask your mother,' I said, now spread-eagled across the floor in an attempt to retrieve pieces twenty-four through thirty-six of Coco's 400-piece kitchen set from the shaggy tendrils of the rug.

How, I ask you, does a tiny nine-month-old consigned to a four-by-four playpen manage to destroy an entire room in less than thirty minutes? The girl had talents I never even knew existed.

I gave Matt a quick debrief on the whole horrific 'Nana' episode, and could see him trying not to laugh.

'Come on, it was just a coincidence.'

'Here I am. I've given up my job, my life, my ironclad rule about never, ever leaving the house in flats, and what do I get rewarded with? "Nana."'

'You're not really going to let this get to you, are you Ally?' he asked.

'Actually, I think I am.'

'You're being ridiculous.' He reached out his arms to pull me up off the floor.

'And speaking of heinous displays of disloyalty, what about you?' I spat. 'A date night with your own wife obviously doesn't sound appealing, hmm? Perhaps you'd prefer a night out on the tiles with "Nana" instead?'

'We'll go somewhere. I'll book us a table,' he said, with a sigh.

'Fine. Do it. Just don't book Basilico. I don't want to be stuck next to a table of ageing Z-listers.'

He laughed. 'As opposed to the cool, cutting-edge suburban hipsters we're hanging out with now?'

I gave him the death look and he was smart enough to drop it.

That night, I had an awful sleep. I woke up drenched in sweat, after a horrific dream about a fashion show where none of the models turned up and I had to walk down the runway wearing nothing but Lisa's pink satin crotchless panties. Coco and Matt had sat beaming at me from the front row, wearing T-shirts with Judy's smug-bloody-smiling face plastered on the front, Coco shouting 'Nana! Nana!' at the sight of me.

*

The plan had been to go somewhere fabulous, but in the end both of us were too knackered to drag ourselves further than the next suburb, so we ended up at Santo's Ristorante up the road – one of those Italian jobbies with a tongue-in-cheek retro theme going on, all red-checked tablecloths and melted candles stuffed inside old wine bottles.

Matt, ever the gentleman, pulled open the door of the restaurant to let me enter first.

'Hang on, before we go in, I should probably mention the rules,' I said.

'Rules?'

'We're strictly forbidden from talking about Coco tonight.'

He smiled. 'Anything else?'

'Um, let's see. Money, work and bills. And it's probably safest if we steer clear of Judy too.'

Matt nodded, curtly, and with that we headed to our table, a cosy little setting for two, with a picturesque view of the tankers thundering down the six-lane highway outside.

At first, conversation flowed. We settled on a farm-stay holiday somewhere in the Kangaroo Valley for next Easter (I would research possible options online), scheduled a trip to Bunnings over the weekend to pick up a paint chart so we could choose a new colour for the front fence, and agreed that it was about time we had the dishwasher looked at because it kept making a horrible grinding noise every time you switched it on. All before the entrees had arrived.

After that, there was a whole lot of silence.

The whole not-mentioning-Coco thing was proving tougher than I'd thought. In one smooth move, it erased everything faintly witty or amusing from my repertoire, leaving me with essentially . . . nothing. I even willed the stupid mandolin player with the builder's crack to come over and play us a tune.

What the hell did we used to talk to each other about?

Matt was struggling too. 'So, have you been having a good time with the mums at playgroup?'

Ah, yes, I met a Dylan McKay look-alike who turns my insides to mush and who just happens to be the husband of one of the other mothers, and I just spent $173 on a bondage kit. How has your week been?

Nervously, I twiddled the hard, melted wax stuck to the bottom of the chianti bottle, as the waiter cleared our zucchini fritters and laid out fresh cutlery for our mains. The silence stretched on, and rather than looking Matt in the eye, I fashioned a rather nice little wax family instead, one of whom had a toothpick wedged firmly between the eyes. I'm still not sure which member of our little family my subconscious meant that one to be. Really, it could have been any of us.

'So, has Judy mentioned her leaving date yet?' I ventured.

He raised an eyebrow. Oh yeah, that's right. She was off-limits too.

'God, why is this so hard?' I wondered, without immediately realising I'd actually said it aloud.

'I don't know,' he said with a heavy sigh.

'We used to have fun, remember? Do you remember fun?' I asked him.

'I do.' He reached across the table, past my little wax family, and took my hand.

Something turned in my stomach – a scary flip, one I'd never felt before. 'Matt, do you think we're –?'

My words were cut off by the arrival of Mr Bumcrack himself, who had decided that now was the perfect time to delight us with a rendition of 'O Sole Mio'.

'Evening folks. You look ready for a little romance,' he said in a completely unromantic and decidedly un-Italian way, before planting his oversized rear on the chair next to us.

We watched him play. We ate our linguine alla carbonara. We ordered coffee. Matt gave him a tip when the performance came to an end, and then it was time to go.

I never did get finish asking Matt that question, and he never asked me to. I guess some things are better left unasked.

Walking back to the car felt like wading through mud, my heart dragging like a dead weight behind me with every step. Date night had been a failure. Rather than make us feel closer, it had only served to highlight just how far we'd drifted apart. I bet the other mums finished off date night with a playful romp in the bedroom. Safe to say that wouldn't be on the cards for us tonight.

Matt was walking Just half a step ahead of me, holding his key out ready to beep the car open with the remote control. Anyone watching us would think we were walking together, but from where I stood it was clear we were walking alone.

The house was pitch black when we pulled up. Strange. Judy had a very irritating and expensive habit of leaving every light in the house on, no matter the time of day or night.

I wasn't the only one who noticed. Matt half walked, half ran to the front door and his hand fumbled as he tried to put the key in the lock. My heart closing in around my throat, I was one step behind him, poised to tear past him up to Coco.

And then I heard it.

The unmistakable sound of giggling – romantic-type giggling – coming from the living room.

Matt flipped on every light switch in rapid-fire succession and the room lit up like a football stadium. Judy's head popped up over the back of the sofa, followed by a bald head with two of the bushiest nostrils I'd ever seen, on a man wearing an Argyll sweater.

'What the hell's going on?' Matt cried.

'This is my friend Gerald,' said Judy, laying her hand on Bushy Nostrils' Argyll-clad shoulder. 'From the internet course.'

Bushy Nostrils nodded curtly to us.

Could it be true? Was it really possible that Judy had got herself a boyfriend? And if so, what the hell was the protocol here? Did we kick Bushy Nostrils out? Send Judy to her room? There's really no rulebook when it comes to your 67-year-old mother-in-law bringing home her toyboy lover for a bit of nooky on the sofa.

Minutes later, we were all sitting around the kitchen table having a cup of tea, no-one saying very much at all. Matt couldn't look at his mother. Harnessing all my PR skills, I did my best to keep the mood light and breezy and steer the conversation as far away as possible from any topic involving OAPs and highly inappropriate sexual shenanigans. 'So, did you learn anything interesting at the internet course today?'; 'What about that new Mel Gibson film? I hear it's going to be his come-back.' It was utterly exhausting.

After Gerald had rather hurriedly finished his tea and we'd all said a chaste farewell at the front door, Matt turned to his mother: 'How could you do this to Dad?'

'Matthew, your father's been dead for fifteen years.' It was the first time I'd heard her use that tone with him, the one she normally reserved for me or the famously unhelpful staff at the takeaway Indian joint.

Matt shook his head, all silent repugnance. But Judy wasn't having a bar of it. 'Do you know how long it's been since I've been out with a man? Had an enjoyable evening with a member of the opposite sex?'

You and me both, honey, I felt like adding.

'Well I think it's disgusting,' he said.

'What? That I've met a nice man? Or that someone in this house is actually communicating with a member of the opposite sex?' she spat back. 'I think people in glass houses really shouldn't throw stones.'

'And what the hell's that supposed to mean?'

'You know exactly what it means.' And with that she stormed upstairs and slammed her bedroom door like the surly teenager she'd apparently become.

I looked across at Matt and promptly burst out laughing. Finally, at least one of us was having fun.

16

#craft #prostitots
#sausagesizzle #shutupandsmile

'You haven't put yourself down for a duty,' barked Drill Sergeant Nikki the minute I arrived at playgroup the following week, thrusting a dog-eared clipboard into my hands.

'A *duty*?'

'Just check the roster and choose something.'

I scanned the bit of paper clipped to the board, which ran top to bottom with a list of playgroup jobs. All the easy ones had already been taken: Harriet had put her name down for laying out the refreshment table; Sharron had swiped clean-up duty; and Bree had nominated herself as today's official fruit chopper-upper. Well, at least we could all rest assured it would be done in the most hygienic way possible. Slim pickings remained: Sing Song, an experience I didn't think any of us cared to revisit, and Craft. Now, while some mothers' hearts might leap at the prospect of a little macramé or papier-mâché with the kids, I wasn't one of them. I'd been crap at art at school, and over the years my feelings about any sort of hands-on activity that started out with a whole lot of mess and ended up with a public viewing (aka judgement) had developed into something verging on the phobic.

The clipboard, the expectations, the dreaded craft cupboard I'd managed to avoid all these weeks . . . they were pushing every panic button I had.

I raced back to Nikki, who was now in the kitchen tallying up the number of cartons of long-life milk still left in the fridge.

'I don't think I can,' I squeaked in a tiny voice.

She turned around. 'Sure you can. What have you got?' she asked, grabbing the clipboard from my trembling hands.

'Craft, easy.'

Yeah, maybe for some.

'That only comes round every three weeks. Actually, Craft's today.'

At this point she must have taken note of the globs of sweat dripping down my face and the look of abject terror in my eyes, because she suddenly dropped the drill-sergeant mask, stood up and put a kindly arm around my shoulders.

'Look,' she said, guiding me ever-so-gently towards the craft cupboard, 'the kids don't even know what they're doing. Just choose a bit of a theme, and go with the flow. As long as it's messy and gets in every bit of their hair and clothes, they'll have a blast.' She opened the doors of the great crafting cupboard and shoved me inside. 'Trust me,' she said, shutting the doors with a bang.

It was like a bomb had gone off at Mardi Gras. There were feathers, glue, crayons, glitter, paint and sequins as far as the eye could see. Just looking at it made my head hurt. A theme? How the hell was I supposed to make a theme out of this hot load of crap?

As I mentally ran through my options, my throat began to constrict and it became harder and harder to breathe.

Somewhere outside I heard Nikki give the kids their marching orders: 'Hurry up with that morning tea, everyone! Craft's next!'

Hell, hell. Think, think!

Then, in a blinding flash, it came to me: makeup lesson!

I ran out of the craft cupboard, grabbed my handbag, turned it on its head, and emptied out every manky stick of mascara, ground-down tube of lipstick and half-congealed pot of concealer, as well as a whole load of other crap I hadn't even remembered was in there. Remnants from my previous life just waiting to come to the rescue in my new one lay sprawled across the craft table.

'Craft's up!' I announced with near-hysterical relief as a horde of excited toddlers crowded around me. 'Okay, today's theme is going to be a little different . . .'

I sat them down at the table and began.

*

Twenty minutes later, Bree sidled over, eyeing little Crystabella as she attempted to attach falsies to her eyelashes with paper glue. 'It's hardly craft,' she sneered.

Yes, hello, actual Life Skill. You're welcome.

'Look,' I said, holding Coco's hand behind her back. 'I've even taught them how to do it one-handed so they can touch up their makeup when they're half pissed.'

Bree didn't seem entirely convinced. 'They look like a bunch of prostitots,' she sniffed.

Really, she was probably just worried about how enthusiastically her beloved little Hunter was taking to the whole thing.

There was only one other slight blip in my otherwise perfect Mini Makeover Tutorial. As I was busy shading in Milly's patchy eyebrows, the sound of Harriet's piercing cry filled the air. 'Oh my God, has someone given him tree nuts?' she screeched, pointing at the huge, plumped-up lips that were now threatening to swallow Archie's face.

Christ, not this again.

Everyone crowded around him. I gave his lips a poke. Then a wipe. Nope, not tree nuts: turned out it was just my Lip Inflator lipstick in my all-time favourite shade of Roaring Climax. I sighed audibly with relief, while Harriet sneered at me wordlessly and whisked Archie off to the corner for a soothing breastfeed. But I'll bet my last dollar she was straight off down the shops to buy some Roaring Climax for herself later.

After all the mums had left for the morning and taken their happy little prostitots home for a nap, it was just Nikki and I. She swept the cookie crumbs and bits of squashed banana off the floor, while I did my best to remove the industrial-strength eyeliner now smeared across the back of every chair.

There was companionable silence for a while, then she looked up at me. 'I forgot to ask, how was date night?'

Hmm, how to respond . . . Wonderful? Blissfully romantic? Best night of my life? 'Disaster.'

'Don't sweat it,' she said with a giggle. 'The first time Cameron and I went out after the twins were born, I started leaking milk all over the front of my top as soon as the waiter uttered the words "dulce de leche". And then I fell asleep in my minestrone.'

I laughed. I wasn't used to women like Nikki, women who were happy to reveal their soft little underbellies. The ones I was used to were far more likely to go out of their way to prove just how rock-hard and impenetrable their abs and their outer shells were. 'Here, punch me, hard as you like, and we'll see who's left hurting,' they seemed to say. This was a new experience for me, and not an altogether bad one.

*

Judy was out when Coco and I got home, presumably carousing with her hairy-nostrilled lover, so we pulled out the snazzy red KitchenAid Matt and I had been given as a wedding present but never actually gotten round to opening, and spent the afternoon baking mini cupcakes. I thought we might take them to the park the next day to share out with Coco's friends.

The end results were pretty impressive: we'd done Mrs Fields proud. 'And I won't tell anyone our little secret if you don't, mmm?' I said to Coco with a smile, as I tucked the cardboard box behind the bin.

She grinned her funny little three-toothed smile back at me, then returned to the job at hand; smearing lurid pink icing on top of the cupcakes and across the surrounding benchtops.

I was beginning to enjoy the new pace of our days. While our schedule was technically more jam-packed than it had ever been, there was somehow more time to be together, just being. The days didn't feel so much like a slow, painful grind up a steep mountain anymore. They were more like a pleasant unfolding. Some of the time, I felt like I was actually enjoying myself.

I was just getting started on dinner when I heard Matt unlocking the safety gate in the hall. 'A reservation fee of $875 for a place in the Kindergarten class at St Swithuns?' he said, almost choking on the words as he walked into the kitchen, holding up a letter with a very smart, gold-embossed logo at the top.

'Yes, and you're welcome,' I said, tossing a handful of mushrooms into my new state-of-the-art Thermomix. 'I know you'll sleep better at night knowing that your only child has her future secured at the best primary school in the country.' Perhaps now wasn't the time to tell him the aforementioned Thermomix had cost me more than the St Swithuns reservation fee and the first couple of years' school fees combined. I couldn't be sure how impressed he'd be that not only could it create mouthwatering savoury dishes, but it could ferment its own yogurt too.

'And look here,' he said, jabbing at the piece of paper with his finger. 'It says they want an extra $255 every year for the next few years just for doing us the honour of holding her place!' He stressed the 'five' like it made some huge, enormous difference.

'Come on, Matt, you and I both know I used to spend that in a week on shoes,' I said.

'But you were working then. We're on one income now. Things are different, can't you see that?' he barked back.

'What I can see is that you're deluding yourself if you think these things don't matter. It's not just about her educational needs, but her social ones too. St Swithuns is going to help her, you'll see.'

'Oh God, now you're even starting to sound like one of them.'

'Starting to sound like who, exactly?' I spat back, snapping the lid shut on my Thermomix.

'Those playgroup nutters. You're turning into some sort of Stepford wife. I don't even recognise you any more.'

'Well take a good hard look in the mirror, Mama's boy, because sometimes I don't have a damn clue who you are either.'

We stared at each other. Stalemate.

'And another thing,' he said quietly, deliberately. 'I think we should consider cutting out the internet supermarket shop. The delivery bill is really adding up.'

Okay, now he was just being ridiculous. 'And how exactly do you expect us to eat?'

He raised an eyebrow.

No. He couldn't have meant what I thought he meant.

'You know I don't do supermarkets.' I had it on very good authority (Flora, who had also trained as a healer) that the supermarket scrum interferes with my very delicate chakra.

'Well it's either home delivery or your two takeaway cappuccinos a day. You choose.'

What the hell kind of choice was that?

'Oh and something else arrived for you in the post too,' he said before I could respond to his ridiculous ultimatum. He tossed a mysterious brown package my way. I turned it over. No return address.

Judy wandered in, flushed and a little breathless from her afternoon with Gerald. 'What's that, then?' she asked, nodding towards the package. 'No idea,' I said, ripping the paper off with a flourish.

My seven-piece beginner's bondage kit. One 'tickly palm' spanking paddle, one lace-edged satin blindfold with Velcro closure, two padded wrist cuffs, two ankle cuffs, and a handy pink bag to store them all neatly away after use. Judy walked, tittering, out of the kitchen.

I looked across at Matt. 'I swear to God, I thought it was lunch-boxes.' He stared open-mouthed back at me.

Mental note – next time I order sex toys, must organise a PO box.

But later that evening, after I'd put Coco down, I discovered the bondage kit carefully deposited in the top drawer of my bedside table. Hmm, maybe Dita was right. Maybe it was time for a little bedroom tune-up.

I crept towards the bathroom, ready to do a little primping before bed, just, you know, in case, when Judy waylaid me in the hall. 'I was just wondering,' she said, stumbling a little over her words. 'Where you bought that set from?'

And just like that, in a puff of smoke, the steam was blown clean off what had potentially been a hot night of passion.

When, when, *when* would I ever have sex again?

*

So today was the day of the Annual Happy Mummies Sausage Sizzle, otherwise known as the perfect excuse to wrangle hard-earned cash from unsuspecting DIY enthusiasts outside the local hardware store so we could re-stock the playgroup craft cupboard.

Harriet and Jenna arrived with armloads of shopping bags filled with budget pork sausages and home-brand sliced white bread: 'You lot owe us fifteen bucks each.'

We set about assembling our folding picnic table and firing up the portable Weber alongside the local Scouts group and the ambulance service, and prepared to do battle. Our cunning plan was to undercut the competition by fifty cents a sausage, to draw attention away from the fact that both the Scouts and the ambulance lot were not only offering gluten-free options but complimentary fried onions to boot.

'Here, have a sausage,' we said, thrusting one at every poor, defence-less soul that walked past our stand at 7.45 in the morning, whether they liked it or not. 'That'll be $2 please.'

The husbands had come out in force to support the fundraising efforts of the Happy Mummies, and were decked out in aprons and brandishing tongs and industrial-size bottles of tomato sauce like their lives depended on it. It was excruciating. I couldn't look at a single one of them. None of the other mums had said it, but I could only presume they had all received their special deliveries in the post too, which filled my mind with mental images I'd really rather have done without.

'That ambulance lot are using curried pork and pineapple. The kids love 'em. We're really gonna have to up our game,' Elliot said to me gravely from behind his 'Mr Good Lookin' Doin' Your Cookin'' novelty barbecue apron.

'Yes indeed,' I replied, as if I was a foreign correspondent reporting from the front line on the six o'clock news.

Anal plug, anal plug, anal plug, anal plug.

Cameron arrived, having taken Ashleigh to an early morning soccer game. 'They lost five nil, but Ash played her best game of the whole season,' he said proudly (not only was he a great dad but a great stepdad too!). He donned his 'King of the BBQ' apron and took up position behind the Weber. As he chatted and laughed with the other parents, I felt myself unable to stop gazing at him from beneath my regulation Happy Mummies peaked cap (emblazoned, naturally, with the group logo 'Happy Mummies Rock!' For the love of God, wasn't it enough that I was here when I could be lying in bed with a bloody mary and the weekend papers?). He was like one of the sausages sizzling on the grill, ripe and tasty and filled with all sorts of things you know are bad for you but taste so damn good.

I wondered whether he'd been enjoying his ankle-to-wrist bed restraints.

Nikki nudged me. 'Matt's great, isn't he?'

'Huh? Who?' How dare she interrupt my lustful fantasies about her husband.

'Matt, he's such a sweetheart. Did you see he just bought that little kid with the crew cut two sausage sandwiches because he didn't have any money on him?'

'Oh yeah, he's always the soft touch,' I said.

It was true. Unless, of course, it involved me spending money on shoes, scatter cushions, home delivery, non-surgical cosmetic procedures or basically anything that brought an ounce of happiness to my day. Regarding those items, he was a tight-fisted bastard who could squeeze the last drop of pleasure out of the smallest of life's joys.

I watched as he slathered tomato sauce on one then the other of the crew-cut kid's sausages and then challenged him to a playful arm-wrestle.

Okay, maybe bastard was too strong a word. But the tight-fisted part was still true.

*

'Please remind me again why we're doing this?' asked Matt as he tried to master the mechanics of 'The Triangle', a complicated manoeuvre that involved him straddling my buttocks from behind, splay-legged, while I cradled Coco in my arms and we all smiled blissfully into the camera.

We were forty-five minutes into our happy family photo shoot, and Pascale-Augustine, bless her French cotton socks, was doing her utmost to get us on task.

'Because I want to remind myself every day as I gaze at your picture on the wall how much I love you,' I replied, giving him a firm shove in the gut so that he'd remove his elbow from my back.

And later:

'Higher, higher,' Pascale-Augustine urged as she squinted through the lens. 'And higher still!'

I could tell from the slump in Matt's posture that he wasn't even going to attempt to nail the leap-in-the-air-with-joy pose, and was in actual fact beginning to lose the will to live.

He wasn't the only one. The mega-watt smiles I'd started out the day with now felt more like pained grimaces, and every now and then

I'd had to check Coco's eyes to make sure they weren't stuck together again, giving the impression she'd lost two rounds to ten with Anthony Mundine.

The whole thing was a complete joke. All of the Lusty and Large outfits I'd brought with me to the shoot had instantly been deemed unusable. Black, apparently, 'does not verk so vell in zee natural light'. Not wanting to hamper Pascale-Augustine's creative process, I resisted the urge to ask why the hell, in all her fifty-four million emails to me over the past three weeks, she had neglected to mention this one pretty elementary fact? I mean, show me a woman of childbearing age who doesn't naturally gravitate towards the all-black section of her wardrobe when she knows she's going to get her picture taken.

So that meant I had to be photographed in Matt's once-white, now-grey t-shirt and ripped jeans, which I'd driven over here in. Suddenly my mother's *Dynasty*-style shoulder pads and poodle perm didn't seem quite so bad.

'I want happy, loved up, you're in love,' Pascale enthused. Ah, nothing quite says happy families like needing stage directions from a complete stranger in order to demonstrate your love for each other.

We did playful.

We did cool.

We lay on the floor. We cuddled.

We tossed Coco between us through the air like a basketball – because that's the kind of thing we did every day in the real world!

We even kissed.

'Don't worry – I'm very good weet de Photoshop,' Pascale-Augustine promised as we crawled out the studio door ninety minutes later.

*

The next day, I chose not to relive our family-photo-shoot nightmare by recounting it to the other mums at the Happy Mummies park get-together.

It was Thursday, so we knew to give Bree a wide berth: it was one of her air days. She stood sour-faced and scary behind Hunter at the swings, calculating under her breath how many calories she was burning with each push as he giggled and kicked his feet in the air.

Sharron sat on a picnic mat on the grass with Ruby, the two of them surrounded by an assortment of activity books in deceptively fun colours, with titles like *Algebra Is Fun!* and *How to Get Ahead of the Class . . . and Stay There*, all of which would guarantee Ruby's position as the most hated child in kindergarten.

The other mums busied themselves nearby with their weekly ritual of passing around plastic bin-liners filled with hand-me-down clothes. So, business as usual, really.

I slumped over my now-cold and, if Budget Matt had his way, quite possibly last-ever cappuccino and watched the ceremonial clothes exchange. Harriet was swooning over a tatty old pair of shorts that Jenna had gifted to Archie, while Jenna licked her fingers and attempted to rub a dirty mark off the hem. Vegetarian spag bol, perhaps? Regardless, both looked entirely satisfied with the transaction.

I was trying my hardest, I really was, but some things I just didn't get. Take this clothes-swapping business. Here they were, driving their top-of-the-line Range Rovers, and putting their multitude of kids down for the sort of schools that cost more than my father had earned in his entire lifetime. Most of them had sublime little million-dollar holiday homes tucked away on the coast or on the side of a glorious sun-soaked mountain. And yet, they were happy to dress their kids in second-hand crap covered in stains from another child's dinner. Then, just to make the hand-me-downs even more appealing, at the very moment of handover they would reveal that their entire household was infested with nits or the cat couldn't shift its fleas.

It was like they were all playing a game of 'Who Can Out-Thrift Who?' Thankfully, no-one had picked me for their team.

And then, as I looked from the Happy Mummies clothes exchange over to Sharron, busy telling Lisa she was actually the very opposite of a pushy parent and that Ruby refused to read anything but university-level books, and finally to Bree, always on a mission to convince us she enjoyed nothing more the taste of air, it occurred to me that I wasn't the only one with a Master Plan: perhaps I had more in common with these women than I'd thought.

17

#HappyMummylife #HotDaddy #worstmotherever

And so I settled into the Happy Mummies routine: coffee shop Mondays, playgroup Tuesdays, coffee shop Wednesdays, park or indoor play centre on Thursdays.

This was interspersed with the not insubstantial amount of time I spent obsessing over Cameron. I'd even dug out the state-of-the-art squat cage from the bottom of Judy's cupboard. I hadn't actually used it, mind, but I'd certainly thought about it, and I figured that was at least a step in the right direction.

I couldn't help noticing that Cameron had started coming to playgroup every week, and at some point during each session he invariably ended up next to me. It was the same routine every time; he'd saunter in with Nikki and the twins, circle the room doing a bit of cursory chit-chat with the other mums, pop the twins in the sandpit or at the craft table or wherever they were likely to make the most trouble, and then wander casually over my way. We'd then spend the rest of the morning giggling and flirting over our tepid cups of tea like a pair of teenagers.

I wondered whether anyone else had begun to notice. I knew that Nikki wouldn't be a problem – she was far too busy playing Sergeant

Major with her long-life milk audits and organising of the morning tea roster to register that her husband's attention was directed anywhere other than her and the twins. But Bree, Lisa, Sharron, Jenna and Harriet – they were all just as switched on to Hot Daddy's movements as I was. Surely, they'd clock something was up?

And I knew I should feel guilty. Cameron was married, so was I, and Nikki and Matt were not exactly ogres. But on the back of what felt like a lifetime of bone-crushing boredom and self-loathing, these little bursts of Cameron-coated sunshine felt like the only thing I had. And that's all they were, after all – little glimmers of light in an otherwise dull and gloomy abyss. They weren't causing anyone any harm, so why should I give them up?

Meanwhile, back on the home front, things were looking up. Judy was spending more and more time with Gerald and less and less time hovering over me, which delighted me no end but left Matt simmering like a resentful adolescent in the depths of a full-blown emo phase.

Judy, not immune to her beloved youngest son's misery, had now resorted to covert tactics every time a date with Gerald was on the cards. She'd come downstairs with pink lipstick smeared across her two front teeth and trailing old lady perfume, and offer up the same breezy line every time: 'Just popping out to meet a few friends to go over some internet biz tonight.' Geez, it was like we were back at school again, only this time Judy was the hot young teenager sneaking off to have some fun and we were the disapproving old fuddy-duddies stuck at home, being lied to.

But the whole role-reversal joke was beginning to lose its lustre, and I knew Judy would want to swing things back her way some time soon. I just wasn't sure how.

Before long, I found out.

Judy suggested we go out for lunch the following Sunday, just the five of us.

'Why on earth would she think I'd want to do that?' Matt asked me, incredulous.

Being female, I understood exactly what Judy was up to.

We went to one of those atrocious family-friendly pubs replete with indoor play area, video games room and an ocean of slot machines artfully designed to keep every member of the family happily emptying their pockets for hours on end. It was the sort of place Matt and I used to laugh about together on a Saturday morning over our baked Spanish eggs and cinnamon and buckwheat pancakes at some cool little inner-city café. Yep, karma really was a bitch.

The venue had been Gerald's suggestion – apparently his grandkids couldn't get enough of the place. Oh God, were we a blended family now? Was this our future? I wasn't sure how my husband, who very much subscribed to traditional '70s family values in which Mum and Dad stayed together forever even if they couldn't resist baring their teeth at the sight of each other, would handle it.

As we queued up at the all-you-can-eat buffet behind a frazzled couple with seventeen squabbling kids, I watched how gently Gerald tended to Judy: the way he offered up the best soy-and-linseed roll in the basket, carved her the slenderest cut of meat just the way she liked it, and leapt to protect her when one of the squabblers in front of us began kicking his brother in the shin. Something about it made my heart ache.

Gerald talked about his grandkids. We heard how little Henry had a bit of a speech impediment that made him shy around the other kids but really seemed to be coming out of himself now that he'd discovered drama, and how proud they'd all been when he was chosen as understudy to play Fagin in the school play. And how his little sister Olivia was desperately angling for a rabbit. It was obvious he loved them.

Next, it was Judy's turn to gloat. We heard how her own wunderkinds were set to take over the world just about any day now: 'David's had the most brilliant idea for a gadget that allows you to wear your own pet. Can you imagine? He's just trying to get a patent for it. And Lawrence, of course, has just been made assistant to the assistant manager at his local co-op.' It was enough to make me want to hack up my cheesy leek-and-potato mash all over the plastic tablecloth. But Gerald listened attentively and nodded and smiled in all the right places. Funny, but I didn't even think he was putting it on.

Less and less, I was noticing the hairy nostrils and thinking how cruel Mother Nature could be in her distribution of hair. More and more, I was noticing what a genuinely nice man Gerald was.

'Complete tool,' whispered Matt to me as he watched Gerald's careful attempts to crack open the plastic-y topping on his crème brûlée without making the whole thing explode across the table.

'He's a nice man, Matt. You really should give him a chance.'

God, was this really me speaking? Maybe Matt's brainwashing theory was right and I really was turning into a Stepford wife (must google what that actually was) without even realising it?

We dropped Gerald home at his flat in Killara (several failed eyesight tests in a row meant he no longer had his licence, but that was okay because he'd really learnt to love walking again) and he thanked us for a wonderful lunch, despite the fact he'd paid.

'Well, thank Christ that's over,' Matt said to no-one in particular when Gerald was far enough out of earshot.

Judy said nothing and neither did I. Both of us knew her cunning little plan to win Matt over was starting to work, even if he didn't know it yet himself.

*

Later that evening, Matt asked me to help him prepare for an interview he'd be doing with Sky Business TV the following day. He'd be talking about the rise of online streaming in home entertainment – from TVs and gaming stations to laptops and now smartphones – and so we did a few practice run-throughs in the bedroom, like we usually did before his press interviews.

'Don't you think you should be focusing more on the national broadband changes and its effect on rural areas when you get to that bit?' I asked him when he dodged what I thought was a pretty straightforward question the interviewer was likely to ask.

He looked at me for a moment. 'Don't you miss it?'

'Um, that's not answering my question,' I said.

'I mean it. You're so good at this. Surely a tiny part of you misses it?'

'Not really,' I said.

*

But the next day I wasn't feeling so sure. As I stood between Harriet and Bree in the assembly line outside the toy cupboard, handing a plastic car, followed by a play kitchen and then a smiling three-legged goat, into the hands next to me, I started thinking: is this really it? Is this the sum total of my life now? My job, my identity, my nice clothes: everything I'd worked so hard and so long for – had letting go of it all without a fight really been worth it? Had it brought Matt and I any closer? Or did the skundies still stand between us like a huge unresolved question mark?

And then Cameron arrived, instantly wiping all these horribly existential questions from my mind. I felt myself perk up. His gorgeous smile and cheeky little in-jokes were just the boost I needed.

Nikki was in charge of Sing Song today and had roped Cameron in to help her out. My heart sank as he rallied the kids into what promised to be an enthusiastic and lengthy rendition of 'Fruit Salad – Yummy Yummy', replete with plenty of jumping and butt-wiggling across the hall. I lingered in the kitchen, washing up the mugs and teaspoons as slowly as I could in the hope that he might pop in, even just for a few moments.

Dammit. By stooping down on my knees and peering through the scullery window I could see that he'd now been sidetracked by Jenna, who, having exhausted everyone else's ear about the whole thing, was now rabbiting on tearfully to Matt about how Elliot had ruined Hamish's chances for life by secretly signing him up for a place at his old grammar school, The Everglades, and not the Steiner school, as she'd wanted. So now, instead of learning how to meditate, connect with his feminine side and curdle his own cheese, he'd be transformed into one of those burly hugger-rugger types who communicate by grunting and get mocked at parties for their bad dancing and severe haircuts.

'How could he do this to me?' she wailed, clinging to Matt's arm.

Her life, apparently, was no longer worth living. At this point it took all my willpower not to leap through that scullery window and tell her that a two-million-plus house on the better side of St Ives, a timeshare in a Noosa beach shack (read: mansion fronting right onto the sand), a fine, upstanding husband in decent employ, and a brand-new top-of-the-line Mercedes convertible were hardly good enough reasons to top yourself, and were in fact things that most people would kill *other people* for, but it somehow didn't seem like the right moment. I couldn't help noticing a smug smile plastered across Harriet's face as she quietly gathered up all the dirty mugs and plates and listened to Jenna's outpouring of grief. In the unspoken but never-ending competition for Earth Mama supremacy between her and Jenna, for once Harriet had come out on top. Archie's spot in the 2019 class of Steiner Primary was secured; his cheese-curdling, basket-weaving future was all sewn up.

Shit. It was nearly eleven thirty; time was almost up. I let out a sigh. Oh well, only another week till I'd see Cameron again.

'Pass me the tea towel and you've got yourself a drying assistant.' Hooray! He'd arrived!

We compared notes on the most disgusting methods for concealing vegetables in your kids' dinners, talked about a new fashion photography exhibition that was coming up at the MCA that we were both dying to see, and marvelled at the mind-boggling and never-ending popularity of The Wiggles ('it's like they come out of the womb singing those damn songs!') despite the fact they weren't even a group anymore.

Or were they? Neither of us could actually remember.

'I've met The Wiggles, you know. The original line-up,' I said, dropping my tone to a serious level.

'You name-dropper – I bet that's how you introduce yourself at every party,' he laughed, swiping me on the bum with his wet tea towel.

With psychic smarts I'm sure she didn't even know she had, Nikki chose that exact moment to make her presence known.

'Okay everyone, time to pack away,' she hollered out in the main hall. 'We'll see you all next time. Don't forget it's Hawaiian Week – bring your grass skirts and maracas!'

But that was fine. I'd had my fix for the day. To hell with missing work. To hell with Matt and his stupid skundies. The sun was out and I was with a gorgeous man, albeit a very married one, and had a whole afternoon of snuggling on the sofa watching *Yo Gabba Gabba* with my delicious daughter to look forward to. Things weren't so bad, right?

I headed out to the hall to get Coco.

Coco.

Where was Coco? *Where the fuck was she?!*

I ran to check all the obvious places – under the trestle tables, on the school stage, behind the boys' urinal. She wasn't in any of them.

It was then that I noticed the heavy hallway doors swinging wide open on their hinges – something that was strictly forbidden, and usually very closely monitored, by the Happy Mummies. It felt like a clammy hand was clutching at my heart as I remembered that the school sat on the junction of two very busy roads.

A sort of piercing, primal scream escaped from deep inside me, and my world screeched to a halt.

And then a funny thing happened – everyone else's world stopped too. In less time than it took to exhale, every parent in that room was on the same page as me. And although I didn't see a single pair of lips moving, word spread like wildfire through the group. One of ours was missing. 'Rockabye Your Bear' was swiftly shut off, teams of mums were rounded up to scour the playground and roads (roads!), arms were around me, and faceless voices were asking me gentle probing questions – Where had I last seen her? What had she been doing?

I don't know, I don't know, I don't know! I was too busy bloody flirting with Cameron, wasn't I?!

It was Nikki who found her.

Thank God she'd bypassed the roads and wandered straight into the middle of a Year 2 scripture class. The teacher hadn't even noticed that a chubby little ten-month-old had crawled into their midst and sat down quiet as a mouse on the mat beside the other children to hear how David had met Goliath.

'She's here, she's fine,' said Nikki, depositing Coco back in my arms.

There was a collective sigh of relief, and I promptly burst into deep, snotty sobs.

For once I was grateful for Nikki's bossy, militant ways. With no input from me, it was decided that I would leave my car at playgroup, and Coco and I would go back to Nikki and Cameron's. It was my third trip in the people mover, but this time I barely registered the bumps or squeaks or the fact that I was bouncing around in the back like a ping-pong ball between the snotty-nosed twins. I didn't notice anything, in fact, except Coco's face and hair and breath next to me.

Nikki and Cameron helped us out of the car.

I'm not sure whether Id ever imagined what the inside of Nikki's house would be like, but if I had, my money would have been on perfection. Everything in order, books lined up on the shelves in colour-ascending order; hospital corners stretched so tight you could bounce your dinner off them; not a hair, not a toothbrush, not a teaspoon out of place. I mean, what else would you expect from a Type A army majorette sort?

Instead, what greeted me as I stepped through the door into their open-plan kitchen and living room was complete and utter chaos. Toys were strewn across the floor, cushions had been removed from all the sofas to create a series of cosy, interconnecting forts that snaked right the way out onto the deck, the walls were pockmarked top to bottom from what I could only imagine had been games of indoor golf, and a stack of dirty dishes towered precariously in the kitchen sink.

Notably absent from this scene were carved letters on the wall spelling out where we were. No need. The whole place screamed 'home' from its every pore.

And I loved it.

Cameron headed straight to the kitchen and poured me a glass of something strong and sweet, depositing it in my hand without a word, while Nikki brushed a pile of Cheerios off a couple of cushions on the living room floor and tossed them onto the sofa. She handed Coco a huge chocolate-chip cookie from an open jar on the coffee table, and patted the spot on the sofa beside her. I flopped down.

'I bet that would never have happened to you,' I said.

'What are you talking about?' she guffawed, looking back towards the kitchen. 'I'm the worst mother around. Tell her, Cam.'

Cameron nodded away vigorously from behind the breakfast bar. 'Besides,' she said, turning back to me. 'You wouldn't be a proper mother if you didn't lose your kid at least a couple of times.'

I couldn't help but laugh through my tears.

She pointed to an empty fish tank filled with murky green water on the console table behind us. 'See that? Used to house Kermit the goldfish, who sadly passed away last Thursday morning. I popped him in the toilet before the kids woke up, as you do, only I forgot to actually flush.' Oh no. 'Yep, Bodie found himself peeing on Kermit's corpse. The poor kid will be scarred for life. And when Ashleigh was younger, I forgot the tooth fairy so many times she went into school and tried to convince her entire class that the tooth fairy's actually meant to leave IOUs. Need I go on?'

Huh. Well, that was unexpected.

The blender came whizzing to life behind us. Cameron was fixing the kids banana smoothies. 'Ally, you want one?' he asked.

Yeah, I did.

Coco and I stayed all through lunch until it was almost time for Cameron to pick up Ashleigh from school. Conversation moved from spectacular parenting fails to the impossibility, after you'd had kids, of holding on to the person you once were and the couple you'd once been.

'But the thing is, it does get easier,' said Nikki as she passed Snotty Twin One the Foxtel remote so he could fire up *Peppa Pig*. 'Now that the boys are out of nappies and sleeping through the night, Cameron and I are actually making plans again, going out. We've even been to the movies.'

The last thing I wanted to think about was the two of them going out, having fun. Easiest solution: bring it back around to me. 'God, I can't remember the last time I saw a movie,' I sighed.

'Well, let's go, the four of us,' said Nikki. 'It'll be fun.'

Hmm, a double date with Nikki and Cameron wasn't quite what I'd had in mind. It'd be a bit like going on a date with your teenage fantasy and his mother. My little crush on Cameron was something I wanted to protect and keep to myself for as long as I could. The last thing on earth I wanted was for us all to become friends.

But like the double-faced cow that I am, I nodded and smiled enthusiastically. 'I wonder if that new Brad Pitt one's out yet,' I cooed.

None of us was sure, so we decided I would google it before the week was out.

*

When Coco and I finally dragged ourselves home later that afternoon, we found something waiting for us on the doorstep. A blue zip-up cooler bag and a white shopper with the name of the local supermarket stamped on the side. I was pretty sure I hadn't ordered anything online in the past few days and I couldn't for the life of me imagine what it might be.

I gingerly unzipped the lid and peered inside. The smell of warm roast chicken filled my nostrils. I pulled back the carefully folded silver foil. Yes, it was indeed a roast chicken. And there was gravy, and pan-fried brussel sprouts, and mashed potato, all tubbed up in neat little individual containers, and in the white shopper, two bottles of fancy-looking Japanese beer and a bottle opener. A small folded-up note in writing I didn't recognise said: 'Enjoy.'

I slumped down right there on the doorstep, next to the chicken, holding Coco tight, and wept.

It was, without a doubt, the nicest thing anyone had ever done for me.

18

#moviedate
#Dylan #Brenda #90210
#nothingcomesclose

For some reason I never got round to telling Matt about our movie plans with Nikki and Cameron. I kept meaning to, but every time I remembered it, something came up and it slipped my mind again. In the end, Matt went off to work on Thursday morning still clueless about the whole thing.

It had been one of those crazy days that felt like it would never end. Coco had refused to go down for her afternoon nap and was being as grizzly as a bear with a sore foot, and Judy had managed to bugger up our internet connection in her effort to recalibrate the something with the something-or-other – a vital security measure she'd picked up at her training course that apparently we couldn't possibly do without.

'If you could just find me the wi-fi password, Alexis, I'm sure I could get it up and running again.'

If I could have found the damn wi-fi password, I'd have been more inclined to shove it down her throat.

At just after four my phone pinged. It was Nikki.

Sorry hon, can't make movies tonight. Cameron still keen if you guys r? x N

Hmm. I had to think about that one for a second. What would Angelina or Gwyneth or any of my other celebrity Twitter besties do?

No probs. We'll see him there @ 7. xx A

I did try ringing Matt: several times in fact. As luck would have it, he never picked up.

In the end I sent him a text, then hastily pulled out a tub of lamb curry from the freezer to defrost by the sink, and raced upstairs to get ready before I chickened out.

I dressed deliberately low-key in jeans and a slouchy cashmere V-neck. The last thing I wanted was for Cameron to think I was making any sort of special effort.

He was already outside the cinema when I arrived, leaning up against the wall in a very Dylan McKay-esque fashion and flicking through his iPhone. My stomach lurched at the sight of him and I had to remind myself how to put one foot in front of the other as I walked towards him. He shoved his phone in his back pocket when he saw me and leaned in to offer up a chaste peck on my cheek. The bristles on his chin grazed my skin, and he smelt musky and oh-so-different to Matt, like a mix of saddle-leather and soap. The whole ride-'em-cowboy effect completely undid me, and as a result his kiss ended up somewhere around my ear.

'Sorry,' I mumbled, feeling my cheeks burning bright. I was a mother, goddammit. This sort of childish shit was supposed to be long over by now.

'No, I'm sorry,' he said. 'We've messed up your plans. Nikki had to help Ash with a history assignment for school.' He glanced over my shoulder. 'Where's Matt?'

'Stuck at work,' I said with a doleful sigh. 'Looks like it's just you and me.'

He pulled out one of the three tickets in his hand. 'Guess we won't be needing this then.'

I watched as he sauntered over to a balding man standing at the back of the box-office queue and tapped him on the shoulder. He handed him the spare ticket. When the guy opened up his wallet to give him some money, Cameron waved him away. 'Enjoy the movie,' I heard him say. Ticket man beamed, pathetically grateful to be saving $18. Could Cameron be any more charming if he tried?

I would tell you what the movie was like if I had any idea. It was something about pirates and lost treasure and the Spanish Civil War, I do know that, but I was far too busy being completely over-aware of Cameron's every breath, every miniscule movement beside me, to follow what was happening on the screen.

He didn't hog the armrest like Matt did, nor did he force me to spend the first half of the movie listening to him chomp loudly through a mega box of sweet and salty popcorn. I spent at least thirty minutes side-eyeing the tiny gap between our arms on the armrest, willing him to move his arm just a little bit closer, until eventually he did and the hairs on our forearms were touching. For the next forty-five minutes I didn't breathe.

God, this was like high school.

After the movie we went for a coffee that turned into a couple of glasses of wine. We talked and talked and didn't show any signs of running out of things to say. One topic just spilled over naturally into the next, our words crossing, our sentences merging. More than once we said the exact same word at the exact same time, making us both crack up. At one point, I even showed him the cheesy outtakes from our disastrous family photo shoot on my phone, and we laughed together at the ridiculousness of it. And the whole time I could feel the toe of his shoe under the table, resting suggestively against mine.

'I'd never do that,' he said. 'I know exactly how I'd like to shoot you.'

He held my gaze for just a beat too long, the smile fading from his lips, and suddenly the little tune we'd been playing together all this time changed pitch.

By 10.45, every other table in the café was empty and the waitress told us she was closing up for the night.

It was, quite honestly, the best first date of my life. Without the whole both of us being married and having kids part, that is. Maybe *because* of it. Who knows?

When I got home, I crept up the front steps and opened the door as quietly as I could, but obviously not quietly enough.

'How was the movie?' Matt called out from the kitchen.

'Fine, good,' I said, trying to mask my jittery over-excitement with the slowest and most casual of ambles into the room. God, was it completely obvious? Was it written all over my face?

Matt was sitting at the table, busy making tiny red scrawls on what looked like an extremely dull pile of paperwork. For such a big guy, it always amazed me what neat little handwriting he had.

'Did your friends enjoy it?' he asked without looking up.

'Actually, it was just Cameron. Nikki had to help her daughter with something.' Even saying his name out loud gave me butterflies.

'Not that idiot from the dinner with the dicky bow-tie?' he said, still not taking his eyes from his paperwork.

'He was being ironic, Matt.'

I rolled up my sleeves, ready to rinse out a few of Coco's bottles and leave them to drip-dry next to the sink. Of course, tonight being Judy's shift, they'd already been chemically sterilised and properly dried and were now standing neatly to attention like little soldiers along the windowsill.

'What he was being was a prat. And I'm surprised you, of all people, with your finely honed antenna for all things even faintly ridiculous, failed to see it.'

'Oh, sweetheart, I'm not looking to have an affair,' I said, coming over and circling my arms around his neck. 'It was only a movie.'

He shifted uncomfortably in my embrace. 'Yeah, I know that,' he said. 'Just funny you never mentioned it.' With that, he untangled himself and headed upstairs.

We made love that night. It was possessive and hungry, like we were both trying to prove a point or get the upper hand.

It was the best sex we'd had for ages. The only sex we'd had for ages. And for once, thoughts of Cameron didn't even cross my mind.

19

#returntonormal
#playdate #TeamNikki

A repeat performance? A tender kiss? A knowing smile between two married folk who had finally, after what felt like months of careful avoidance, oiled the coils of their saggy mattress? I'm not sure exactly what I was expecting the next day, but it certainly wasn't what I got.

As I clung to my last precious moments of sleep like a dying man, I could hear hushed chitchat around me, followed by the unpleasant sensation of the mattress making a sudden, downward dive under the weight of a heavy object. I squinted through the darkness and could make out Judy, in her floral terry bathrobe, perched on the edge of my side of the bed, a squirmy Coco on her lap, and Matt buttoning his shirt in front of the mirror.

If I ignored them for long enough, perhaps they'd all just go away.

I felt like shit, my limbs aching, my throat as scratchy and dry as if I'd been on a three-day bender. God, wasn't it only yesterday that I could stumble in drunk at two in the morning and still bounce out of bed bright-eyed and bushy-tailed for work the next day? Back then there was nothing that a couple of strong coffees and lashings of makeup couldn't fix. It was going to take a little more than caffeine and concealer this time, I thought, as I eased myself up to a semi-sitting position.

'What's going on?' I croaked.

Matt flicked the light switch, and the sudden, harsh brightness forced me straight back under the duvet.

'Coco's been up since three o'clock. Didn't you hear her?' Judy said.

'Has she really? Didn't hear a thing,' I muttered back through the duvet. Okay, I might have faint recollections of Coco-type murmurings sometime in the midnight hours, but they had seemed to taper off pretty quickly and, quite honestly, it was about time she started learning how to settle herself at night.

'We've been downstairs watching back-to-back episodes of *Bananas in Pyjamas* for hours. She couldn't get back to sleep.'

No wonder. Clearly Coco was with me in finding the idea of grown-up men walking around in banana suits a tad creepy.

My little midnight wanderer began to crawl across the duvet towards me.

'She seems pretty chipper now,' I said, pulling her deliciously warm morning body in for a cuddle.

'Hmm, well let's see how that translates a few hours from now.'

God, how I hated it when the old battleaxe was right.

By 10.30 we were in full-scale, no-holds-barred tantrum mode. Coco was thrashing around in her high chair and screeching at the top of her lungs like a prisoner chained to a gurney as I tried to spoon strawberry yogurt into her mouth. Meanwhile, there was a weird buzzing noise in my ears that felt like a prelude to my head exploding clear off my body. Wasn't it only two glasses of wine I'd had last night? Hard to remember, drunk as I had been on lust and carnivorous thoughts.

My stomach lurched at the thought of it. Oh God. Cameron-photos-Hot-Daddy-armhair-touching.

The buzzing sound suddenly reached a new level of intensity. God, was this a guilt-induced aneurism? No, it was just my mobile phone vibrating its way across the coffee table.

'Hey, it's me,' trilled Nikki in a far-too-loud voice. 'We're just round the corner from you. Fancy a playdate?'

I said yes before I even had time to fully process her question. Why, why, *why*? How was I supposed to sit opposite her playing happy mummies when less than twelve hours before I'd been playing footsies with her husband in a dingy coffee shop?

Oh God, maybe she knew, and I was about to experience one of those awful Ronaldo-style you're-trying-to-steal-my-husband type punch-ups.

But surely such things didn't happen in the 'burbs?

'Great. I've got to nip to the post office first, but we'll be with you in about fifteen,' she said.

I was momentarily distracted from her words by the sight of my mismatched pyjamas and the thick, creamy pink trail that started somewhere above Coco's right eyebrow and ran down to the floor and up the full length of the wall behind her.

Cue the speediest tidy-up known to man.

I wiped down the yogurt-y walls, squirted a hefty dose of Toilet Duck into the downstairs toilet, shoved a plastic cup containing what looked suspiciously like Judy's dentures inside the vanity cupboard, pushed my collection of parenting books (*The Three-Martini Playdate: A Practical Guide to Happy Parenting*, anyone?) to the back of the shelf and replaced them with all of Matt's boring Booker Prize winners and political biographies, tossed the piles of clean and not-so-clean washing occupying every corner of the living room into the bottom of the pantry, whipped the fifty-million take-out menus off the fridge door and hauled out my yogurt maker and crockpot from the kitchen cupboard and positioned them smack bang in the middle of the bench top: all in the time it normally takes me to locate the teabags.

Phew. Nothing like a deadline to get your arse into gear, I thought, looking around with satisfaction. The place looked better than it had in weeks. You could actually see the floor. There was a cheery rap at the door. I looked down. Shit. Unfortunately my little speed routine hadn't allowed me time to change out of my jammies, brush my teeth or pull a brush through my hair.

Nikki breezed in, twins in tow, oblivious to the state I was in and full of apologies for not making it to the movies the night before. 'I hate these bloody teachers. I swear to God, they're out there laughing at us right now. "So you thought the papier-mâché reptilian was a challenge? What about a medieval battle scene out of pipe cleaners and icy-pole sticks? Oh, and did we mention it was due yesterday and will go towards your kid's final HSC mark?"'

So it seemed she had things on her mind other than a Ronaldo-style punch-up. She went on and on with her apology-slash-teacher-slamming. I didn't have the heart to tell her that bowing out of our double date and giving me the opportunity to spend an entire evening alone with her husband was the greatest gift she could have given me bar a full, uninterrupted night's sleep. Maybe even greater.

I perched stiffly on the edge of the sofa, Diet Coke in hand, trying to perfect the look of somebody who was actually listening. I must have been pretty convincing, because the words didn't stop and Nikki was soon working herself up into a frenzy over the gall of her daughter's teachers. And probably, let's face it, still a little high on the glue she'd inhaled the night before during the construction of the Medieval Icy-Pole Fortress. Her pitch edged higher and higher, and she was dunking the pomegranate teabag she'd brought with her today into Matt's favourite 'World's Okayest Dad' mug with such ferocity I thought it would shatter over both of us.

And where was my darling Coco in all this? The Olympic-level tantrum session was over and done with, thank God, and she was now busy seeing how far she could pull Snotty Twin One's blonde hair before it came out of his head. I had to admit, this whole heart of stone business was beginning to concern me a little.

So, this was it – our first ever one-on-one playdate. And if www.raisinghealthykids.org was to be believed, I only had about another three thousand of these things to look forward to if I was to have any hope of giving Coco a decent sense of social confidence.

The thing is, the whole thing was just so damn exposing. I didn't think I'd ever felt so naked, my whole life was laid out bare for her to see. Sure, this wasn't the first time Nikki had visited my home, but this was different: I hadn't had a full week to hide away all the more embarrassing parts of my life – there's only so much staging you can do in fifteen minutes. Okay, the house was moderately tidy. But did she really need to see the pictures on the bookshelf of me at the office Christmas party, dressed up as Wonder Woman and knocking back tequila shots over the top of Batman's (Alejandro's) head, or Matt's ~~stupid~~ beloved collection of Pink Floyd and Sex Pistols and The Dead Milkmen on vinyl? And where, for the record, did that hideous novelty candle on the sideboard come from?

I suspected this was Judy's work. She and her crimes against interior design were taking over my life and destroying my reputation, like an insidious weed, and I hadn't even noticed.

In my old life, home visits usually occurred at the tail end of a long night out, and whoever came over was usually far too drunk to notice what was going on around them in the home décor stakes. At three in the morning, with a belly full of caipirinhas, even the most hideous stencilled feature wall or lovingly découpaged sideboard seems quite acceptable (and I know this for a fact, having forgiven – nay, even lusted after – a fair few in my time).

But here in the stark, sober light of day, with Nikki rabbiting on and Coco now busy attempting to scalp Snotty Twin One, I couldn't help noticing how horribly dated, how suburban wannabe, the place was, with its fringed soft furnishings and faux-modernist glass-and-timber combos. Was it time to call Marco the interior designer back again, I wondered? Or maybe I should try something different, and go for a bit of a shabby chic vibe instead?

And then, just as I was deep in thought about linen slipcovers, dhurrie rugs and driftwood picture frames, the twins got bored. Stale rice crackers and rolling around on the floor with a lethal ten-month old were no longer cutting it. Things swiftly went from bad to worse. The twins became inquisitive. They pulled out my precious pile of *Vogue Italias* from the shelf under the coffee table and spread them out across the floor to create a makeshift slide for their plastic dinosaurs. They tried to poke bits of rice cracker into the slender necks of my beloved Murano vases, before proclaiming our house 'dead boring' and begging for Happy Meals for lunch.

'No, there's plenty of stuff you can do here,' I said in my best, jolly, no-I-really-want-you-to-stay voice, pulling out a box of cooking things for them to play with. They looked at me from under the rims of their matching 'Farts Now Loading' peaked caps, eyebrows cocked. Come on, buddies, I urged silently, surely you can push a little harder than that for your nuggets and chips.

But no, it seemed we'd reached a stalemate. Thankfully, Coco chose that moment to do a poo, and I escaped upstairs to change her nappy. Not since Judy arrived had I felt so happy to leave my own living room.

When I headed back downstairs, I found Nikki on the sofa, reading a crumpled up bit of paper. She didn't look up as I came in.

'You really didn't like us much, did you?' she asked, holding up my dog-eared, ten-point Master Plan to conquer the bitches at Happy Mummies.

Fuck. Where the hell had she found that? More importantly, how the hell to respond?

'Well I, uh, didn't really know you . . .' I stammered, the weird ear-buzzing starting up for real this time.

She burst out laughing. 'It's okay. We didn't like you much either.' She patted the spot next to her on the sofa. 'But don't worry. We like you now.'

What followed, once the twins had worked out how to download illegal movies on Matt's laptop, was an altogether not-too-painful forty-five minutes of chitchat about everything from the unlikely friendships you form once you have kids, with the sort of people you'd never normally meet in real life, and competitive crafting ('it's a thing, Ally, don't let anyone tell you otherwise') to how best to introduce acai powder into your family's diet without them noticing. We even touched on work – a topic I tried my hardest not to think too much about.

'You know that feeling that whatever you do, it's not even close to enough?' Umm, yeah. 'Well I feel like that every minute of every single day. Not cutting it at home, not cutting it in the office. The kids are out of control. I've forgotten what my husband even looks like. And I'm late for Every. Single. Meeting. But the minute I try and pull back at work, they reel me back in.' Nikki's gaze drifted over to the twins. 'And then I look at you guys – devoting yourselves full-time to your kids the way "proper" mums are supposed to, giving of yourselves where it really matters, and it makes me feel somehow . . . less than . . .' There were tears in her eyes and she tried to blink them away.

Woah, I was having none of that. Feeling 'less than' was exclusively my department. 'Trust me – giving of yourself to your kid each and every day does not make you a first-rate mother,' I said. 'In fact, probably just the opposite. I bet you spend more quality time with the twins in the thirty minutes after you come home from work than I do all day with Coco.' Was it possible that I was actually giving parenting advice to Mama Superior? 'Besides, look at you – you're single-handedly running playgroup. Happy Mummies wouldn't exist without you.' She threw me a wry smile. 'Okay, fine, but it certainly wouldn't be nearly so well organised. Look, if you really want to get yourself out of work, it's simple. You just have to find yourself an underage bimbo who does your job far better than you in half the time with twice the technical know-how and in a far shorter and more fetching skirt, and they'll kick you straight to the kerb like yesterday's sushi. That's how it happened for me.'

The second the words were out of my mouth I regretted them. What was I thinking? The last thing I wanted was to give the Happy Mummies a reason to pity me.

She reached for my hand. 'Oh, Ally,' she said, more kindly than I wanted her to. 'But I don't know how many hot young things are itching to get into conveyancing – more like lecherous old geezers with unhealthy porn addictions and no concept of personal space.'

And with that, we both burst out laughing.

The one topic it seemed we were both carefully avoiding was Cameron. There was one slightly iffy moment when she told me he'd be away in Phuket for the next week, shooting stills for a David Jones commercial, and how she was considering using the opportunity to get a semi-permanent done to remove the greys from around the front of her face 'because I'm pretty sure a worn-out, grey-haired old fart is not what you want welcoming you home after a seven-day shoot with models in bikinis'. But after making all the right noises about how completely unnecessary it was and how lucky Cameron was to have a real woman, blah blah blah, I managed to move off the subject.

When Snotty Twin Two stumbled down the stairs clad in my pink satin blindfold, dragging Snotty Twin One behind him via my lacey padded ankle restraints, Nikki announced it was time to go.

'This was fun,' she said on the doorstep, once we'd managed to separate the twins. Snotty Twin One immediately turned to pee into the water feature behind her. 'Put your doodle away, Bodie!' Turning back to me: 'We'll have to do it again.'

Was it? Would we? I didn't really have much to measure it against. And while her idea of fun was obviously vastly different to mine, maybe Coco and I had actually pulled it off. I looked down at my co-pilot to see whether she too was feeling pleased with the morning's progress, and she gazed back at me, a fistful of fine blonde hairs trailing from her tight little grip.

Nikki and I said our goodbyes and I was finally free to collapse in a heap on the sofa.

I thought about my Master Plan to conquer the Happy Mummies, my detailed list of cunning machinations to win them over. Plotting to get ahead, to get what you wanted, had been nothing out of the ordinary in my old life. Hell, it had been positively encouraged. But I couldn't help wondering how the Three Bitches – how Alejandro –

might have responded if they'd ever actually seen my plans written down in black and white like that. Would they have been as forgiving as Nikki?

I rang Matt to give him an update.

'I'm just running into a meeting,' he said in an 'is this really important?' tone.

Well, yeah, it was. 'Coco and I just hosted our first playdate and I think we had fun,' I announced triumphantly.

'That's great.' There was a painfully long pause while he waited for me to tell him the real reason I was calling.

'Um, that's it,' I said.

'Okay, well, I'll see you tonight.' I was left holding the phone, dial tone drilling into my ear, feeling faintly ridiculous.

He was right, of course. When did having a mum and a couple of obnoxious kids over for a cup of tea become important news? Once upon a time, I'd only phone him to report things of actual consequence, like that I'd be jetting out early the next morning to take the red-eye to New York or that I'd just shared mojitos and a bowl of guacamole with the lead singer of some ridiculously hip new band. Nowadays, I wouldn't even know a hip new band if they had it tattooed across their faces.

'Park later?' I said to Coco.

No response. Hmm, just like her father, unable to fake enthusiasm even for my sake.

20

#onesielove #sugarcravings #sprung

As I glanced at Matt beside me on the sofa – his eyes glued to the TV, gut spilling over the top of his unzipped pants, and one extraordinarily hairy toe sticking out of a hole in his left sock (I suppose, as SAHM extraordinaire, I was meant to darn that or something) – I reflected that our one isolated night of passion hadn't done much to help The Cause. It was like it had never happened. He saw me watching him and misread it completely, putting an arm around my shoulder to pull me in for a cuddle.

'What do you feel like watching?' he asked. I pushed him away, suddenly overcome with the urge for something sweet.

Since I'd imposed a strict ban ten days ago on all refined sugars entering the house, pickings were slim. Thankfully, I'd had the smarts to set aside a secret stash: enough mini Mars Bars, Cherry Ripes and milky-top Freddos to keep a small nation riding a sugar-induced high for weeks, which I'd kept safely hidden away in a place no-one would ever find them: on the top shelf of the cupboard behind the packets of mueslis, grains and whatnot.

But what was this? Doing a frantic hand-sweep from left to right across the full length of the shelf, my fingers came across nothing but a single empty Freddo wrapper. It sat there in my hand, Freddo smiling up at me with a toothless, taunting grin. I got on a chair and shoved all the stupid birdseed aside, just to be sure. Yep, the shelf was empty as a nun's box. Of course, whoever had done this knew they'd have the last laugh. After declaring a jihad on all things not pulled straight from the earth and served up half-raw and completely unpalatable, I could hardly kick up a stink about having my chocolate stash raided. Evil bastard.

But I would not be deterred.

'I feel like some dessert,' I announced to Matt in my best and-it-would-be-great-if-you'd-go-to-the-shops-and-get-it-for-me voice.

'What? Huh? But I thought we were . . .' He looked so confused, bless him. After having been forced to ditch all his beloved chocolate-covered muesli bars and trans-fat-enhanced breakfast cereals in pursuit of a cleaner, healthier lifestyle, he was now having a U-turn suddenly thrust upon him.

'Come on, don't you feel like it too?' I wheedled. If I was going to break the stupid paleo fast, he was damn well going to do it with me.

He shifted uncomfortably in his unzipped pants. 'I don't think so, Ally. It's all those slow-cooker meals. They're swallowing me whole,' he said. 'I sit in the middle of meetings and feel like my belt's about to burst right open.'

Okay, fine, no dice. Once upon a time he would have gone up to the shops for me anyway.

Fine. I'd just have to do it myself.

It was pushing the ungodly hour of nine o'clock – a time by which I was usually fast asleep – and at this point in the evening, nothing was going to separate me from my cosy ugg boots and bright pink zebra-print onesie. I had originally purchased this, it should be noted, in an ironic humour kind of way, but had subsequently discovered it to be the greatest, snuggliest item of clothing known to man. I considered changing into something more appropriate for public viewing, not wanting to scare the neighbours and all, but decided that it was hardly likely I'd see anyone that mattered at this hour. And really, if the grouchy neighbours did spy me through their lace kitchen curtains, they hardly fell into the 'people who mattered' category. I leapt into the car in a flash of pink-and-black zebra-print and sped up the road to the corner shop.

Once there, I scanned the fat-free frozen yogurt offerings while trying my best to ignore the tub of Ben & Jerry's Couch Potato calling out to me beside them. Oh, the dilemma. I didn't want to live in size fourteen (okay, fine, sixteen) jeans forever. I was just doing the all-too-familiar arm dance between the virtuous option and the one I really wanted, when I heard a familiar cough. I glanced up from the freezer aisle to see Cameron.

Shit. Bloody perfect.

I flung myself behind the personal care section and thought of all the nice, attractive outfits I could have been wearing to casually bump into him at nine o'clock on a Thursday night at the convenience store (evening gown, perhaps?).

And then it dawned on me. Hang on, wasn't he meant to be in Phuket?

As I peered out between the tampon boxes and extra-ribbed condoms and watched him drop a six-pack of beer on the counter and ask for a packet of cigarettes, my mind spun trying to find plausible reasons why he might be here in the 'burbs and not cavorting across the sand dunes with a bunch of supermodels. Maybe Nikki got her dates wrong and the trip wasn't this week after all. Or perhaps he was organising her a lovely, secret surprise for her birthday. I watched as he collected his change and left.

There was, at least, one small ray of sunshine to cling to: he hadn't seen me. After a safe amount of time had passed, I crept out from my hiding spot and gingerly placed the tub of Ben & Jerry's on the counter. The server raised a questioning eyebrow at the sight of my onesie, but I refused to be shamed and handed over my cash with my head held high.

Just as I was turning to go, Cameron reappeared.

'Ally, what are you doing here?' he asked, looking genuinely shocked.

Oh God, oh God. I pulled the voluminous zebra-print fabric closer around me in a pathetic attempt to minimise the full scale of its horror. 'Oh, you know, just picking up some dessert for Matt,' I said, grabbing a nearby packet of Huggies. 'And some things for Coco. Good wife and all.'

He laughed nervously and asked the shop guy for a lighter.

There was a weird protracted pause while shop guy tested out fifty million different lighters to find one that actually worked, and Cameron and I stood there silently, not knowing quite what to say.

He had a little stubble on his chin, which only added to the whole rakish caught-out-doing-something-I-shouldn't charm, and the sight of it made my stomach do strange things.

'Um, I didn't know you [told blatant, out-and-out lies to your wife about travelling overseas when quite clearly you're still right here] . . . smoked?'

He grabbed the lighter and shoved it deep in his pocket. 'Only when I'm stressed. It's my dirty little secret – please don't tell,' he said with a wink.

And what other dirty little secrets have you got hidden away? I wondered, as he nodded a curt goodbye and disappeared.

It was a question I was still asking myself forty-five minutes later at the kitchen table, as I carefully ran my spoon around the full circumference of the bottom of the Ben & Jerry's tub. I could think of a million perfectly valid reasons why he might still be here and not in Thailand, but it was his demeanour that really bothered me the most. He had acted like a guilty man. I had no problem with him keeping secrets from his spouse. After all, who didn't? But why did he have to keep them from me as well?

The Great Cameron-Hiding-Out-in-Sydney Mystery took over my entire weekend. While I should have been enjoying a rousing stomp around Narrabeen Lake with Matt and Coco, followed by a duck-feeding session with a bunch of clearly spoiled and over-fed ducks who waddled right past our stale crusts and straight over to the lady doling out fresh ciabatta, what I was actually doing was racking up an ever-expanding list of plausible reasons why Cameron should be on a covert shopping mission to buy beer and cigarettes up at the local Pack 'N' Snack, like a badly behaved teenager, when he's meant to be on a foreign beach cavorting with glamazons.

The answer, I decided, lay with my new BFF, Nikki.

*

The following Tuesday at playgroup, I bided my time and waited for the perfect moment to pounce. I stood by, cool as a cucumber, while Nikki helped Bree inspect Hunter's hair for nits, and then listened patiently as she delivered a half-hour sermon on how you can save a bucketload of money on expensive treatments by suffocating the little fuckers in copious amounts of cheap home-brand conditioner. The nits, not the kids, that is. My time finally came near the end of the session, when the whole lot of us were roped into craft clean-up duty (today's paper-bag puppet-making, with all its requisite glitter, paint, glue and markers, necessitating a full-scale team effort).

Bree attacked a spot on the table that I'd just cleaned, while Nikki started stacking a load of chairs, one on top of the other, nearby. It was now or never.

'So, Matt and I have a new obsession – Ben & Jerry's new Couch Potato flavour. Sounds gross, but you've got to try it.' Bree gave me a look that said she'd just as likely imbibe nails. 'We can't get enough of the stuff. We ran out of it on Thursday and I had to do an emergency run up to the Pack 'N' Snack.' I gave a small, breezy laugh to lend my tale a bit of humorous authenticity. Then, casually enough not to cause alarm bells, but loud enough for Nikki to hear: 'Funny . . . I saw Cameron up there too.'

Nikki's eyes flickered my way.

'Yeah . . . that's right. Last Thursday, I think. He was buying beer and . . . umm, beer.'

She edged closer, barely flinching under the weight of the umpteen chairs in her arms. 'You couldn't have. Cameron's been away shooting in Phuket. He only got back on Sunday. It must have been someone else.'

Bree nodded. 'Maybe you should get your eyes tested, Ally. Plus, you really should stay away from those desserts. Particularly after six. No chance of burning them off. They convert straight into fat cells while you sleep. And you know what they say about baby weight.' Looking straight at my pouchy belly: 'The longer it's on, the harder it is to shift.'

Oh yeah, I've read that one too, I thought, grabbing the last of Lisa's flapjacks and stuffing the whole thing into my mouth.

Hmmph. So there you have it. It was official. Cameron had lied.

Then again, what was the big deal? Surely the odd lie here and there was part of any healthy marriage. Perhaps he just needed a few days away from the craziness of family life. He wouldn't be the first person to fake an important business trip to steal a couple of nights away in a hotel in the city to bathe / poop / indulge in a TV binge session alone and uninterrupted for once. Hell, I'd consider doing it myself, except that I didn't have an actual job.

Or maybe Cameron had got back from his trip early and didn't want to disturb Nikki and the kids. That could happen, I suppose.

Please let it be so. The alternative was unthinkable. I looked more closely at Nikki. Wasn't she even the teensiest bit concerned?

It was enough to fry my already addled brain. For a few days I decided I hated Cameron. Who needed a lying, deceitful crush-Daddy when I had a boring and delusional one of my own sprawled on the sofa back home? I decided to give Cameron the cold shoulder next time I saw him.

But when I did, it didn't take him long to charm his way right back in to my affections. I hated myself for being so easily won over, but my anger was no match for Cameron's charming ways.

Plus, it should be noted that apart from a few cheery words of greeting to the group when he arrived, he was nothing but fully focused on the twins the entire morning. He couldn't even be tempted away from his Lego tower building by the offer of one of Bree's dehydrated banana chips, hard as she might have tried. I watched as she shoved the plate under his nose for the second, maybe third, time. In the end, he gave in and took one, but shoved it in his pocket the minute she wasn't looking.

Then Harriet appeared, all flustered and angsty, her hair piled high on her head in a messy wet bun.

'What's wrong?' asked Nikki at the sight of her.

Harriet let out a huge dramatic sigh. 'Toby announced last night that I've got to join him at a work dinner with his boss tomorrow night.' More pained sighing. 'In the city.' At the words, her face crumpled in on itself and it looked like she was about to burst into tears. The mums went into instant empathy mode, clucking around her like a bunch of mother hens and stroking her damp hair. I looked at them, confused.

'But really, what's the big deal?' I asked.

Harriet turned her weary eyes my way. 'You don't get it, Ally. She's one of those corporate high-flyer types, all private jets and razor-sharp suits and shiny, perfect, cosmetically doctored teeth. I've got nothing to wear, nothing to say, I haven't even seen a *normal* dentist since God knows when. Sure, she's a mum and she's got kids, but it's nothing like this.'

She cast her hands wide to take in the scene of mess and devastation before us. 'What on earth is she going to think of me?'

The other mums nodded and murmured sympathetically, clearly agreeing with every word she had just said.

But from where I stood, it was clear they were all just looking at it wrong. I squared up to her. 'Sure, Toby's boss might be racking up the air miles and single-handedly running the business world, but does she know the name of her kid's teacher? Who his best friend is? Can she even remember his name? Under the stylish clothes and the perfect teeth, she's probably a seething mass of resentment towards her wet-blanket stay-at-home husband and spends her nights secretly logging on to hookup.com.' Harriet laughed snotty tears. 'And don't worry about the clothes – I've got loads of that business-armour-type stuff. You can just borrow something of mine.'

Before I had a chance to escape, Harriet had me wrapped in her bony arms. Over her shoulder, I could see the other mums giving me that warm, fuzzy look of acceptance I'd been waiting so long for. 'Thanks, Ally,' Harriet whispered into my ear. 'What would we do without you?'

Finally, *finally*. She shoots and she scores!

Feeling pumped and ever so slightly overcome by this sudden and wholly unexpected show of appreciation, I raced outside for a breather. I wrestled Coco into her arctic all-in-one number as fast as I could and headed for the sandpit, zooming straight past Cameron without so much as a glance.

A few minutes later, he and the twins joined us. For a while, neither of us spoke as we watched the kids hurl things at each other in the sand-pit, me still punishing him with my full-scale silent treatment and him either shocked into silence by the pure force of my will or fully focused on spending quality outdoors time with his offspring. *Okay, fine, two can play that game*, I thought, as I watched him carefully trickle just the right amount of water into Snotty Twin One's (Two's?) rocket-shaped bucket from his watering can. I tugged at the zip of Coco's all-in-one to ensure she was still basking in a warm tropical glow in there, then lovingly crafted a stack of little sand patties for her, which she squashed, one after the other, with the back of her spade.

'Mooooooore,' Snotty Twin Two wailed at his father, rocket bucket shoved firmly into Cameron's belly, head thrown back in frustration.

Cameron let out a sigh. He leaned into me so that our shoulders were just touching through our puffa jackets. 'You know, I really enjoyed myself the other night.'

'Me too,' I replied stiffly with a sort of half laugh, half snort.

'I hope you haven't forgotten what I said. I really meant it when I said I'd like to shoot you.' Only, the way he said 'shoot' made it sound like something else entirely, something far more interesting. Oh God, was that the sound of my wall of silence coming crashing down? Shoot me, shoot me right now, I thought pathetically.

'I really shouldn't,' I stammered back. 'You know: Matt and all.'

'I didn't say I wanted to shoot Matt.'

No, well, you wouldn't really, would you? That would defeat the entire purpose. Oh God, oh God, what to say? It all seemed so rushed, so sudden. When did we go from mild flirtation over the refreshment table and footsies at the coffee shop to discussing full-scale, full-frontal nudie photography? And would he be frightened away if he saw my flabby baby apron and my boobs swinging perilously close to my belly button the moment they were unleashed? It wasn't like sex with your husband, you couldn't actually do it in a darkened room with minimal body contact, I supposed. Or maybe he hadn't actually meant naked. Maybe I was reading waaaaaay too much into it. Ahhh!

Just as I was about to say something – anything – Nikki appeared. We leapt apart like a pair of guilty school kids, but in typical Nikki fashion she didn't bat an eyelid. 'Here you are. I've been looking for you two everywhere. You must be freezing out here!' she said, rubbing her hands against the cold.

No, actually, 'steaming hot' would be a better way to describe it.

She motioned towards the hall. 'Can you come inside for a sec? I've got a group announcement to make.'

Lord above, what now? Had someone forgotten to bring the paper plates? Left the milk out on the counter? Or, God forbid, neglected to return their dirty mug to the sink?

I stomped resentfully back into the hall, Coco slung football-style under my arm. Really, the cheek of the woman. How dare she interrupt a pivotal moment in my burgeoning relationship with her husband like that!

She shepherded us all into a semi-circle around her. 'I've just heard some rather shocking news.' My ears pricked up at her tone. Maybe it wasn't the milk this time. 'Ms Pricklethwaite has just informed me that come the end of next term we're being cast aside for a new kiddie boot-camp. Sorry to be the bearer of bad news, folks, but after —-two years, Happy Mummies will be closing down.'

The room went silent as her words sank in. It was like someone had died. Bree gazed, beady-eyed and furious, at some invisible Ms Prick-lethwaite poltergeist hovering above our heads. Jenna let out one of those horribly inappropriate giggles you make when you've just heard some really bad news, like that someone has a terminal illness or they'd lost their job and their home in one fell swoop. Meanwhile, Harriet – cross-legged on the floor, with Archie draped across her chest sucking away at her left boob, his big old gumboots kicking up a storm on the timber floorboards – blindly reached up her hands for someone to hold.

Lisa was the first to speak. 'But why? She can't just go and do that. We've been here forever.'

'Yeah! Who does she think she is?' There was an angry hum as eve-ryone started putting their two cents in.

Nikki held up a hand to curb the onslaught. 'Yes she can, and she has,' she said.

'Why don't we just go somewhere else?' someone else asked.

Nikki shook her head. 'For what we can afford to pay? We'd be looking at some crappy church hall out the back of beyond, and I don't think any of us want to be doing that kind of drive every week. Besides, it goes against everything that Happy Mummies stands for: we're about community, we're local, this is where we belong. But Ms Pricklethwaite says the bootcamp's going to pay three times what we do. They're pri-vately funded but we rely on fundraising. There's no way we can ever compete with them.' She looked around sadly. 'The game's up, folks.'

There were gasps all round.

At first, I didn't know what to think. My gaze moved from Coco huggle-throttling one of the nameless toddlers who, like her, treated this place like a home away from home, over to the refreshment table piled high with all the homemade cakes and slices, so lovingly filled with dried fruit and seeds and other tasteless muck that promised to keep our kids healthy, and finally upon the shell-shocked faces of everyone around me.

Then I began to feel pissed off. Very pissed off.

Nikki couldn't be serious. After all the work I'd put in here with these ridiculous women, when I was finally, *finally* having a modicum of success, she expected me to go and start somewhere else? My eyes flickered to the back of the room where Cameron stood, arms folded, veins tensed and bulging. Our eyes connected, just for a moment. And of course, there were other very good reasons to keep Happy Mummies alive too.

There are times in a person's life when you know it's time to step up. For me, this was one of those times. I took a deep breath and moved forward to the front of the group so that I was standing opposite Nikki.

'How much are they talking?' I asked, all business.

'Six thousand for the first year, and seven and a half every year after that.' For the first time ever, her voice sounded tiny and defeated. In some weird way, I knew she felt she'd failed us.

But just my asking for hard figures had sent a current of possibility sweeping through the group.

'We could put on a sausage sizzle. That always raises some hefty funds,' offered up Harriet.

Seriously, in what currency? Unicorn money? Our last fundraising effort had raised a total of $362, and that wasn't even factoring in the money most of us were still owed for that disgusting home-brand bread and dog-food sausages.

Somehow I didn't think a sausage sizzle was going to cut it this time. What we needed was something bigger: much bigger. And I knew exactly what to do.

'I might have a solution,' I said, turning to the assembled group. 'But I don't want to tell you what it is. Not yet, at least. Leave it with me till next week so I can get some stuff figured out, and I promise I'll reveal all then.'

'What is it? How can we raise that kind of money?' The questions started pouring in from all sides.

I waved a hand for silence. 'Look, all I can tell you is this.' Everyone leaned in. 'As most of you here know, I can't craft, I can't sing and I can't even make a particularly nice cup of tea. But what you probably don't know is that I have a very particular set of skills. Skills I have acquired over a long career.' Oh God, why was I going all Liam Neeson all of a sudden? Fortunately, from the wide-eyed faces looking back at me I figured none of them had actually seen *Taken*. They were lapping up my every word. 'Skills that might be just what're needed to save Happy Mummies. All I'm asking is that you be patient with me and have a little faith.'

They began nodding, at first almost imperceptibly, gradually getting more enthusiastic. Nikki, Lisa and Sharron looked intrigued. Bree scowled. Cameron gave me a small smile and uncrossed his arms. Phew. That was the most I'd ever said to the group as a whole in all my weeks at Happy Mummies. What I felt like now was a stiff drink, a very long straw, and half an hour lying prostrate in a darkened room with a moist towel over my face. There's nothing quite like asking a roomful of people to put all their eggs in your one little basket to leave you wanting a lie-down.

When the group had disbanded, Bree sidled over to me. 'I can only presume your little plan's going to have a vintage theme.' Umm, perhaps. Haven't quite worked out the specifics yet. 'Seeing as you do so like your things second-hand, don't you, Ally?' Her eyes trailed over towards Cameron as she wandered off.

Second-hand. Huh?

Then it dawned on me. *Fuck. FUCK.* She was onto us.

21

#memories #priceless #bankruptcyasmallpricetopay

But before I could worry about how I'd single-handedly rescue the Happy Mummies from extinction, and whether or not Bree was about to reveal her suspicions about me and Cameron to Nikki, I had other matters to attend to: namely, going to collect our Sunnylove family photos. Time had distanced me from the horror of the shoot, and I was actually feeling quite excited. Plus, Pascale-Augustine had had three solid weeks to work 'zee Photoshopping mageec' so I figured she must have at least one decent shot by now.

I picked up Matt from the train station after work, and before I'd even had time to put the car into gear he began laying out the ground rules. 'Now, whatever happens, however smooth their sales spiel, we are not going to spend more than $200 tonight. I know how these people operate. Repeat after me, Ally. Two hundred dollars. Not a cent over.'

'Two hundred dollars, not a cent over,' I repeated robotically, eyes fixed firmly on the road.

Whatevs. So long as there was at least one photo where I didn't look too much like a hippo in her final trimester of pregnancy, I didn't care how puny our budget was.

It was quiet when we arrived at the Sunnylove studio, not a soul in sight. Perhaps we'd got the date wrong? I flicked back through my phone for the last email I'd received from Pascale-Augustine. Nope, definitely tonight.

There was a bright yellow buzzer on the reception desk with a little handwritten sign beside it saying 'If I'm alone, give me a buzz!' Cute. I made a few loud, deliberate coughs, just in case. Nada. I pressed the buzzer and it released an angry blast.

From behind the desk, a door swung open and a young girl in an emerald-green airhostess-type dress and snazzy neckerchief (were they a thing now?) appeared with a dazzling smile and two glasses of champagne on a tray. I perked up at the sight of the champagne while Matt silently mouthed 'Two hundred, tops' at me.

'Sorry to keep you waiting – I was just getting the room ready,' the girl said.

The room? It sounded like we were about to get a Brazilian or a neck massage, not pick up some photos.

'We're just here to collect our shots,' I explained, as you would to a very slow and very stupid child.

'Yes, that's right,' she said brightly, beckoning us through the mysterious back door. 'Come on through.' We were ushered into what looked like a tiny darkened cinema, with plush seating for about fifteen. 'I'm Raquelle. I'll be your hostess for tonight.' Ah, that explained the airhostess uniform! 'Take a seat and we'll get you started.'

She held the tray out towards us, we both took a glass, and she disappeared as quickly as she'd arrived.

Matt plonked himself down on a seat towards the middle of the room and looked back at me, an expression of bewilderment mixed with impatience on his face. I shrugged back at him. Hell, I had no idea what was going on here either. Maybe we had to wait for some other people to arrive.

We sat quietly in the gloomy darkness, sipping our champagne. If it hadn't felt so awkward, it would have actually been rather relaxing.

I thought about the last time I'd sat in a cinema. It had only been a couple of weeks ago, but it may as well have been a whole other lifetime. With Cameron, there had been none of the exasperation, no unspoken 'let's get this damn thing over with – there's an important game I don't want to miss on the telly later – oh, and while we're at it, did you remember to pick up my dry-cleaning?' vibe.

While I was bunkering down with these grumpy thoughts, the strains of Whitney Houston's 'The Greatest Love of All' started to fill the room. I glanced at Matt. What was going on? A pair of spotlights suddenly bore down on the big screen in front of us and there, in full, glorious technicolour, was the most wonderful thing I'd ever seen – my beautiful daughter, radiant with joy as she flew through the air between our loving arms. And then, in perfect sync to the emotional ascent of the music: Coco's face, in its myriad different shades – serious, playful, silly, contemplative – burst across the screens all around us. It was too much to take in. I sat there open-mouthed, my eyes craning from left to right so as not to miss a single fabulous frame.

'Taramasalata? Stuffed olive?' whispered Raquelle, suddenly appearing at my side with a platter of dips and crudités. I blindly took a cucumber stick and dunked it into a bowl of hummus. She topped up my champagne.

The music then switched to something more upbeat, signalling it was now time for the fun part. The family shots. I braced myself for mama hippo, but was delighted to see she was nowhere in sight. I looked positively normal, attractive even, and so did Matt. Pascale-Augustine had really outdone herself. It was like watching our own little private movie and we were the stars.

And I can't lie – we were nothing short of breathtaking.

I looked across at Matt to see if he was feeling it too, and saw huge, fat tears streaming down his cheeks. There was an awkward moment as he tried to juggle his babaganoush-coated carrot stick and champagne in one hand and wipe his snotty nose with the other. Nope, not just me then.

Invisible hands then deposited a pair of iPads and snazzy digital pens in our laps. The photographs on the screens came back on repeat and all we had to do now was swipe on our iPads for the ones we wanted. I shoved Matt's budgetary edict aside and began blindly swiping just about every shot that came into view before it disappeared forever. It was like a very expensive game of Whac-A-Mole, and a really rather enjoyable one at that.

Once the show was over, Raquelle ushered us back out to reception. We sat in a pair of comfy armchairs while she crouched on the floor beside us, her knees knocking against mine and her arm curled around the back of my chair.

'I know you're just going to luuurve your pictures,' she purred. 'Of course, you can take the risk of hanging these incredible works of art, these precious mementos of your lives together, yourselves. Some people do,' she said with a disapproving sniff at the mere thought of such a thing, such people. I found myself sniffing too. 'But nothing will ever match the arrangements custom-designed by our professional hanging service. At $275 an hour, it really is a massive bargain.'

I was just about to say 'No, thank you, I think we've spent enough,' – really, I was – when Matt spoke up, still snotty and nasal from the emotional onslaught of the past hour. 'Let's book it in.'

In the end, our bill came to $2415, not including the personal hanging service bit. But as Raquelle pointed out, it really was a massive bargain.

On our way out, I gave Matt a look. *Not a cent over $200? Know how these people operate, huh?* He studiously avoided it, blowing his nose into an already well-soiled tissue. I reached out to hold his hand as we walked to the car.

*

Judy and Gerald were at home when we got there, snuggled together on the sofa like a couple of lovebirds, as they watched an old *Downton*

Abbey episode. It struck me how quickly they'd grown into a twosome. Having Gerald here in our living room seemed so normal now that I'd barely registered him when I walked in. It was like they'd fast-tracked all that getting-to-know-you, should-we-or-shouldn't-we-do-this-thing crap, and gone straight to the good part, the bit where you don't have to be saying or doing very much at all to be having a great time. Maybe I was still on a weird high after our private movie session, but I couldn't help feeling pleased for Judy. After all, if a crotchety old moose like her could find happiness, maybe there was hope for the rest of us too.

Raquelle had given us a fat little pocket-sized look-book of all the photos we'd chosen, so we could spend the next few days poring over our own fabulousness before the full-scale installation arrived. We proudly presented the look-book to Judy and Gerald, who fell about laughing at the sight of it.

'It doesn't even look like you,' said Judy, through her tears. 'Are you sure you've got the right pictures?'

With that, the look-book was firmly shut, never to be spoken of again. Perfect coupledom Judy and Gerald might have achieved, but good taste was clearly something that would always elude them.

*

I could barely contain myself for the next three days, waiting for the pictures to arrive. Early on Friday morning they did just that, accompanied by a twitchy little man in a pair of pristine white coveralls with ironed creases down the front.

'I'm Trey, your visual stylist,' he said, offering his fingertips for me to shake.

My what? Oh yeah, the picture-hanging guy.

Trey promptly ordered the three burly young things lounging beside him on the front step to get the huge cardboard-covered packages out of the back of the van and into the house, which they were forced to do pass-the-parcel style over the safety gates in the hall. To their credit, they didn't utter a word of complaint. But it did seem to be taking an awfully long time. Had we really ordered this many photos? I felt a tiny little bean of foreboding embed itself somewhere deep in my lower belly.

As the hot young things stacked the canvases ten-deep across the hall, Trey examined my walls. From the almost imperceptible head-shaking and quiet tut-tutting he made as he moved from room to room, I could tell they weren't quite meeting his standards. He obviously didn't read *InStyle* magazine. If he did, he'd know that this room was almost an exact replica of the living room in Charlize Theron's New York penthouse. He stopped short before a framed poster of a 1980s Paul Weller mid-screech, strumming the bejesus out of an electric guitar. Ah yes, except for a few bits, that is.

That damn poster was the bane of my life, it really was. Matt had picked it up after a concert at The Hippodrome some time towards the middle of last century when he still actually went to concerts, and however many times I'd tried to convince him it would look marvellous tucked away in the downstairs loo, the damn thing had ended up smack-bang in the middle of the living room. I was not about to shoulder the blame for this one. 'That was *not* my choice. Entirely my husband's doing. He's always harping on about never having had the chance to join a band, to express himself musically. Something to do with an oncoming mid-life crisis, I suspect.'

Trey turned to the beautiful oil painting of Waterloo Bridge at sunset that I'd picked up on my first ever trip to London – all summery pinks and mauves, interspersed with a dash of vibrant orange – a truly exquisite piece.

'And whose midlife crisis can we attribute this one to, hmm?' he asked.

Cheeky bastard. How dare he charge me $275 an hour for this!

In the end, it was decided that they all had to go. To be replaced with huge life-sized canvases of Coco, Matt and I, photoshopped to within an inch of our lives, plastered across every wall. Seeing ourselves up close like this, with our weird, flawlessly glowing skin and Hollywood smiles, I couldn't help thinking we looked ever so slightly deranged.

Then Trey unveiled his pièce de résistance. Pulling the curtains shut and flicking a switch on the wall, the biggest canvas of all – Matt beaming into the camera as Coco hurtled through the air towards him – began making a weird humming noise a bit like an engine running, and a strobe lighting effect burst through the whites of Matt's teeth.

Coco erupted into stormy tears at the sight of it.

Fine, money down the drain, but I could take them all down when Trey left, I thought to myself.

As if he'd just read my mind, Trey then whipped out a hand drill from the toolbelt round his waist, and bore some seriously evil-looking, thumb-sized brackets into the wall. 'This way you don't ever have to worry about your little angel knocking your pictures off the walls.' He gave a picture of Coco balancing a rubber duck on her head a firm wiggle to demonstrate his point. 'These babies aren't going nowhere.'

Trey declared the whole picture installation a resounding success.

'I don't know,' I said, gazing around at my own eyes leering at me from every corner of the room. 'Don't they all seem a little too . . .' I searched for the right word. 'Much?'

'Not at all,' said Trey sniffily. 'Maybe it's just your walls that are a little too small.'

For the rest of the day, I sat frozen on the sofa, transfixed by the eerie love shrine all around me. It was quite possible, I decided, that Point Seven of my Master Plan had been overkill.

*

Judy and Matt arrived home at the same time that night. They stood at the doors of the living room, slack-jawed and speechless.

'And that's not all. Wait till you see this,' I said. I flicked the strobe lighting switch, the engine started up, and the scary teeth picture came to life once more.

Judy gasped and Matt put a hand to his mouth. Then, just as quickly, he pulled me in close and buried his face in my hair. 'Don't you just love it?' he whispered.

See? I thought with a smug smile. *It is entirely possible I can get things right, some of the time at least.*

Now, back to that Rescue Plan . . .

22

#braindrain #saveHappyMummies #Judytotherescue

'I don't get it,' said Matt when I told him about my grand scheme to save Happy Mummies from extinction. 'Since when do you care if playgroup closes down? You hate those women.'

We were getting ready for bed, him scrabbling under the covers to find his tracky-dacks and me rubbing Echinacea-enhanced cream into the dry, itchy skin between my fingers (winter eczema – when would this hell ever end?). I watched eagle-eyed as he pulled off his boxers. The dirty washing basket was close, but was it close enough? It certainly wasn't as close as the floor. Would he? Wouldn't he?

Bah! They were in the basket. I had to admit, a tiny part of me was disappointed.

Next, without exchanging a word, we both turned our attention to the mountainous pile of clean clothes on the middle of the bed and started folding. Since becoming a four-person household, ignoring all the washing until the end of the week, as we used to, had become near impossible. Leave it for so much as a day and it started taking over. As I passed Judy's voluminous lace-trimmed old-lady bloomers across to Matt and he popped them on top of the neat little pile he'd made up for her on the edge of the comforter, I couldn't help wondering what the other mums were doing with their husbands in bed right now.

'I don't hate them,' I said, folding my own undies, which – who was I kidding? – were just as voluminous as Judy's. 'Besides, don't you want Coco to have a little motherly support if and when she decides to become a mum herself some day? Happy Mummies is an institution. If I can help keep it alive, I should. Besides, it's really no biggie.'

He looked at me like I'd lost my mind. 'No biggie? You know better than anyone how much work this is going to take. And don't forget, these women are housewives; they'll have absolutely no idea what they're doing. You'll have to hold their hands every single step of the way.'

'Actually, many of them are surprisingly accomplished. Wait till you see what, uh . . .' I cast around for a suitably impressive example of the Happy Mummies' handy skills. Jenna and her maternity knits? Lisa and her wondrous flapjacks? 'Just you wait and see. We'll surprise you. It's going to be massive.' Even to my own ears, I didn't sound particularly convincing.

Matt passed two corners of a queen-sized sheet to me so we could do the fold-up dance together. 'Really? Accomplished, you say?' he said with a stupid, condescending smirk as our hands met in the middle. 'You know, Ally Bloom, I believe you actually like them. I think they've become your friends.'

'Don't be so ridiculous,' I spat back, grabbing the sheet from him. 'You know I couldn't possibly be friends with people who insist on wearing open-toed shoes in autumn, and without, I might add, even a lick of nail polish.' I shuffled awkwardly to conceal my own Haviana-clad feet, with their scabby, bare toenails, beneath the valance.

'Friends'. Pah! What would he know? This was purely business. I was under no illusions as to why I was pulling out all the stops to save Happy Mummies: it couldn't close because I was too bloody lazy to start up again with a new group of women elsewhere: and the thought of missing out on my weekly one-on-ones with Cameron was enough to make me want to strangle myself with the waistband of Judy's bloomers. Plus, there was the little matter of my growing addiction to Lisa's flapjacks – she'd even started bringing along an extra plateful every week just for me, bless her. It would probably break her heart to deny her of that pleasure now. Poor, deluded Matt. What would he say if knew the real truth? Then again, he was partly to blame for this whole thing. He'd been the one, after all, who'd insisted we move to the 'burbs in the first place. Wasn't fantasising about sleeping with one's hot neighbour / tennis coach / friend's husband all part of the suburban idyll? And besides, with no decent cafés or shops to amuse me, how else was I expected to fill my days?

The next morning, with less than twenty-four hours to go before I had to present my ideas to the playgroup mums, I knew I couldn't put it off any longer; it was time to get to work. I fired up PowerPoint, popped Coco in front of ABC4Kids (educational), made myself a cup of tea and got down to business.

After five minutes of staring at a blank screen followed by about forty-five googling 'What's really up with Beyoncé and Jay Z?', and 'When do the spring sales officially start?', I heard Coco calling out for me. Well, to be more accurate, she was calling out for 'Nana'.

Where had my brain gone? Was it true, what they say – had it seeped out of me along with the afterbirth the day I'd had Coco? I was pretty sure I used to be fantastic at this sort of thing, I'd had a razor-sharp focus. Perhaps what I needed was a break: clear my mind. I shut down the computer and set about making Coco and I gnocchi with cheesy tomato sauce for lunch. It definitely felt like a big-old-bowl-of-carbs sort of day.

Exhausted by the stress of the morning, I decided to have a little lie-down when Coco went for her nap. I snuggled under the duvet and resolved to give the Rescue Plan my full, undivided attention later that night after Coco had gone to bed.

*

I woke up two hours later to discover that Coco had figured out how to remove her nappy and was busy decorating the wall beside her cot with its contents. She looked up at me, pleased as punch, as I stood frozen in horror in the doorway. *Seriously?!* I had been thinking about doing a bit of a feature wall in that spot, but this really wasn't what I'd had in mind. I thought about grabbing Coco from her cot and closing the door on the whole sorry, stinking mess, but somehow didn't think that would pass Judy's unspoken 'perfect housewife' test.

Moments later, just as I was snapping on the rubber gloves, Judy walked in. 'How funny,' she said, gazing fondly at the faeces-covered walls. 'That's exactly what Matt used to do when he was little.'

Marvellous, I thought. I can pop that one right up there under 'monobrow' in the growing list of delightful genetic gifts he's passed on to our daughter.

*

But in the end it was Judy I was forced to turn to in my hour of need.

'Come to bed,' Matt implored, as I sat, stubborn and martyrish, at the kitchen table in front of the open laptop.

'Not now. I've got to do this,' I growled back.

He kissed the top of my head and let his hand linger on my shoulder for a moment, obviously waiting to see if I'd change my mind. The weight of it was incredibly distracting and I shook it off.

At midnight, I was still sitting there staring at the screen, now in that weird, panicky, self-pitying state where you don't know whether to smash the computer into a million pieces or slump on top of it and sob your guts out. Just then, I heard the familiar slip-slap of Judy's slippers in the hall; she was clearly on the way to the loo for her umpteenth wee of the night.

She popped her head in to see what I was up to. When I told her, she announced chirpily: 'Oh no, forget a PowerPoint presentation. What you need is one of those whizz-bang new video-editing apps.

We learnt all about them at our training course last week. Have a look at CyberLink Power Director. Marvellous app. Turns all your presentations into proper little movies. You'll probably earn yourself an Oscar.'

I turned slowly around to face her. Right, I thought. For once the old witch could make herself useful. 'And how, exactly, might I do that?' I said, knowing full well that I was about to enter painful and unpleasant Judy-overload territory.

'Well, it's quite straightforward really,' she replied, angling her body over my head towards the open laptop, so that my face was nestled deep in the murky pits of her dressing gown.

There followed several hours of failed download attempts and long, drawn-out explanations from Judy on the mechanics of CyberLink that had me wanting to bash my head against the CaesarStone benchtops five hundred times without stopping.

'My teacher tells me I've got a real knack for this stuff,' she trilled. 'Gerald said maybe we should think about starting a little business together. You know, going to people's houses and helping them when their computer's crashed and whatnot.'

Someone please shoot me now.

By 3.30 am, I was starting to see double, which meant there were now two Judys standing before me, rabbiting on about the joys of technology like a pair of crazed Mark Wahlberg–Energizer Bunny hybrids. Where the hell did the woman get her energy from? I was pretty sure the only one of us who'd had a nana nap today was me.

But, most importantly, the damn thing was done. The Happy Mummies had better get ready to be blown away.

*

But the next day I woke up a mass of nerves. What if they all hated it? Thought I was insane? Worse still, what if they actually liked it, but Matt was right and at the end of the day they couldn't cut it and the whole thing was a complete and utter – and very public – failure?

I'd already had enough experience with that to last me one lifetime, thanks very much.

When I got to playgroup, I felt all eyes on me. My stomach was a tangle of knots and I wondered how on earth I'd keep down the blueberry-and-cream-cheese bagel I'd had for breakfast. I raced over to Nikki, who was laying out platters of strawberry and banana kebabs on the refreshment table, and gave her a quick run-through of my plan.

She didn't utter a word in response, just gave me one of her firm, military-style nods and clapped her hands to get everyone's attention. 'Gather round, ladies. Ally's got an announcement to make.'

Hang on, I wanted to shout, that's not how it works. What did she think? Where was my feedback? And did she really have to make it sound so bloody official?

The women moved towards me like a single, ominous mass and I felt tiny beads of sweat break out on my upper lip.

'I know. Why don't you do it?' I hissed at Nikki, thrusting my laptop into her arms.

'What are you talking about? This is your gig, Ally,' she laughed before shoving it back at me and herding me towards the front of the group. Ugh, that blueberry bagel was really starting to make itself known.

I looked around at the expectant faces before me, all hoping, believing, that I held the answer to the Happy Mummies problem. 'Um, yeah, so, about that grand scheme I was telling you all about last week . . .'

Silence. Bloody hell, where were all the screeching toddlers and fisticuffs over toy cars when you needed them? And why was I feeling so queasy? It wasn't like I hadn't done this a hundred times before – in my old life I'd presented to far tougher crowds than this more times than I'd had hot dinners and never even batted an eyelid. But this time was different. Something about their expressions – so willing and hopeful – made me feel . . . what was the word I was looking for? Responsible.

Coco tugged at the hem of my pants and I reached down to pick her up. She cooed in my arms and reached round to shove a fistful of my ponytail into her mouth, just like she always did.

Deep breath in through the nose, out through the mouth. Okay, let's get this thing over with.

After the final slide had been shown and I'd read out the last part of the presentation, I shut the laptop with a bang. 'So, there you have it, folks,' I said.

The silence was deafening.

I glanced around. Sharron appeared to be mumbling something to herself under her breath, while Bree looked like she'd just bitten into something very, very nasty.

'You want us to put on a craft fair?' Lisa said at last, enunciating the words 'craft fair' slowly and carefully as though making sure she'd heard them right.

'Yes, but this will be no ordinary craft fair,' I explained. 'It will be an event like no other, a salute to the dying art of handicraft. We will be trailblazers. People will come from far and wide to experience the true meaning of 'crafted with love' – it will be a chance to get off the mass-produced roundabout of the consumerist world we live in . . . but with a fashion-forward edge, of course . . .' Now this was more like it. I could feel the old bullshit-pump spluttering to life somewhere deep inside me and its murky juices beginning to flow through my veins.

'How can we be trailblazers? We're just a bunch of mums,' said Harriet, bringing my happy flow to a grinding halt.

Jenna stepped forward, all huffy indignance. 'Speak for yourself. I've always thought my knits would look great in the fashion pages of *Vogue.*'

'There you go – that's the attitude,' I said. 'And you're right. You are mothers – we're all mothers – and that's exactly what our USP is going to be. The whole motherhood thing is completely hot right now – think Jessica Alba with her Honest range of cleaning products made with hair of goat and beetle placenta or what have you, and Kim

Kardashian flashing around pictures of her one-year-old finger-painting her million-dollar Birkin. We couldn't have come along at a better time if we'd tried.'

'But we're not Jessica Alba. And none of us have Birkin bags. Who's really going to want to buy this stuff?' asked Harriet.

I let out a chortle-snort. Seriously, were they not paying attention? 'No-one, of course.' They stared back, now more confused than ever. 'But once Jenna's crocheted jumpers are properly marketed as the unique one-offs they really are and Lisa's famous flapjacks are prettied up enough that you literally want to eat them through the plastic, trust me, everyone will be buying.'

Hmm, still no dice.

I tried another tack. 'Look, do you really think Moda's zebra-print bags are worth $850 a pop or that the Tiffany key ring your husband gave you for your birthday is worth two hundred bucks? It's all about perception and packaging. You can put a steaming pile of turd into that little blue box, tie it up with a shiny white ribbon, and voila: it suddenly looks like it's worth a small fortune. Perception and packaging. The key is that each and every one of you –' I looked deep into the eyes of each woman standing before me in turn – 'has to believe it.'

Were they convinced? There was much fidgeting and mumbling and looking down at unpolished toenails, so it was pretty hard to tell.

After what felt like forever, Nikki did her military hand-clapping thing again. 'Okay, so who's in with Ally's plan?'

Gulp.

Nothing.

I peered towards the back of the room, where Cameron was standing, arms crossed, leaning back against the wall and watching me with the sort of slightly bemused smile you might give a crazy person. He gave me a little wink, unfolded his arms and moved one high above his head. Soon after, a second arm appeared on the other side of the room, then a third, and after a few agonising moments I was looking out across a roomful of raised arms.

I saw Jenna lean in to Bree, arm held aloft. 'What have we got to lose? It's not like anyone else has got any bright ideas.'

Okay, so it might not have been the resounding triumph I'd hoped for, but my plan had passed. Which meant, of course, only one thing: my new world and my old one would be colliding whether I liked it or not.

23

#saveHappyMummies
#crafternoon #photoshootMums
#worsethanabunchofsupermodels

By 9.25 am on Monday, those niggling little questions Matt had planted in my mind a few nights before had firmly taken root and were now fast turning into crater-sized balls of self-doubt. As I looked across the table at the Happy Mummies, arguing over who would do what and whether macraméd toilet paper could legitimately be described as 'craft', I wondered whether he'd been right: had I bitten off more than I could chew here?

I raised a hand to shush them. The key to success, I explained, was identifying your particular talent, whatever the hell that was, and then busting the shit out of it. 'And remember – you've got to believe in it 110 per cent. Perception and packaging,' I said solemnly.

First up, Jenna. We decided that she would expand her original idea of crocheted breastfeeding tops to include tanks, halters and generous beach cover-ups. She needn't worry about the odd hole or dropped stitch, as they would only add to the charming home-grown vibe we were going for. I was pretty confident the designs themselves would be a hit among the crowd of editors, stylists and photographers I planned to invite to the fair, as the concealed pockets would provide perfect spots to pop their mobiles, keys and any illicit drugs on a night out or a day at the beach. With the help of Jenna's sister-in-law and some ageing aunt who was tucked away in a retirement village in Pennant Hills and would therefore relish the chance to have something to do all day, Jenna would aim for a total of seventy-five pieces, which we'd sell at $100 each.

'You have got to be kidding me,' spluttered Bree.

Jenna threw her the evil eye. 'I think that sounds about right. These are one-offs after all,' she said, dreams of *Vogue* covers clearly still dancing before her eyes.

Next, we moved to Lisa. Her first suggestion, naturally, was to do a scaled-down version of her infamous PDP party and set up a couple of tables of sex toys ('They're not sex toys, Ally. They're pleasure accessories. And did I mention they're all fully recyclable?'). How could I explain the very fine distinction between tongue-in-cheek sauciness and desperate smut? Plus, nothing quite screams sad loserville like a bunch of out-of-shape housewives walking around in public, shopping for strap-on dildos. It had to be shut down. In the end, thankfully she agreed to ditch the recyclable pleasure accessories and produce a bumper crop of her wonderful flapjacks instead, which she'd package up all retro chic in cute little jam jars with gingham ribbons.

Done, tick.

Harriet was next. She told us that she'd be happy to forage through her local bushland in search of fallen gumnuts, banksia pods and the like, from which she'd fashion a range of unique and fully biodegradable children's toys. Apparently that's how she made all her boys' playthings.

'Nature is their toyshop,' she informed us solemnly.

Man, I couldn't even begin to imagine how disappointing Christmas morning must be in their house.

Then it was Sharron's turn.

'I'm not even sure I'll be around that weekend. Ian's talking about doing the Kokoda Trail.'

Seriously, the Kokoda Trail?

'Look,' I said firmly, 'you need to prioritise this. Think about it. Ten, fifteen years down the track, if Ruby still hasn't got a lid on that lisp, who's she going to turn to? These kids, the ones you see scaling the walls here today, they're going to be the sum total of her support network. Hunter over there, licking biscuit crumbs off the floor – he could be Ruby's one and only chance to go to her high-school formal. Perhaps you can live without the Happy Mummies – more time on the tennis court, or whatever – but ask yourself: can Ruby?'

Tears streamed down Sharron's face. 'Fuck Kokoda. I'm in.'

She not only committed to supplying six dozen each of her famous mint-chocolate-chip, raspberry, peanut-butter, strawberries-and-cream, and sweet-potato-and-caramel cupcakes, but also promised to head up tidy-up duty once the fair was over, too.

And then there was Bree. Apart from her admittedly impressive skill at surviving on nothing but air for twenty-four-hour stretches, she hadn't showcased any particular talent in all the time I'd known her. This was not something I felt inclined to point out, particularly as today was Monday, aka Air Day, and I really didn't want to piss her off.

'Maybe you could do a lemonade stand?' Harriet suggested gently.

Bree looked back at her as though she was a bit of gum to be scraped off the bottom of her shoe. 'Actually I do have something,' she said carefully. We leaned in. 'I've perfected a recipe for vegetable soup that burns more calories to eat than it actually contains.'

And so 'Bree's Negative-Calorie Hunger Buster' was born. It would be the veritable jewel in our crown. I guess still waters really do run deep.

Just as I was feeling more kindly towards her, Bree turned to me. 'And what about you, Ally? Won't you be making anything?'

My heart froze. Visions of me, drowning beneath a sea of felted balls with a noose made of pipe cleaners around my neck, flooded my brain. Organising this event was one thing. It had never occurred to me that they'd expect me to actually contribute.

'Ally's management,' piped up Nikki, shooting Bree a frosty look. 'She doesn't have to make a thing. Her job is to make sure this whole event actually happens.'

In moments like those, I almost hated myself for cavorting with her husband.

Between the other mums, we managed to add to the line-up: loom-kinis (bikinis made entirely of loom bands – a glowing example of how some of these women had way too much time on their hands); baby bloomers in vintage fabrics; tin-foil art; and decorative garden gnomes crafted to resemble each and every member of the family. Nikki told us that Cameron would be happy to do a pop-up photography stall where people could get tasteful family pictures taken.

So I reckon we had it all tied up.

After less than fifteen minutes of going over the logistical details, we then dedicated a full hour and a half to arguing over what name to give ourselves. In the end, we settled on Made With Love. Meh. Personally I preferred my suggestion – Chicks With Knits – but it was deemed a little too out there for our refined North Shore sensibilities (and apparently implied that we all suffered from head lice), and by that point I was too bored with the whole thing to argue.

*

By lunchtime Wednesday I was losing the will to live. I had spent the entire morning trying to get one shot of everyone together that we could use for the press release: a picture that neatly summed up what Made With Love was all about. The idea was that we'd all go au naturel: just a bunch of happy, normal mums pitching in together and doing what it took to save a local institution.

Cameron had agreed to take the photographs, but I was pretty sure that was just so he didn't have to be in them as our token male.

After swearing blind only yesterday they wouldn't be doing anything special to prepare for the shoot, they all turned up this morning with full professional makeup jobs and blowouts and bursting out of their push-up bras. Lisa had even gone to the trouble of having her hair tinted a curious shade of burgundy. 'Just felt like a change.' Ridiculous women. Don't they know this photo was probably going to be used at the size of a postage stamp, I thought, as I swished my hand through my poker-straight, newly Keratined locks.

Much time was then wasted arguing about who would stand where in the shot. All of us, naturally, wanted to be somewhere near the back, where our carefully made-up faces would be on full display but our bodies would be completely obscured by the unlucky cows standing in front. It all started falling apart when Cameron suggested that a couple of us sit cross-legged on the ground at the front and Bree realised she'd walked out of the house without putting on her undies – something to do with bad panty line. Evidently she'd never heard of a G-string.

In the end, we decided to use a photograph of the kids holding up our snazzy new 'Made With Love' banner instead, which sounded like a straightforward enough plan once we'd found sufficient quantities of Smartie cookies and snakes to coerce them into standing still for fifteen seconds.

But things took an unexpected turn. Women who had only moments before pleaded for the chance to hide at the back of the shot went into full-scale *Dance Moms* mode, elbowing each others' kids out of the way and thrusting their own offspring front and centre.

'I really think Hamish should go there,' said Jenna, shoving Ruby aside so she landed splat on the floor. 'He's in his Country Road flannels today, which I think you'll agree really capture the earthy, homegrown essence of what Made With Love is all about.'

Remind me why I wanted to do this again?

On the upside, Coco left photoshoot-hell with her first ever birthday party invitation. Lisa's little Milly was turning three on Sunday, and would be celebrating with a mermaid-themed party and sausage-sizzle in Lisa's backyard. Too sweet! When I got home I stuck the invite on the door of the fridge, where it sat in all its glittery pink glory among the well-thumbed menus for take-out Chinese and pizza. I vowed to buy Milly something fabulous to mark the occasion, while silently thanking God that she was a girl and I wouldn't have to fork out my hard-earned money for a stupid truck or digger or something.

24

#birthdayparty #presentfail

Lisa had insisted that Judy come, and Judy had insisted that Gerald come, and for some inexplicable reason Gerald had insisted on bringing Speech Impediment Henry along too, a freckle-faced boy of about twelve, who spent the entire afternoon wandering around the garden kicking holes in the grass with the spikes of his soccer boots. Meanwhile, Judy flittered around in a floral print muu-muu and matching headband, twittering on to anyone within earshot about how lovely the whole affair was, how different to the low-key shindigs (her word, not mine) they used to put on for the kids back in the day, while Gerald attempted to make awkward small talk with a still sullen and resentful Matt over a warm bottle of beer. So here we all were in Lisa's backyard, all spruced up in our Sunday best and ready to party, my not-so-happily almost-blended family.

I don't know what Judy was on, but from where I stood, this little shindig was hardly something to write home about. From the moment I'd cautiously stepped onto Lisa's overgrown lawn, it was clear it wasn't going to be anything like one of the kids' parties you see on *The Real Housewives of Beverly Hills*. There would be no hot waiters with bare, oil-slicked chests walking around with trays of cocktails or circus entertainers impressing the kids with their dazzling contortions and whatnot (Gideon in an Afro wig trying and failing to make animal balloons really did not count).

Lisa's fun under-the-sea theme consisted of little more than a rather morose-looking blow-up mermaid that hung from the rafters beneath the upstairs deck and whacked everyone in the head with her tail every time they walked by, and a lonely pirate, sword raised and snarling to attention, in the agapanthus beds.

'Esky's under the table, help yourself,' Afro Gideon said as he walked past me, his latest attempt at a balloon poodle erupting in his hands and setting off a rapturous round of applause from the hordes of kids, most of whom, judging by the uncontrollable brown bumfuzz on their heads, were his. Like I said, we were a long way from Beverly Hills.

I found Cameron on all fours in the far corner of the garden trying to rig up a teepee out of a pair of picnic chairs and a Dora the Explorer bedsheet. Jenna's Elliot reclined next to him on a sunlounge, barking helpful words of advice, with a low-carb beer resting on the arc of his gut.

'You surviving?' Cameron asked me with a wink.

'Only just,' I replied.

'The trick is to keep yourself really, really busy,' he said, getting up to grab a couple of clothes pegs off the Hills Hoist. 'Two hours of torture passes a lot faster when you find yourself plenty of jobs to do. Plus, there's far less need to engage in small talk.' My despair must have been obvious. 'I'm here for you if you need me,' he added.

I glanced back at Matt, who was watching me carefully from the far side of the garden. It was hard not to compare them – the two significant men in my life: Matt, standing stiff and unyielding between Judy and Gerald, with his Arctic-white calves and matchstick ankles, the logo on his T-shirt stretched so wide across his belly you couldn't actually make out the words, while Cameron glided around in all his tanned, lean, supple deliciousness, looking like he'd just leapt off a hundred-metre cliff after grappling with a couple of mountain lions.

And here I was, like some doomed Cassandra, torn between the pair of them.

The teepee now complete and ready to be enjoyed, the kids ran straight past it towards a huge bouncy castle at the other end of the garden. Cameron shrugged and got to work on setting up a cricket match. Guess he really meant what he'd said about keeping busy.

Meanwhile, in keeping with her burgeoning social life (and early surrender to peer pressure), Coco was gleefully crawling after the others towards the stupid bouncy castle. As the older kids challenged each other to see who could dive-bomb onto it from the furthest distance, followed by an all-out war, where they attacked each other with blow-up baseball bats, I hovered around the edges, trying not to be too helicoptery about the whole thing while nevertheless trying to discourage Coco from joining in and risking irreversible spinal damage.

It was no easy task. Coco was now in the full throes of her pulling-herself-up phase. Everything in sight – tables, chairs, strangers' legs – provided the perfect opportunity to see the world from a far more interesting standpoint, and the edge of the bouncy castle proved irresistible. She beamed up at me with her three-toothed smile, bouncing up and down on elasticated knees, while huge, sugar-hyped children hurtled towards her and flung themselves straight over her head. She was having the time of her life, and I felt like I was about to have a hernia.

Sharron sidled over with a platter of Mediterranean flatbreads and dips. 'Gosh, I guess it's true what they say,' she said, nodding towards Judy and Matt, as I helped myself to a stack of crackers and tzatziki. 'Men really do marry their mothers. The likeness between you two is just uncanny.'

I stared back at her, dumbfounded, before spinning my gaze towards Judy in her head-to-toe floral number and then down at my own bang-on-trend Aztec playsuit. How could this be? I bought this outfit at Zara, for God's sake. I muttered something about Coco and nappies and how it was about time for a change, and stumbled across the lawn and into the bathroom as quickly as my trembling wedges would carry me.

I shut the bathroom door, deposited Coco on top of the closed toilet lid and turned to face the mirror. There were bags under my eyes, a chin that was not so much double as just one continuous part of my chest, and two deep lines arching down from the top of my nostrils to my lips. Maybe it was the lighting in here, but I'm sure they hadn't been there this morning. What were they called again – marionette lines? Puppet lines. Trust the French to give such a romantic, whimsical name to a grotesque side-effect of ageing that I knew couldn't be removed without some seriously expensive and painful surgery. I put my hands behind my ears and pulled back the skin of my face as far as it would go. There it was – the old me!

I spent the next ten minutes analysing my pulled-back face from various different angles. Was it finally time to push aside my dread of hospitals and book that plastic surgeon? Meanwhile, Coco yanked all the toilet paper off the roll beside me and arranged it in a mountainous heap between her chubby thighs. *Honestly*, I thought, craning my neck up into the harsh fluorescent light, *that Sharron can go fuck herself.*

When I finally dragged myself back out to the yard, it became clear that a Situation had unfolded in my absence. Harriet was standing frozen at the gate with a huge present under her arm and Jumping Axe Kick Toby, unflinching and defiant in a fetching pair of lime-green tropical-print shorts, beside her. Ian stood at the far end of the garden behind the built-in barbecue, eyeballing his nemesis, with a sausage wobbling aggressively between the prongs of his tongs. Presumably this was the first time the two of them had come face to face since Toby had flattened Ian in the Woolworths car park. Seriously, what had Lisa been thinking inviting them both here? Even I knew she'd broken a cardinal Happy Mummies rule. Who did she think she was? Mahatma friggin' Gandhi?

Sensing that World War III was about to kick off, Nikki instantly flew into crisis management mode, reminding us all that this was a child's birthday party – that is, not the place to let blood or guts fly. She leapt to Lisa's side. 'Why don't we go inside and Milly can open her presents? The PRESENTS.'

'Ah yes, the PRESENTS,' Lisa trilled back in the weird high-pitched voice of someone who was only just realising that her under-the-water birthday-party-sausage-sizzle could fast become the low point of the Happy Mummies social calendar.

But anyway, we were about to do presents. This was the moment I'd been hanging out for all day.

For the record, I hadn't deliberately intended to outdo everyone else, but I knew that my gift would blow all the others out of the water. I'd had so much fun choosing it, spending half a day trawling the delectable shelves of The Fairy's Grotto in Mosman. And while I wasn't exactly thrilled to see that my gift had been stuffed in the middle of a teeming pile of tat on the coffee table, crushed beneath a sea of cheap wrapping paper and homemade cards, I refused to let it bother me. At the end of the day, it would only make the big reveal all the more satisfying.

Naturally, Lisa made Milly open all the crappy presents first, cooing and squealing with delight (Lisa, that is, not Milly: Milly's glazed, slack-jawed expression never faltered) over an endless series of rainbow-hued ponies and grotesque little dolls decked out like hookers. All the while, Toby and Ian stood at opposite sides of the room glaring thunderously at each other. The huge pressie that Harriet had walked in with had had me a bit worried, so you can imagine my relief to see that it contained nothing more than a set of pint-sized plastic golf-clubs. Puh-leese. How old did she think Milly was – sixty-three?

And then finally, it was my turn. Milly ripped off the hand-embossed wrapping paper I'd chosen with such loving care like it was a bit of old newspaper around her nuggets and chips. She hauled out the glittering mermaid costume, hand-sewn by a team of near-blind seamstresses on a Tuscan mountaintop, with a bodice and tail encrusted with hand-sewn Swarovski crystals and two rows of pink and white pearls swinging at the neck, and flung it straight on top of the pile of plastic crap before reaching for the next present.

Huh?!

Catching sight of the agonised look I threw her way, Lisa reached out for my gift and did a too-little too-late examination, without, I might add, a single coo or squeal. 'Um, I'm not sure what to say, Ally,' she said, running her calloused fingers along the delicate gold thread of the mermaid's tail. 'You shouldn't have?' A question rather than a statement. What the hell was that supposed to mean?

'Maybe you're right,' I said sourly, getting up and grabbing the first thing in sight – a bowl of chips that someone had upended a box of Ribena into. Me and my pride would need a few minutes in the kitchen with these soggy pink chips to recover. A hundred and forty-five dollars. Not to mention the $12.50 for the hand-embossed wrapping paper. And the ungrateful little slack-jawed cow hadn't even bothered to take off her stupid Disney mermaid costume and try it on.

Nikki followed me in. 'I take it this is your first time,' she said.

'And hopefully my last.'

She let out a little chortle as she reached down to empty the dishwasher. 'Look, there are some hard and fast rules about these things that you should know. It doesn't matter what the theme, what the party host spends on putting their shindig on: you never spend more than $30 on a gift. Ever. Not only does it make everyone else look bad and they end up hating you, but once your weekends start filling up with these things – and trust me they will – you'll bankrupt yourself before Coco hits high school.'

Why did it always seem to be Nikki who had to explain the rules of the game to me? And why was I so dumb that they always needed explaining?

'There's something else too,' she said, passing me a tea towel to dry a stack of lunchboxes that had come out of the machine still wet.

Shit, I knew it. Bree's told her everything. Here it comes.

'I wanted to thank you.'

Okay, not exactly what I'd expected. 'What for?'

'Cameron told me he's taking your picture.'

I was flabbergasted. Why would he have told Nikki about it?

'Uh, yeah,' I said, squirming. 'There was some talk about it. Nothing's set in stone though.'

She took the lunchboxes from my hands. 'Well, whatever. Cameron's business is still in its early stages, you know how it is, and I just really appreciate your support. You're a good friend, Ally.'

'No problem,' I mumbled back.

Oh God, oh God. I was officially the worst person in the world. Not only was I bankrupting my own family in an effort to impress a three-year-old, but now this?

Why was life so hard?

I stumbled back out to the living room, only to find it deserted, Milly's huge pile of presents abandoned in the corner amid a sea of discarded popcorn and empty juice boxes, a twinkle of Swarovski crystal peeping out from the middle. Ugh. Time to go and find Matt.

But where was he? I headed out to the backyard, where I saw that Bree had him ensconced in what looked like a very deep and meaningful conversation over by the trampoline. What the hell was she up to? Coco and I hid behind the acacia bush and watched them.

When at last Bree moved off, I sprang to Matt's side, my heart racing. 'So what were you two talking about?'

He looked breezy and relaxed, not at all like he'd just been given news that would have him speed-dialling the divorce lawyer.

'She was just telling me how much they all liked you, how you've totally changed the dynamics at playgroup. I really think you've made an impression there, Al,' he said proudly as he took Coco from me.

Yeah, right. I knew her type. Hell, I *was* her type. Butter him up first, get him to trust her and then, when he was least expecting it, boom! Straight for the jugular.

I vowed not to leave Matt's side for the rest of the afternoon. I positioned myself right in the bosom of my almost-blended family, warm glass of wine in hand, and watched as freckly Henry continued his soccer-booted assault on Lisa's lawn. He was making pretty good progress, having pockmarked the entire back section. I felt almost proud, him being practically family and all.

Jenna sidled over to Henry. 'So where do you go to school?' It was an innocent enough question designed to make an awkward pre-teen feel like he was part of things, but one that sent splinters of alarm through everyone here who knew. The hairs on the back of my neck stood up. There was no way out; he'd have to answer. Jenna stood waiting, her smile fading a little as time dragged on. Henry, one muddy boot still wedged in the grass, tentatively opened his mouth. I willed the words to come. No doce. Then, just like that, they all started to come out at once. 'W-W-W-West Pymble P-P-P-Primary. In Year S-S-S-Six.' Listening to it was agony – like watching a cardboard box, all sharp planes and corners, tumbling awkwardly down a long set of stairs.

I glanced back at Gerald, and saw him silently mouthing each and every syllable along with his grandson. *Slow down, you've got this*, his look seemed to say. When, at last, Henry had finished speaking, Gerald stood back proud and triumphant, and my heart broke into a thousand tiny little pieces.

Later, when the parcel had been passed, the tail pinned onto the mermaid (for the record, in Beverly Hills they prefer to pin the label on the Prada), the dads had beaten the bejesus out of the particularly stubborn piñata, and the sugar-free cake had been consumed, we were officially free to go. I was exhausted, physically and emotionally.

'You did it,' whispered Cameron as he handed me a goody bag containing a pile of tempting paleo treats for Coco to smear all over the back seat of the car. Phew. He was right; we'd survived. 'You wait till she starts school,' he added with a smirk. 'Then you've got two or three of these things a weekend to look forward to.'

Wonderful. Another thing to add to my list.

25

#crossfitforlife #perfectdistraction #PRskillz

With the fanfare of Milly's birthday over, it was now Judy's turn. Despite her incessant reminders in the days leading up to the big event ('Ooh, I hate it when this time of year comes round again, I really do!') I still only remembered at the last minute, in just enough time to add a Celebration Sponge to my supermarket order and grab a gift voucher from the local beauty salon, which we presented to her along with a rousing rendition of 'Happy Birthday', while she exuded 'oh, I'd completely forgotten it was today' coy embarrassment.

By happy coincidence, our last-minute, slapdash gift turned out to be very timely indeed, as Gerald had booked a hotel room in the city and would be whisking her off for what he claimed was 'a nice dinner and a bit of a show' but what we all knew was really a dirty weekend. He was quite the dark horse, that Gerald. I was impressed. Matt, meanwhile, could barely look his mother in the eye.

'I hope she's thought about protection,' I said to Matt with a smirk.

He shot me a venomous look. 'And I hope you're bloody joking.'

'Relax, Matt. She's well beyond her baby-bearing years. Unless of course, she really is the Blessed Virgin Mother you've always suspected her of being.'

'Up until this whole Gerald fiasco, perhaps,' he said with a wry smile.

It was kind of adorable how he put his mother on this impossible-to-reach pedestal. I wondered if Coco would gaze up at me like that some day.

'You could look at your mother's relationship in a whole different light, you know,' I said. 'How many people get a second chance at love? Your mother's one of the lucky ones. Gerald's a good egg.'

'He votes Greens. My father would have hated him,' said Matt.

'Moot point, methinks,' I replied.

But right now I had bigger things to worry about than whether Judy was going to morph into one of those miracle grandmothers you see on *Today Tonight* who pop out a baby twenty years after menopause, or how we'd all survive the next election if Gerald and Judy ever got married. No, I had far more pressing matters to attend to: namely, embarking on the next stage of my Happy Mummies rescue plan – reaching out to all my old contacts. This was not something I was particularly looking forward to, but given that my grand scheme had no hope of working without them, I knew there was no getting around it.

I shut my bedroom door, flopped onto the bed and began scrolling back through all the names and numbers on my phone that had once made up the entirety of my life. The list was long: over five hundred editors, stylists, bloggers, vloggers, PRs and general hangers-on. I figured that even if only a quarter of them came along on the day (or, more likely, made every promise of coming but ended up bailing after five minutes, walking away with a couple of lines for their blog or magazine pages) that would be enough. They had deep wallets, I had a long memory, and it was time they returned the favours for all those free handbags I'd gifted them in the past.

I'd been hoping to do the whole thing by email, this being the digital age and all, where everyone conducts their business without ever having to hear a voice or make actual human contact. But after two days had passed and I hadn't heard back from a single one of them, I figured I had little choice but to go old-school and pick up the phone.

I decided to start with the easy ones.

'Russell, it's Ally,' I said to the freelance idiot from *Who* magazine who was actually responsible for me being in this whole married-mothering-playgroup-rescue-mission mess in the first place. 'The last time I saw you, you had your face shoved in the cleavage of that under-age blonde at Groucho. God, I wonder what she's up to now,' I said, all breezy, conspiratorial giggles.

'Probably folding my underpants. She's my wife.'

Oh God, oh God, foot in mouth . . . and *why*? 'So, anyway, I'm putting on a very exclusive handicrafts event. Very high-end, top-notch stuff. I was hoping you might cover it.'

'I don't do craft. But my wife does. She's the Senior Features Editor at *Home Hearth Love*. You know, the leading craft magazine in the country?' I could hear his sneer seeping down the phoneline. 'Would you like me to ask her for you?'

'Yes, please.'

Right. Next up, the editor at *Panache* who I'd promised my left kidney to.

'Yes?' she snapped into the phone, the sound of rapid-fire typing continuing unabated in the background.

'How are you, Leanne? It's Ally Bloom. Remember, the kidney?'

Silence.

'Never heard of you.'

Bang. The phone went dead.

Holy fuck. If memory served me correctly, she'd even come to my hen's night.

Surely it never used to be this hard?

Ironically, it was Lola who proved the most receptive of the lot. After lapping up my half-arsed congratulations for winning PR Genius of the Universe at the Creative Excellence Awards, she asked what I'd been up to.

'Um, you know, this and that, rearing a human. Not much really.' Before I had a chance to let her mortification about the pathetic state of my life really take hold, I bowled straight into my Made With Love spiel.

Lola was surprisingly keen. 'Oooooh,' she trilled. 'A craft fair – how adorbs, how quaint. We'll all be there, for sure – me, Helena, Celeste, Robbie, and maybe Alejandro and Colin too. Oh no, hang on, Colin's out. It's Jose now, isn't it? Whatevs – yay! We'll get to meet all your mummy friends!'

Yay indeed. I could hardly wait.

After three hours of soul-destroying grovelling, and umpteen reminders about who I actually was to people who'd celebrated several milestone events in my life alongside me, I managed to secure two write-ups on Made With Love in the news pages of national magazines, a brief mention in the calendar pages of the weekend paper, and four blog posts. Kitty at *The North Shore Times* was even considering putting us on the front cover of her upcoming 'Community' issue. Pretty good going, I thought, for a rusty old SAHM.

At Happy Mummies the following day, I found them all crowded around Jenna's iPad, poring over Kidstuff Daily, a newsy blog aimed at the sort of women who spend their days worrying about how many additives are in their kid's muesli bar and where to find an Olympic-trained swimming coach to give them the basics in doggy paddle. Needless to say, it was one of the Happy Mummies' favourite sites.

'Can you believe it – they've described us as "mums on a heroic mission" and said Made With Love is "a couture craft extravaganza and the must-see event of the season",' said Harriet, reaching for her Ventolin so she could breathe through her excitement.

Well, yes, I could, actually, considering those were the exact words I had spoon-fed the writer yesterday.

'And that's not all,' I said. 'Next Monday, you can look out for a write-up in *Sydney Weekly*, plus, with a bit of luck, you'll all be the cover stars on next week's *North Shore Times*.' They looked back at me in amazement as though seeing me for the very first time. 'If all goes according to plan, we should have a good couple of hundred of the city's movers and shakers coming to this event, plus of course all the local yokels, which means Kiddie Bootcamp can kiss itself goodbye.'

When I said it out loud like that, it actually seemed entirely possible.

And the next day, there was more cause for celebration, with an editorial in the local rag and the news that Sharron had deigned to put up a little thing about us on her blog, The Mindful Mama (accompanied by a huge photo of Ruby in a cheongsam – just, you know, because). 'Well, I've got over 7,580 followers, so that should help the cause a little,' she sniffed.

Lisa leaned in towards me. 'Yeah, and every last one of them bought and paid for. You can do that, you know.'

Later, while I was still riding high on the wave of my own fabulousness, Judy came home all flush-cheeked and chirpy from her dirty weekend with Gerald.

'How was the show?' I asked.

'The show? Oh yes, lovely,' she said. 'But you know, that's not all. Would you believe it, Gerald's booked us on an African safari. Whatever will I wear?'

And just like that, my wave of elation dried up.

I couldn't believe it. My own husband couldn't even be bothered to drag himself online to order the box set of *Game of Thrones* and Judy gets a frigging safari!

'He knows I've always dreamed of going,' she sighed.

My God. Was it possible everyone had a better life than me – even Judy?!

Riddled with depressing thoughts about my new life, and painfully aware that in less than two weeks I'd be coming face to face with the super-fit cronies from my old life, who considered cellulite a far greater tragedy than a life-threatening disease, I decided to kick off a bit of a fitness regime. Better late than never.

I knew from flicking through last month's *Cosmo* up at the hairdresser that crossfit would be my best bet for speedy results. But the thought of putting my out-of-shape body into cardiac arrest in a room full of complete strangers put me off somewhat, so instead I decided to start nice and easy with a gentle stroll around the neighbourhood, pushing Coco in her pram. Not too onerous, and the perfect opportunity for a little quiet thinking time.

But Judy cornered me as I was dusting off my Nikes in the hall.

'Ooh yes, what a good idea. I think I'll come with you. Build up my fitness for Africa.'

There it was again. Africa. The woman couldn't stop herself if she bloody tried.

She dashed upstairs and reappeared moments later, brandishing a pair of purple free weights that were, by happy coincidence, a perfect match for her lilac velour tracksuit.

The three of us headed up the street, Judy pumping her free weights up and down so enthusiastically I thought she might take flight. Even Coco was embarrassed. I tried to walk a step or two ahead of her, but no joy: she kept catching up. I was exhausted before we'd even reached the end of the block.

The weather was warming up and, by the looks of the weirdly empty roads and oodles of free parking around the train station, I figured it must be school holidays. Which meant only one thing: gaggles of depressingly skinny teenage girls in bikini tops and cut-off jean shorts would soon be taking to the streets with the sole mission of destroying what little was left of my self-confidence.

'Look at us, Alexis. Three generations of Bloom women,' said Judy, working those arms higher still. Yep, I thought, nestled in the bosom of the Bloom family matriarchal structure whether I liked it or not. 'You know, I'm really sick to the back teeth of hearing about these women who throw good money away on expensive gyms. If you're doing your job as a mother and housewife properly, there's no need for fancy gyms,' she announced.

I looked at her, all sweet innocence. 'Great! So what you're saying is I've got the perfect excuse for an expensive gym or, better still, a very hot personal trainer?'

She threw me the thin-lipped, disapproving Bloom glare (which, since I was one of them now, I instantly recognised) then pump-pumped up the street ahead of me.

But that was okay. I didn't need a personal trainer – this was about fresh air and clearing the mind and filling my body with all sorts of lovely endorphins that would see me sailing through the next few days. Besides, if *Cosmo* was to be believed, strong was the new skinny, and judging by the hefty biceps I'd developed by hauling Coco up and down a thousand times a day, I was already way ahead of the game in that department.

My mind was gently floating back to my old fantasy about Judy and the tranquillity water feature, when I saw them. Waiting at the bus stop were six girls decked out in regulation crop-tops and tiny shorts, their long, blemish-free legs out on open, hostile display.

One of the string beans, I realised, was Tessa, our babysitter from the PDP party. She was lounging back on the bench like she was sunning herself on a beach in the Bahamas, and laughing about something with a girl with a headful of braids. Just as I was debating whether to shout out a greeting, Tessa gave me a scornful once over and turned her head away. *Hey!* I wanted to shout. *Those stupid braids your friend's wearing, those nod-to-the-'80s acid wash Daisy Dukes – I practically invented those things!* Then again, I thought, looking down at the daggy collared golf T-shirt that Matt usually wore to pull the weeds, and my faded leggings with the gaping hole in the crotch, would they even believe me if I did?

'Come on, Alexis,' shouted Judy, pump-pumping her purple arms like her life depended on it. 'You'll never get fit if you amble along at that pace.'

26

#DylanandBrenda #whathaveIdone?

I decided to take things up a notch on the fitness front and walk to playgroup. Matt would be working from home, but he had lots of important phone calls to make so he wouldn't be able to join me.

'Don't worry, Alexis. I'll come along,' Judy announced as I was halfway out the door, attempting to make a stealth getaway.

Great. Now my slow amble up the hill would turn into one of her exhausting races to the top.

With a sigh, I stepped aside so she and her snazzy free weights could get a head start.

'I expect there will be a lot of walking when we're in Africa, tearing around after the animals and all,' I heard her lilac tracksuit say from somewhere up ahead.

Ugh.

I arrived at playgroup hot, sweaty and in a completely foul mood, a good five minutes after Judy. Coco had managed to empty her entire zip-lock bag of Cheerios all along the pavement on the way there – an enormously fun game, but one that left her hungry, crotchety and ready to consume the morning tea I did not have. Oh well. We were ten minutes early, so she'd just have to wait until the other mums turned up and she could wrangle something from one of them: parenting takes a village and all that.

My stomach lurched when I saw that Cameron was there early too. He was setting up a pair of long craft tables in the hall and looking typically brawny and irresistible in the process. I hesitated before saying hello, suddenly hyper-aware of being there with him in the full glare of daylight without all the other mums swarming around.

After a moment or two, he spotted us. 'So how are the playgroup-saving Bloom ladies today?' he said by way of greeting. It suddenly occurred to me what a very bad idea it was to adopt the Happy Mummies' unspoken no-deodorant rule. I clamped my arms to my sides and smiled back at him from a suitably safe distance.

Judy unstrapped Coco from her pushchair. 'Think I'll take this little one to the sandpit,' she said breezily, before disappearing outside.

Oh God. We were now totally alone. With my arms still superglued to my sides and my voice about three octaves higher than usual, I began babbling away in answer to his earlier question. 'All's going well, we've had a couple of good write-ups so far and with a bit of luck –'

'Ally, I don't give a fuck about the craft fair.' His eyes fixed on mine and took on a heady look, one I hadn't seen before.

'Oh.' Gulp. The air between us suddenly felt charged with possibility. Man, I could really do with that deodorant right about now.

I could feel my face turning beetroot, little beads of sweat popping out on my upper lip. 'Well, I suppose I'd better get started on unpacking the craft cupboard. Everyone's going to be here in a minute.' Pathetic. *Pathetic.*

I half-ran, half-fell into the dreaded craft cupboard but I could feel the presence of Cameron behind me.

'Here, let me help you,' he said, reaching over my shoulder for a box of jumbo markers on the top shelf.

'No really, it's fine, I've got it,' I said, jabbing at the box with my fingertips and trying not to let the sensation of him being so close completely unravel me.

There was a fumbling, bumbling moment as our arms crossed, a tangle of markers and polite apologies and edge-of-a-precipice potential. And then, before I'd even fully registered it was happening, his lips were on mine and I was falling down a deep, bottomless, Cameron-shaped hole. He must have kicked the cupboard door shut, or maybe it was me, because we were suddenly engulfed in darkness, in our own steamy little world.

'God, you're so sweaty and real and . . . you're like a drug, I can't stop thinking about you,' I felt him breathe the words into my face, my neck, my eyelids, the stubble round his mouth scratching against my skin. He smelt so good. My legs felt like they were about to give way, and I reached out blindly behind me for support. I knocked over all the little jars of glitter and glue that I'd lined up so carefully on the shelf the week before. Oh God, this was better than I'd imagined in my wildest, horniest dream. He was Dylan McKay and I was finally, *finally* Brenda!

'I've been waiting to do this since the first time I laid eyes on you,' he said. Oh boy, oh boy, oh boy. I felt deranged, on fire, my hands clawing at his hair, his chest. I didn't even care that I had BO. I might even have called out 'Dylan!' at some point.

'How long since that husband of yours has kissed those beautiful lips?' he asked, before covering my mouth with his own. He tasted musky and salty and sweet, all at the same time. I felt something deep inside me waking up, unfurling. If only he'd just shut up with the running commentary and get on with it. 'Such a waste. You're just the same, you and I. One foot in, one foot out,' he said, punctuating the words with a trail of tantalising little bites along my neck.

Huh?

I pushed him away. 'What do you mean by that?'

He leaned back against a stack of folding chairs, his breath coming out in short, jagged bursts. 'What do you think?'

My eyes started adjusting to the dark and his outline became clearer. The deep lines on his face, around his eyes, were suddenly more defined.

Is that what I was? One foot in Matt and Coco's camp, and the other hot-footing it with Cameron in the craft cupboard?

'I'm nothing like you. I love Matt.'

'Come on, Ally, don't overthink it. You know you want this as much as I do,' he said, pulling me back towards him and running his hand up inside my T-shirt.

Then, with Cameron crouched down before me, rolling the nipple of my left breast between his teeth and tongue, I had a vision.

It was a vision of underpants.

Skiddies underpants, to be specific. They were there before me, like a bold, bright beacon of pulsating light. And I loved those skiddies underpants. Well, I didn't love them exactly, but I finally accepted them and understood what they really meant. They didn't mean Matt and I had lost sight of each other; they just meant we'd changed, we'd moved on. That next stage, the better, grown-up one I'd been fighting so hard to get to all this time . . . we were already there. And okay, maybe it was a bit grubbier and a little heavier in the jowl department than I'd been expecting, but it was real and it was *us*, and I really, truly with every fibre of my being didn't want to lose it.

And Cameron wasn't Dylan and I would never, ever be Brenda Walsh.

The cupboard door swung back on its hinges with a crash.

Judy.

'It's not what you think,' I stammered, my T-shirt bunched up around my neck, Matt's hands still cupping my breasts.

But it was too late. She'd already deposited Coco on the ground in front of us and vanished in a puff of lilac velour.

Oh God! I yanked down my top, raced out after her and ran smack-bang into Nikki.

'Sorry, I'm late,' she said cheerily, helping me back to my feet. 'Had to pick up some worm pills for Bodie down at the pharmacy. He's been scratching his bum all morning. You ready?'

'Ready for what?' My mind was still spinning in circles, trying to get a handle on everything that had happened in the last couple of minutes. I hoiked my bra strap back into position and peered past Nikki to see if I could spot where Judy had gone.

'How could you forget? You're presenting your grand plan to the school committee this morning. Ms Pricklethwaite and the others are waiting for us in her office.'

Oh yeah, that. 'Can't you do it? Something's come up. I've really got to go and find Judy,' I pleaded, already one foot out the door.

Nikki gave me her best stern, military glare. 'Ally, this is your baby. Come on, let's go,' she said, grabbing me by the shoulders and frog-marching me towards the principal's office. 'Cameron can look after Coco, can't you, honey?' She smiled across at Cameron, who had some-how managed to extricate himself from the craft cupboard and was now calmly trickling almond milk into Sharron's English Breakfast tea.

'Of course,' he said, his face the very picture of innocence. Even I, the master of two-faced lies, was astounded at his coolness.

So there you have it. While every fibre of my being was racing down the street after Judy and forcing her to let me explain everything before she reached Matt, I was here, stuck in a wobbly plastic chair across the desk from three stern-faced old biddies. I felt like a naughty schoolgirl who'd been sent to the principal's office for bad behaviour. Which was entirely fitting, I suppose.

The biddies looked at me and I looked back at them, all of us wait-ing for someone to speak. My mind was a complete blank. I couldn't even remember why I was here. After several moments of awkward silence, Nikki stepped in and did the talking.

Ms Pricklethwaite glared at her over the top of bifocals, when she had finished explaining the whys and wherefores of Made With Love. 'It's a huge inconvenience. There will be mess, crowds. And have you even considered OH&S?' she demanded, looking from one to the other of us.

I glanced at Nikki for help.

'Occupational health and safety,' she whispered under her breath. Then she leaned forward. 'Actually, we've covered all that. We've allocated clear set-up times, packing-away times and clean-up duties. There will be no sign of us once the fair is over. Nothing but a big fat cheque to pay for the Happy Mummies to stay on.'

The three old biddies still looked unconvinced.

Nikki opened her mouth to say something else then closed it again. She slumped back in her wobbly chair and looked at me plaintively. My mind was clearing a little now. Enough to know it was time to pull out the big guns.

I took a deep breath and leaned forward. 'Look, you might think Happy Mummies is just a bunch of mums singing stupid songs and making a mess of your school hall floor every Tuesday morning, but it's so much more than that,' I said. 'These women, the friendships you make, they have the power to save you, to keep you afloat, at a time in your life when you're not even sure how you're going to make it through to the next day. I know that because they saved me. Happy Mummies is worth rescuing, and all we're asking you for is the chance to try.'

Did I believe my own cheesy spiel? I didn't really know. What I did know was that Nikki now had her hand on my arm and was looking across at me so kindly it was all I could do not to cry.

Ms Pricklethwaite observed us solemnly. 'Not one dirty tissue, not one juice box – not one single sign you've even been there at all.'

And so it was agreed. Job done.

The second we were released from the principal's office, I raced to the girls' toilet and vomited all over one of the kiddie-sized loos.

'You alright in there?' Nikki hollered from outside.

'I'm fine. Think it was just some dodgy eggs I had for breakfast.'

How could it have come to this? My life had turned into a bad soap opera, and if I didn't find a way to sort it out quick smart, the next episode would be me, sad and pathetic, trudging the long and lonely road of single-motherhood.

I found Coco with Cameron over at the swings. She was kicking her little legs in the air and having so much fun she cried when I tried to pull her off.

'Thanks for watching her,' I said sulkily to a tiny spot on the ground next to Cameron's right foot.

'Ally –'

I forced myself to look up into his face, waiting for him to say whatever it was he wanted to say.

'I, uh . . . It really wasn't a problem.' His eyes looked tired, and he seemed older than he'd ever seemed before.

Perhaps we both did.

It was time to go.

I said my goodbyes, strapped Coco into her buggy, grabbed a couple of slices of watermelon from the refreshment table to keep her occupied for the next twenty-five minutes and readied myself for the long walk home.

I stood at the top of the road for a moment. Gulp. All downhill from here.

By the time I made it home, I was as ready to face the Judy and Matt firing squad as I'd ever be. Judy would have told him by now, that much I was sure of. But how to fully explain to him why I'd done what I'd done? And more importantly, how to make him understand that it had all just been a horrendous mistake – a trap of my own making that I'd never ever allow myself to fall into again? I had the words of the speech I'd been practising the whole journey home fixed firmly in my mind, but in truth they didn't even go part of the way to explaining what I was really feeling.

Please don't leave. Not now. Not ever.

I turned my key in the lock of the front door. The house was silent. My stomach twisted as I stepped into the kitchen. Judy and Matt were huddled together at the table, a veritable picture postcard of grief. Their hands were clamped so tightly around each other's it was impossible to tell who was comforting who. Matt looked up as I dropped my keys on the counter, the pain in his eyes so palpable I could have reached out my hand and touched it. Judy didn't move a muscle.

This was it. Game over.

I opened my mouth to speak, my carefully prepared words on the tip of my tongue, but Matt got there first.

'Gerald's dead.'

27

#lifegetsreal

They'd found Gerald sitting in his armchair, television still on, his half-eaten dinner on a tray on his lap. I couldn't help wondering if it had been one of Judy's shepherd's pies.

Later that night, after we'd exhausted all of our comforting words and spent hours watching Judy pace the kitchen and stand silent and stoic at the kitchen sink, staring out the window at nothing, Matt and I crawled into bed.

'I suppose in a way you're relieved about all this,' I said, pulling my zebra onesie out from under my pillow.

His response was instant, frightening in its intensity. 'Relieved about it? A man has died, Ally. Are you actually suggesting that would make me happy?' He glared at me, challenging me to respond.

I said nothing.

'For the record, I am not happy about any of this.' With that, he flung his undies, sunny-side up, onto the floor beside the hamper. I looked at them lying there.

Then, in a silent show of solidarity, I tossed mine right on top.

*

Judy wasn't invited to the funeral, and as far as I know she didn't ask to go. I wanted to tell her I was sorry, that I'd seen what she and Gerald had meant to each other. But the words wouldn't come. The huge wall between us, laid down from the minute I'd walked into her life five years ago with my unsuitable attire and my tales of models and rockstars and all manner of unsavoury, drug-addled types, and she'd entered mine with her pastel twinsets and her novelty hand soaps and her barely-concealed disapproval whenever I so much as reached for her precious son's hand, was simply too high to get over.

For the next week, Judy seemed to walk around in a daze, insisting to everyone who asked that she was absolutely, completely fine. 'We only knew each other for a very short time.'

But I knew differently. I made her endless cups of tea that she didn't drink and at one point even offered to let her help me alphabetise the contents of the fridge.

She shook her head. 'What's the point? You'll know from the smell when something starts rotting back there.'

I didn't want to alarm Matt, but I was beginning to get worried.

The following Tuesday, I suggested she get out of the house and join me at playgroup. I didn't particularly care to relive the experience of Judy at Happy Mummies, but both of our worlds had tilted so much since then that I wasn't even sure whether what happened between Cameron and I in the craft cupboard had even happened at all. When I told Judy to put her shoes on, she did as she was told like an obedient child.

When we arrived at playgroup, she stumbled out of the car. Harriet pulled up behind us in her shiny red SUV and, without saying a word, walked over and wrapped her arms around Judy's shoulders.

There they stood, in the middle of the school car park, for what felt like an eternity, me shifting awkwardly from foot to foot beside them, feeling like a complete tool perving on an intensely private moment and willing Harriet to let Judy go. She was my mother-in-law: why the hell couldn't *I* give her a massive hug?

Despite my feelings of guilt, a tiny, awful part of me couldn't help but feel a little bit hopeful. Did Gerald's lonely death in front of *Myth-Busters* mean that I'd be let off scot-free after my little indiscretion? Judy hardly seemed to remember what day it was, so it was quite conceivable that she'd wiped the memory of me cheating on her favourite son among the arts and crafts supplies clear from her mind. Certainly, I'd seen no evidence so far from either of them that she'd passed on the news to Matt.

Thankfully, Cameron wasn't expected at playgroup right until the end, when he'd help Nikki home with the banners she was planning to decorate. This suited me fine: I really didn't feel up to testing my amnesia theory out just yet. Besides, I had too much other stuff to think about. With less than a week to go before the big event, emotions were running high and everyone, in their own little way, was beginning to fall apart.

'Aunt Tilly has gone and broken her hip. She's hooked up to an IV in intensive care and has only managed to finish off nineteen beach cover-ups. On top of that, she forgot the bloody flaps, didn't she!' screeched Jenna, beginning to hyperventilate. Harriet rushed over and began soothing her with a craniofacial temple massage.

'Relax, just breathe it out,' she cooed into Jenna's ear.

Judging by Jenna's death stare, it didn't seem to be working. Upon seeing this, Bree sauntered over and handed Jenna a thick wad of antibacterial wipes.

Folding tables needed to be allocated, chairs needed to be counted, paper plates, cups and napkins needed to be bought, extension cords needed to be located, and an old-fashioned fairy-floss maker needed to somehow, from somewhere, morph into existence. And on top of that, there was the bunting.

'Oh my *God*, where's the bunting?' howled Lisa as random bits of tinsel, tubes of paint and colourful clouds of confetti came flying out of the craft cupboard. 'You can't have a craft fair without *bunting*. And I won't have time to make it – Ned's got his soccer finals and I'm on grounds duty all weekend!' She eyeballed me, all panicked expectation as if I alone held the answer to her life-or-death bunting problem. Oh God, surely she wasn't thinking I'd make it?

I fumbled blindly for an Anzac biscuit on the refreshment table (on today of all days we'd run out of flapjacks!) and stuffed two in my mouth at once. Carbs always helped me think. After I'd chewed my way through them, I said, 'I'll get Nikki! She'll know what to do.'

After hunting high and low, I finally found her in the boys' toilets, crouched down on the tiles and struggling to get a clean pair of undies onto one of the twins, a damp pair scrunched in a ball at her feet, while her little darling smacked the top of her head with a wooden train. She barely seemed to notice.

'I thought we were past all this, I really did,' she said, grabbing a stray ankle and shoving it through one of the leg holes. 'Ashleigh had the whole toilet-training thing completely sussed by two. Sometimes I think the boys are just doing this to piss me off.'

'Isn't there some kind of theory though?' I asked. 'Boys take years longer than girls to work it all out – something to do with the extra bit of anatomy?' I was sure that's what Judy had told me. 'Anyway, forget about that. We've got a bit of a bunting situation going down out here –'

I heard a huge sniffle. Oh God, she was crying.

I crouched down on the tiles beside her. 'Nikki?'

'It's Cameron,' she sobbed. 'He's having an affair.' She buried her head in her arms like a tiny, frightened child.

Fuck, *fuck*.

I did up the zip on Snotty Twin One's cargo pants and motioned for him to run back out into the hall with the others.

He gave me a quick dong on the leg with Thomas the Tank Engine and ran off.

'Well, he hasn't slept with her, I'm sure of it,' I said weakly.

She laughed through her tears. 'And how would you know that?'

Shit. This was it: now or never. I was going to have to be honest with her for once. I went silent for a moment, trying to formulate the right words.

'I don't know what I'm going to do, Ally, what the next step's supposed to be. I can't go through all this again, I really can't.'

I grabbed her by the shoulders and looked her square in the eye drill-sergeant style in a way she'd understand. 'You're going to fight for your marriage and you're going to knock that stupid husband of yours into shape. And you'll be alright. You have to be. I'll help you, I promise.'

What the bloody hell was I saying? I was the evil harlot responsible for all her pain. What happened to telling her the truth?

She wiped the long trail of snot running down her face away with her sleeve. 'That's what I love about you, Ally. You always think that if you just try hard enough you can fix everything. And sometimes you're right. But sometimes you're not.' She stood up and reached out a hand to help me up too. 'Besides, this isn't your problem to fix.'

We stood there in silence for a while.

'You know, I never fully trusted her, even when she was fat,' Nikki said, finally. 'And it's worse since she got skinny – now she thinks she can have whatever she wants, other people's husbands included.'

WTF? 'Hang on a minute,' I said. 'Who are we talking about here?'

'Who do you think? Old five and two.'

'Bree?' I spluttered.

'Apparently they've been at it for months. Remember that time you said you saw him at the shops when he was supposed to be in Phuket? Well, three guesses where he was. All this time he told me he was heading off to photo shoots – booked solid, he told me – he's been with her. I'm such a blind, stupid fool.'

I collapsed back against the sink. 'But how could that be?' The lying, cheating piece of shit. What was so bloody special about Bree? Why did I get the chaste kiss and clumsy boob grab in the craft cupboard, while she got the months-long affair and the sneaky overnighters. Then again, thinking about Matt and Coco and looking at Nikki's tear-streaked face in front of me, thank God it hadn't been me. And on the plus side, at least I would never have to get my saggy bits out in front of him on camera now.

'Look, Nikki, there's something I really need to tell you –'

'Ally, don't,' she said, laying a hand on my arm to cut me off. 'Just don't. I know Bree's probably not the first. And I still want you to be my friend.'

'I want that too,' I said, laying my hand over hers.

She yanked a couple of paper towels from the holder on the wall and blew her nose. 'Come on. We've got some bunting to sort out. Life goes on, right?' She attempted to laugh and I laughed along with her.

Later, after the bunting had been located and the other mums had stumbled off home to get on with their prep for the fair, I watched as Nikki and Cameron packed up the twins in the double stroller, ready to make their own journey home. Nikki strapped Twin One into his seat, while Cameron distracted Twin Two with a bag of popcorn. She passed Cameron a bottle of juice for Twin One, before getting Twin Two into his seat. Cameron tucked a pair of blankets around the boy's knees to prevent the cold from getting in, and Nikki then passed him the banners, which he popped under his arms. She took position behind the wide handlebar and Cameron nudged her aside, careful not to bump her with the banners, so he could push. Throughout this complicated business, neither of them uttered a word.

I guess she was right. Life does indeed go on.

28

#MadeWithLove #FashMumrevenge

In the days leading up to Made With Love, I watched Matt like a hawk. But apart from his usual grumpiness about not being able to unlock the toilet seat and the dishwasher playing up again, there was nothing to indicate anything was amiss. So I concluded that either grief had erased the Cameron incident from Judy's short-term memory or, for whatever reason of her own, she'd chosen to keep my dirty little secret hidden from Matt. Either way, I sent up a silent prayer of thanks to the gods of ill-advised extramarital affairs and vowed never to find myself anywhere near the craft cupboard with that two-timing douchebag ever again.

But early Thursday evening, any lingering questions I might have had about the whole thing were answered. Judy had come downstairs decked out in her lilac velour. This was a good sign. Apart from our playgroup excursion, she'd barely left the house since we'd heard the news about Gerald. Matt must have noticed too; he smiled when he saw her. She asked if I wanted to join her for a walk, but I said no, I had too much to do before the fair. Not a problem, she'd go on her own.

'Have either of you seen my free weights, the little purple ones?' She began digging around in the pile of shopping bags beside the front door.

'Oh hang on,' she said, abandoning the bags and standing upright as though a light had suddenly flashed in her head. 'I must have left them at playgroup that day when, uh . . .' She looked me clear in the face with the startled expression of someone who had been about to blurt out a very big, very bad secret but had stopped themselves just in time.

Matt turned back to his iPad.

So out went the amnesia theory. She remembered perfectly well and had chosen to protect me, to protect all of us. But seriously, *fuck*. The idea of being indebted to Judy was in its own way just as bad – worse even – than having to face the music with Matt.

Matt. Who was at the centre of all this madness, carrying on in beautiful, blissful ignorance. Part of me couldn't help but envy him.

The following night in the five minutes or so between putting Coco to bed and the delivery guy arriving on the doorstep with the takeaway curry, I decided to dash upstairs and take a shower.

As I pulled off my sweater and tossed it onto the bed, I noticed there was something propped up on my pillow, haphazardly wrapped in last year's Christmas paper. Matt appeared sheepishly in the doorway.

'What's this?' I asked him, picking it up and turning it over.

'Open it.'

So I did.

It was Ganesh.

'Better late than never, huh?' he said, with a shy smile.

I couldn't believe it. 'But how did you . . .?'

'And before you ask, yes, I had it blessed. It comes fully loaded with all the good fortune, fine foods, wealth and luxuries we could ever want or need.'

I couldn't even look at him. 'But why? Why now? There's nothing even special about today,' I said, running my finger across the intricate carvings.

'Yes, there is. Don't you remember? It's the anniversary of the first time you let me kiss you. Five years ago today. On the corner of Arthur and Crown Street, outside Tokonoma's. You told me I tasted of chicken katsu and Japanese beer.'

'Yeah, sorry about that. Way to kill the moment, huh.'

From across the room I could see his smile falter a little. 'Don't be sorry. I remember thinking, this woman is extraordinary. She insults me and I can't even dislike her. In fact, I can't get enough of her. Even if you were telling me I had bad breath, I just wasn't ready to let you go. I'm still not ready. Happy anniversary, Ally.'

Before I had a chance to respond, the doorbell rang. The takeaway was here. Matt headed downstairs to answer it, leaving me standing by the bed with his beautiful gift, bound up with all his promises of a new life together, a better one, in my hands.

The guilt almost doubled me over.

*

This was it. The day had finally come. As I spooned lumpy Weet-Bix into Coco's reluctant mouth with a trembling hand, three little words kept playing over and over in my mind: no way out. In less than three hours my two worlds would come crashing together in a gut-curdling explosion of couture and crochet and cotton balls and complete and utter judgement, and no headache, belly ache or freak act of nature would be a good enough excuse to get out of it.

What the hell had I been thinking?

Up until now, I'd done a pretty good job of distracting myself from the cold, hard realities of today, what with having to be extra nice to Judy in light of her grief and her decision not to tear my family apart, and the complexities of the popcorn stand roster to figure out. But now, with my stomach a churning mass of nerves, I only had one little distraction left up my sleeve.

'I'm just going to pop up to the shops,' I announced breezily to Judy and Matt, who were crouched together on the back deck doing something to my potted succulents. They looked back at me, stunned.

'What, you don't mean you're going to the actual –' stammered Matt, pointing a muddy-gloved hand vaguely in the direction of the supermarket, as though pointing to the gates of hell itself.

'Yes. I'm going to the supermarket. Keep an eye on Coco. I shouldn't be too long. But in the event that I don't return in thirty minutes, you might want to consider sending out a search party.' And with that I swept off. Really, they didn't half treat me like an imbecile sometimes.

Once there, I battled my way through the weekend shoppers in search of the personal care section, using my basket as a sort of battering ram to ward off tantrum-ing children and annoying malingerers who stood in the centre of the aisle reading the fine print on the back of the cereal boxes.

Honestly, I thought, as I rammed the corner of my basket into the buttocks of a woman who was hogging the entire aisle as she casually flicked through magazines as if this was her favourite weekend hangout, *who would begrudge paying five poxy dollars to have a nice smiley man deliver everything right to your door, if it meant avoiding this hell?* But today I had no choice. Some things you just can't place in an online order.

I found what I was looking for, paid up and raced back home. It was now 9.15, which gave me an hour and a quarter to get my game face on. And, of course, attend to some other important business. I shut the bathroom door as quietly as I could and got on with it.

'Ally, have you seen my nose-hair clippers?' Matt boomed from outside the bathroom door. I opened it an inch and shoved the clippers into his waiting hand. When I emerged, he stood before me and thrust his nose skywards so I could see right up the full length of his nostrils. 'Did I get them all?' Ah, marriage. It's truly a beautiful thing, sometimes.

He and Judy were both coming to the fair today, in a show of family solidarity I'd really rather have done without. Nevertheless, it would be useful to have extra hands to help me unload the car and keep an eye on Coco.

Next up, find something to wear. This most definitely wasn't the day for low-key leisurewear, much as I'd grown to love it (the sale rack at H&M had, in fact, become my new best friend. Who knew so many different items of clothing could be elasticated?). No, facing up to Alejandro and the crew when they'd probably spent the last three hours getting ready required proper, full-scale battle armour. My heart sank at the thought.

I pulled out my precious archival collection from the cupboard, in search for something that might do the job, hating myself for not thinking about this earlier. Oh God, and where were my Spanx? I dug madly through my underwear drawer and under the bed, but in the end found them in the bottom of the laundry basket, still unwashed from my trip to the office eight weeks ago. Fuck – and I hadn't even shaved my armpits. What the hell was happening to me?

'Come on, Alexis. We're going to be late!' I heard Judy cry from downstairs. In the end, I grabbed a floaty tunic top and a pair of cigarette pants with hidden stretchy panelling down the front. I had practically lived in these at work during my final trimester with Coco. Not ideal, but it was either this or the bondage dress, and I really didn't think of any of us were up for going through that again.

Okay. Let's get this show on the road.

*

The schoolyard had been transformed. Even the bunting looked great. All the mums were in position behind their tables, nervously arranging their craft wares and tucking away stray hairs beneath their 'Happy Mummies Rock!' peaked caps. I suddenly realised I'd forgotten to bring mine today. It was too late to go back for it now. Oh well. What a bummer.

I couldn't help scanning the area for Cameron. Why, *why*? I was relieved to see that he was safely ensconced inside his little pop-up photography studio down the far end of the yard.

The fair officially opened in eleven minutes, which gave me enough time to do a full circuit and get the troops ready for action.

I walked around admiring each of the mums' stands, as if I was the Queen Mum at a village gala day, trying to soothe frazzled nerves with a cheery smile and, when necessary, a few stern words of encouragement. But I wasn't feeling it. Try as I might to look like I'd got my shit together, deep down I was probably more nervous than any of them. After all my big promises about today, what if I couldn't cut it?

I found myself at the 'Negative-Calorie Hunger Buster' stand and could just make out the top of Bree's head, bobbing up and down behind towering piles of her genius soup, while she gave the underside of the table a vigorous scrub. Creepy Egor stood by watching her with the blank look of someone for whom this was a completely normal, everyday occurrence.

'Looks great, Bree. Well done,' I said to the top of her peaked cap, but she was obviously far too busy to respond. Funny, I realised I'd made peace with her weird OCD antibacterial wipe fixation. In fact, I'd actually be quite disappointed if she didn't whip them out. And as I spotted Egor slicking back his man bun when he thought no-one was looking, I actually found myself feeling a tiny bit sorry for her.

The alarm on my phone went off in my hand. Eleven o'clock. We were officially open for business.

But where was everyone? Apart from a few sad OAPs who had been lurking around the edges of the yard for the past fifteen minutes, chomping at the bit to get their hands on the custom-made garden gnomes and a few jars of homemade rhubarb chutney, the place was deserted. Where were my hordes of fashion journos, my photographers, my bloggers, for fuck's sake?

The minutes ticked by. The mums looked at me, eyebrows raised questioningly. I beamed back at them confidently, but inside, my heart was pounding in my chest. *Come on, people*, I silently urged. *We all know how it works. There's no such thing as a free, limited-edition marabou-trimmed bucket-bag. Time to pay up.*

And then, just as I was starting to hyperventilate, they suddenly appeared, gliding towards us en masse over the hill behind the new infants' jungle gym. The fashionistas. Every eye in the place swung towards them, and who could blame us? All that was needed to complete the scene was a bit of slow-mo action and a moody French soundtrack.

They brought a weird, otherworldly energy with them, with their in-your-face patterns and their sharp corners and their wildly oversized accessories. They even smelt different: sort of zesty and fresh and nothing like the musky eau de-must-really-have-a-shower-before-the-end-of-the-day parfum the rest of us were sporting. Helena and Celeste posed, hands on hips, by the bubbler, as if they were models about to be photographed for a back-to-school special, while Robbie peered out through his mirrored aviator shades with the expression of someone who really wished he could change his mind right now and head back to bed.

As for me, my feelings were a mixed bag: relief, gratitude, a touch of embarrassment . . . it was hard to say which one dominated. There was no time to think about that now, though – they were standing right in front of me and there was some serious air-kissing and mutual love-festing to get on with.

But it had been too long and I'd lost the hang of it; a kiss that was intended for Celeste's cheek somehow ended up on the side of her nose. She gave me a funny look, almost pitiful, and then turned to all the mums eyeballing us from behind their stands.

'So, are these your friends?' she asked sweetly, holding her hands up near her face as if to say 'Don't you dare make me touch them'.

I looked over at Nikki, standing proud as punch behind her rolls of finger-painted wrapping paper and feathered headbands, and at Harriet, slapping the wrist of a child who had dared touch one of her hand-crafted banksia figurines.

'No, not really,' I said, shaking my head. 'They're just part of the mums group.'

It was true, of course. But I still hoped none of them heard me say it.

The crowds parted at this point to reveal Alejandro, Enzo trotting sniffily at his heels.

I moved forward to greet him. 'You came!'

He reached for my hand and grazed it with a kiss I couldn't feel. 'For you, my darling, anything.'

'Here, can you put that dog on a lead?' boomed Sharron, hands on hips and decked out in regulation OH&S fluorescent green bib. 'Health and safety,' she added, nodding towards Enzo.

I was tempted to tell her that Enzo was actually a very famous celebrity blogger with a huge cult-like following, but something about the officious green bib put me off.

Alejandro grimaced as though he'd just been made to smell a very ripe Roquefort. 'And yet,' he said to her, eyes scanning the hordes of kids running helter-skelter around us, 'you allow these little monsters to walk around completely unharnessed.'

Sharron gave him a confused look and stomped off. I couldn't help but laugh. It felt good to be back on the other side again; it was like pulling on an old pair of jeans you're convinced won't fit but somehow, miraculously, do.

'Plebians,' he called to her retreating back. 'Really, Ally, I don't know how you've survived this.'

I opened my mouth to respond, but he and Enzo had already wandered off to join the others and coo over the mums' craft offerings, an altogether painful process to watch. As the fashionistas went into paroxysms of ecstasy at each and every stuffed toy kangaroo and marinated olive they encountered, the mums melted in pools of gratitude at their feet. If only they knew this was pretty much the fashionistas' standard reaction to everything. Rule Number Five in the PR game of life: if it's not worth rupturing a hernia over, it basically doesn't exist.

Only then did it occur to me that someone was missing. There was no sign of Lola. *Strange*, I thought, *seeing as she had been so wildly enthusiastic about the whole thing.*

Whatevs. The important thing was that business was booming. The loomkinis were flying off the table. For Harriet's bush toys, there was a queue so thick it was almost impossible to squeeze by. They'd started taking orders right up until Christmas for the gnomes. And Alejandro had nabbed every single tub of Bree's Negative-Calorie Hunger Buster. The little money tins I'd deposited under each of the craft tables were filled to overflowing. All the while, photographers were snapping our pictures and there were already three hundred Instagram posts tagged with the hashtag I'd coined – #Craftoholics.

I rustled up an interview for Alejandro with *Better Homes & Gardens* magazine and then forced Helena and Celeste to pose for a few pictures in front of the garden gnomes for the Happy Mummies Facebook page.

See? Just like riding a bike.

As I was tying macramé hanging-baskets to the back rails of the homewares stand, a familiar face appeared before me. I knew, I *knew* this person, but for the life of me I couldn't remember from where. In her cable-knit cardigan and sensible slacks, she was obviously not part of the fashion crowd, and at the same time she was far too put together to be one of the Happy Mummies.

'Ally, how are you doing?' she asked. And then I saw it – the familiar probing smile. It was Dr Krudnic.

I thought about her question for a moment. 'Actually, I'm feeling great,' I said. And it was true. I really was.

'Well, come back and see me if you need to,' she said before wandering off towards the chutneys and marinades.

I nodded in reply, but I knew I wouldn't. The truth was, I didn't need to anymore.

Alejandro reappeared at my side. 'Well, this is a job well done, Ally. Like always.'

I beamed with pride. He was right, of course. A blind person could see that I'd well and truly nailed this thing.

He leaned in towards me. 'But your little experiment in the 'burbs is out of your system now, no? And you're ready to come back to us.'

What the . . .? I spun towards him. He said it as though this whole thing – getting pushed aside for a younger, thinner, more digitally-savvy version of myself, being forced to retreat with my tail between my legs back to deepest, darkest suburbia – had all been my doing.

'But what about Lola?' I spluttered.

'Bah! The girl's a complete imbecile. Besides, that whole digital-natives wave is so yesterday. Now, we want authenticity, we want community, we want –' He waved his arms as one of the snotty-nosed twins forced a large inflatable hot dog between Enzo's hind legs – 'this.'

Robbie threw me a weary look over the top of his shades. 'She landed a better job at Prada.'

'The little bitch,' said Alejandro, doing that weird air-sniffing thing again before glancing down at Enzo. 'Pardon my French, darling.' Turning back to me: 'Anyway, Ally, I'm willing to put your little lapse in judgement behind us. Go right back to the way things were. What do you say, my little pariah? Are you ready to come home to Moda?'

Moda. The word was like music to my ears. A free pass back to the real world. A return to glory. The chance to escape all this SAHM madness, with its drudgery and its never-ending mess and its interminable, mind-blowing boredom. Deep down, wasn't that what I had wanted? Wasn't it?

Matt wandered over with Coco, who was covered head to toe in fairy floss and looking altogether quite delighted with herself.

I looked from one to the other of them before turning back to Alejandro. 'Give me some time to think it over.'

He and Enzo stared back at me with the same affronted expression, before turning on their heels. 'Well, don't take too long about it.'

'What was that all about?' asked Matt.

'Nothing, really. He was just telling me how much he was enjoying the fair.' Much as my instinct was to broadcast Alejandro's offer to the world with a full-scale Insta, Facebook and Twitter blast, a tiny part of me wasn't ready to. Not yet, at least.

Before I had a chance to think, Coco and I were cornered by a vlogger from the Practical Parenting website wanting to interview me about how I'd come up with the idea for Made With Love and seen it through to fruition. Okay, it might not have been our own reality TV show, but it was certainly a step in the right direction.

'And this morning we have Ally Bloom, Yummy Mummy and mumpreneur extraordinaire,' said the presenter, before launching into a series of riveting questions all about me, me, me.

So, there you had it. I was officially a yummy mummy (and mumpreneur to boot).

And that wasn't all. We were still a good ninety minutes from closing and had raised nearly $7000, enough to cover the next year and a bit for Happy Mummies. The event had been such a hit there was talk of us throwing another fair – even bigger and even better – next year.

I was a triumph. For the first time in my life, I'd actually come out on top. And most amazing of all, no lies, no false promises, no special arrangements had got me there. Plus, I had a chance to return to my old job and the real world and leave all this mummying business behind me. Plan A was back on the table and ready to roll.

So why, then, did I feel so completely crap?

I thought about what Cameron had said in the craft cupboard – 'one foot in, one foot out'. I knew he'd been referring to me and Matt, but in a way it could be applied to other parts of my life too. Take the Happy Mummies. Sure, I'd made my Master Plan to become one of them and stuck to it as diligently as I could, but had I really been ready to trade in my Hermes winged sandals for the Velcro-strapped variety once and for all? Maybe this whole time I'd really been hoping for a way out, and Alejandro and his surprise offer was it.

I was deep in thought behind the lemonade stand when the man himself reappeared, Enzo snuggled in his arms where he was safe from the attentions of pesky children.

'Have you made a decision yet?' he asked, twiddling his pinkie in a glass of lemonade and watching it fizz.

'But it hasn't even been fifteen minutes! I haven't even had time to think!'

He put an arm around my shoulder and pulled me close. 'What is there to think about? We miss you, Ally. Come home, come back to your friends,' he said, the 'rrr' sound rolling in his mouth like a backfiring gun.

Squished against Alejandro's hot, hairy little body, I looked around and realised I already was home. My friends were all around me, pitching in to help make my crazy vision for today a reality. They dropped off roast chickens on my doorstep, helped me find my lost child, taught me about empathy and filled those days that seemed like they'd never end with little bits of hope and laughter, reminding me every single time that I was not alone: I had this. Matt was right. These bonkers, uptight women, who went around thinking Sportscraft was a lust-have label and potty training was a competitive sport, were actually my *friends*.

'You know what, Alejandro,' I said, extricating myself from his arms. 'Thank you for your offer, but I think I'm good. Think I'm gonna stick with this mothering gig for a little while longer.'

He looked back at me, shocked. 'Well, you know I never make an offer twice,' he said, unleashing a furious spray of spittle that landed on my face.

'And I really, sincerely, hope you don't. Because I don't know if I'd be able to refuse it a second time.'

Just then Cameron emerged from his photo booth, a huge camera slung over his shoulder. Somehow, despite being a gargantuan prick who played with innocent and gravely sleep-deprived mothers' affections just for the thrill of it, he still managed to look good enough to eat. He ran a tired hand through his hair, glanced around like he was in search of something or someone, and stopped in his tracks when he saw me.

I looked away.

Alejandro gasped, clutching my arm at the sight of him. 'Lords alive, who is that dishy Dylan McKay lookalike with the camera?'

'His name is Cameron. Absolute charmer,' I said. 'You know, I think he could be your perfect guy. You should go for it.'

And with that, I walked back to my friends.

Later, when the packing up was done and every pompom, popsicle stick and bit of papier-mâché was disposed of, a horde of very tired, very happy Happy Mummies headed back to their cars. That glass of wine on the sofa had never sounded so appealing.

Nikki called out to me over the top of her people mover. 'See you at the park tomorrow, Ally?'

'I'll be there,' I shouted back. 'Both feet in.'

29

#soblessed #NoReally

Curiously, when Coco and I returned home from the park the next day, I discovered I couldn't open the front door. Something inside was blocking our way. I pushed and shoved, but whatever it was refused to budge. Eventually, I twisted a foot around the corner of the door and managed to kick it aside.

It was Judy's suitcase. And it was not alone – there was a series of shopping bags and holdalls lining the full length of the hallway, right up to the stairs. Perched on top of them was an old-fashioned safari hat, finished off with a satin ribbon.

I couldn't believe it.

Judy appeared at the top of the stairs in a cloud of old-lady perfume. 'You're going,' I said.

'Yes, you'll finally be free of me,' she said, coming down the stairs. 'Matt said he'd drive me to the airport. He should be here any minute.'

'No, I meant to Africa.'

'Well, of course. Why wouldn't I be?'

'Well, I just thought, what with Gerald and all . . .' I let my sentence trail off, still unable to say the actual words. Dead. Gone. Over.

'Alexis, he would have wanted me to go. More than anything else in the world, he would have wanted me to go.' She smiled briefly at an invisible something over my shoulder, then quickly snapped back to the here and now. 'Besides, think of all the young whippersnappers I might meet while I'm there. They don't call it Tempting Twilight Tours for nothing, you know.'

I laughed so hard I got tears in my eyes. And then: 'I'm sorry, Judy. Really, I am.'

'You have nothing to be sorry for. Apart from all these hideously awful family photos, of course,' she said, nodding towards a gigantic three-toothed Coco leering at us from the wall.

'You know you can come back. Any time. You can stay as long as you like.'

'I know. But right now it's time for me to go.'

'Coco will miss you. And so will I.' Funnily enough, I think I actually meant it.

Silently and awkwardly, she pulled me into her arms and planted a kiss on the top of my head. It was the closest we'd ever come to scaling the huge wall between us. Not perfect, but a pretty decent effort.

'You and your little family are going to be absolutely fine without me. Like I said, you're a better mother than you think, Ally.'

Ally. Did she just call me Ally?

She opened up one of the holdalls at her feet to put a sweater inside. The bag was already full to bursting and refused to close. I bent down to help.

'It wasn't what you thought, you know, that thing you saw at playgroup,' I said, yanking hard at the zip.

She yanked along with me. 'It never is.'

'Thank you for not mentioning it to Matt.'

'Bumps in the road. Take it from an old bag: the journey's never easy. But that doesn't mean it's not completely wonderful,' she said, as together we managed to close the bag shut. She looked up at me. 'But you're wrong. I did tell him.'

WTF?

For a moment, I was frozen to the spot in stupefied silence.

He knew.

Matt knew. And he loved me anyway.

Then everything happened at once. 'How long till his train gets here? Have I got a few minutes?' I blurted out. Judy nodded, and I thrust Coco into her arms. 'There's something I've got to do.'

I knew that if I ran up the street fast enough I could probably get to the station before his train pulled in. I could surprise him. Tell him everything before he'd even left the platform.

But as I raced up the street I could already see him in the distance, walking towards me, suit jacket straining at the buttons, the briefcase I bought him for Christmas held stiffly by his side. My big beautiful bear.

A confused smile crept across his face when he spotted me, and suddenly I couldn't wait another second to be with him.

It was taking too long. I looked down and realised my beloved Jimmy Choo slingbacks were slowing me down.

A gaggle of leggy teenage gazelles in spray-on leggings and ugg boots was sloping down the road in front of Matt. Before I had time to think about how hard those shoes had been to find, how long I'd waited for them to come in and how much I'd spent on them, I tossed them towards the gaggle. With the quick reflexes of youth, one of them caught the slingbacks neatly in her hands.

She looked at me, confused.

'Look after them. They're limited edition,' I called. I really hoped she would.

The old battleaxe was right. It was time to let go. Time to let go of the idea of being a certain kind of mother, a certain kind of wife, a certain kind of me. It was time to just be.

I ran barefoot straight into Matt's arms. It was a proper embrace, nothing like the token kisses we gave each other on birthdays and anniversaries, or those cursory pecks that were forgotten as soon as they were given when he headed out the door in the morning. This one I would remember forever.

'I have something to tell you,' I said. 'I'm not perfect. In fact, I'm not even close to perfect. And I never will be. But I'm okay with that, I really am. If you are.'

He took my face in his hands, carefully, like it was something delicate, worth treasuring, and looked deep into my eyes. 'Oh, Ally, my perfectly imperfect, yummy mummy fashionista extraordinaire. How could you even ask me that?' He kissed me so deeply I forgot that I was standing on the street corner, barefoot, kissing a man who'd just got off a train. I felt almost sixteen again. 'I love you and I'm not ever letting you go,' he said. 'Besides, I'm hardly perfect either. Look at the way I bulldozed my mother into your life like that.'

'Actually, asking Judy to stay was . . .' Okay, I wasn't about to call it the best thing he'd ever done, because, come on. 'Enlightening.'

I heard a burst of laughter from somewhere behind us. I looked over and saw Jimmy Choo girl, holding her/my slingbacks tightly in her hand, watching us and cackling away with her friends. *Crazy old people*, they were probably thinking.

How right you are, I thought with a giggle.

'But she's going now,' says Matt.

'She is.'

'Happy?'

'Not really. I think I'm actually going to miss her.'

'Well, on the upside, I suppose it means we can be the Three Amigos again,' he said, tracing a slow, tantalising finger down my cheek and along my lip, just the way he used to.

And that's when I felt it – the flip. And the flip, and the flip, and the flip. Granted, it may just have been the hormones, but really, at this point that hardly mattered.

I put his hand on my belly. 'Actually, I think you'd better make that the *Four* Amigos.'

Acknowledgments

One of the best parts about writing a book is the incredible people you meet along the way. I've been lucky enough to meet three such people: my wonderful agent, Sally Bird, who took a chance on a first-timer and found *Confessions* the most perfect home imaginable; publisher Jeanne Ryckmans, who so graciously (and stylishly) welcomed me into the Nero fold; and my brilliant editor, Kirstie Innes-Will, who made the editing process an absolute joy and taught me lessons I shall never forget. Thank you all so very much.

Thank you to all the wonderful mums – for welcoming my family into your lives, making me laugh, and giving me a shoulder to cry on when I've needed it. I promise none of the characters in this book are based (entirely) on you!

To my sister Melissa, thank you for supporting me in more ways than I could ever possibly count, and for convincing me that the impossible is, in fact, entirely possible.

Reading group questions for
Confessions of a Once Fashionable Mum

To download reading notes for
Confessions of a Once Fashionable Mum,
visit www.nerobooks.com.au